"ALL MOST WOMEN WANT IS THE RIGHT MAN."

Audrey strove for nonchalance in delivering her statement, but she felt as awkward as a young girl on her first date.

"Oh? Describe the right man to me," Boyd challenged.

"That's impossible!" Audrey blushed, trying to hedge the question and get out of this conversational cul-de-sac as gracefully as she could.

"Why? Haven't you met him yet?"

Audrey opened her mouth, then quickly closed it again. Her luminous eyes widened as Boyd, seemingly without effort, pulled her from the chair and settled her on his lap, wrapping his arms around her.

Boyd pressed her against his chest and placed his lips in the hollow of her throat. "Fess up, Audrey. The truth of the matter is you have met him...."

ABOUT THE AUTHOR

Sometimes life throws a curve—or maybe even more than one. That's what Audrey Hamilton, the heroine of *By Special Request*, discovers. One thing in life *is* for certain: Barbara Kaye's novels are always entertaining and insightful. *By Special Request* is the seventh Superromance by this talented Oklahoma author. And it comes as no surprise that her loyal fans are anxiously awaiting her next!

Books by Barbara Kaye

HARLEQUIN SUPERROMANCE
  46–A HEART DIVIDED
124–COME SPRING
161–HOME AT LAST
206–SOUTHERN NIGHTS
219–JUST ONE LOOK
257–A SEASON FOR ROSES

HARLEQUIN AMERICAN ROMANCE
19–CALL OF EDEN

Don't miss any of our special offers. Write to us at the following address for information on our newest releases.

Harlequin Reader Service
901 Fuhrmann Blvd., P.O. Box 1397, Buffalo, NY 14240
Canadian address: P.O. Box 603,
Fort Erie, Ont. L2A 5X3

Barbara Kaye

By SPECIAL REQUEST

Harlequin Books

TORONTO • NEW YORK • LONDON
AMSTERDAM • PARIS • SYDNEY • HAMBURG
STOCKHOLM • ATHENS • TOKYO • MILAN

Published August 1987

First printing June 1987

ISBN 0-373-70270-1

PROLOGUE

BENEATH A CLEAR TEXAS SKY the blackland prairie stretched ahead for seemingly endless miles, fresh and emerald-green even in the heat of July. Generous rains had fallen all spring and early summer, and the pastures were in excellent condition. Jesse Murdoch nudged his horse across a rise and down into a small creek's grassy valley, oblivious to the beauty of the landscape. He rode for perhaps half a mile. Then reining in his horse and squinting under the big brim of his black Stetson, he gazed down the creek bank toward a stand of post oak. When he spied the slim figure of a young woman lounging against a tree trunk, her pinto mare tethered nearby, a grin spread across his face and excitement pumped through his veins. Audrey was waiting for him, just as she'd promised. Setting his horse at a gentle canter, he closed the space between them.

Audrey Hamilton straightened when she heard the approaching horse. Nervously she wiped her hands on her jeans; her fingers felt stiff and cold. She found it hard to believe that only a few hours ago she had been filled with happy anticipation. Now she was sure she had never been angrier in all the twenty-two years of her life. Her nerves were stretched to the snapping point, and she prayed she would get through this encounter with Jesse without completely losing her composure.

She studied the man on horseback. His ever-present black hat was shaped in the distinctive style known as a "Montana peak," and he sat tall and straight in his saddle. As he came nearer, she could see that charming boyish grin on his rugged tanned face, and she seethed inside. Lord, he was a handsome one! He oozed effortless charm and confidence. For months she had been so sure that she was, at last, deeply in love. Now her only conscious emotion was shame at having been taken in by such an unprincipled, deceitful bastard!

Unaware of the dark thoughts spinning inside Audrey's head, Jesse rode to within a few yards of her, swung out of the saddle and tethered his horse to a tree. Then he sauntered toward her, his arms outstretched. "Hi, honey. Been waiting long?"

Audrey stepped back, avoiding his intended embrace. The grim expression on her face stopped Jesse in his tracks, and warning bells began clanging in his head. *Something's wrong,* he thought. For the first time it occurred to him that Audrey's father might not have welcomed her alliance with a common cowboy as readily as she had assumed he would. If so, Jesse had no idea what his next move would be. "Well, did you talk to your dad?" he asked warily.

"No." The word was precise, clipped.

"You . . . said you were going to."

Audrey took a deep breath. "I won't be talking to Dad about us, Jesse. I talked, or rather listened to Sam Graves instead."

Jesse frowned. "Who the devil is Sam Graves?"

"Dad's friend, the one you saw yesterday. He's visiting from Wyoming." She placed some emphasis on "Wyoming" and waited to gauge his reaction.

"Oh?" Now a very real fear swept through Jesse.

"Yes." Audrey folded her arms across her chest, turned and walked away a few steps, then turned back. "He saw you and asked me what your name was. I told him, and...it seems he knows you."

Jesse attempted a smile. "Sorry, hon, your friend's mistaken. I never met anyone named Sam Graves."

"Oh, he doesn't know you personally. But he sure knows of you. You see, he's very well acquainted with a family named Revis. Maybe the name Janet Revis rings a bell."

The color drained from Jesse's face. Judas, talk about the bad-luck kid! How many miles could the Revis ranch be from the blackland prairie of Texas? A thousand-plus? Not in his wildest dreams would he have imagined that the Hamiltons would ever hear of the Revises. For the first time in his adult life, Jesse Murdoch was at a loss for words. He could feel his great dreams crumbling like clay at his feet.

Audrey never took her eyes off him. Somewhere in the back of her foolish romantic mind she had harbored the hope that Sam would turn out to be wrong about Jesse, but one look at Jesse's face banished that hope. She felt sick inside. Dear God, she had come within a whisker of being the biggest fool ever.

Poor Janet, she thought, recalling the story Sam had told her. The unsuspecting woman in Wyoming had honestly thought Jesse was sincere, right up until the minute he rode off into the sunset. Jesse had come very close to his goal that time, but he hadn't counted on Janet's father's chauvinistic attitude. Once Jesse discovered that Janet would never own the ranch, that it would go to her uncle in the event of her father's death, he had packed up and left, without so much as a goodbye to the young woman he'd assiduously courted for six months. According to Sam, Janet had had a hard time getting over it.

Audrey's chest heaved in agitation. Maliciously, she was enjoying every second of Jesse's discomfort. "And Janet wasn't the first, was she, Jesse? Sam also told me about the woman in Montana. But she was only eighteen, and her father saw through you right away. Oh, you have quite a reputation out west! You're a good cowhand, so you can always find work, but you have this peculiar fondness for working on ranches whose owners have single daughters. You make me sick!"

Regret, despair and grudging resignation settled over Jesse. He wasn't the least remorseful over having wooed Audrey with avarice in his soul. He was only sorry that another goose that could lay his golden egg had escaped his clutches. He supposed he could try turning supplicant, vow to the heavens that his feelings for Audrey were completely different from anything he'd felt for Janet, but he didn't think Audrey would buy that for a second. That had always bothered him; Audrey was a helluva lot smarter than Janet had been. Damn!

Jesse wanted to shake his fist at whatever fate had sent Sam Graves to the Hamilton ranch. Audrey had been the perfect "catch"—young, beautiful and the only heir to the various Hamilton enterprises, which were considerable. Besides the ranch, the old man owned a company in Dallas and a splendid home there, along with another on the Gulf Coast. Compared to the Hamiltons, the Revises had been strictly potato patch.

Jesse had envisioned a life far beyond his most optimistic expectations. His sojourns in Montana, Wyoming and Texas had taken a precious three years out of his life. He was nearing thirty and anxious to secure his future. Long ago he had decided that the best way to do that wasn't by hard work but by taking advantage of his attractiveness to women.

Desperation overtook him when he saw Audrey turn toward her horse. He had to do something. He couldn't let Audrey walk out of his life. Grabbing her by the arm, he spun her around to face him. "Audrey, honey, you're overreacting to an old man's gossip. I really am fond of you, and we make a good pair."

She laughed harshly in disbelief. "Save it, Jesse. You are incredible! I'm going back to the house and tell Dad to send you packing."

"I wouldn't do that, if I were you. Guess I oughta warn you of something. I can ruin your daddy if I set my mind to it."

"You're also crazy! *You* ruin my father, one of the most important men in this state. You overestimate yourself."

An indolent smile matched the tone of Jesse's voice. "I'm not sure I do. I've been on this ranch some time now, and I've heard things I wasn't supposed to hear, mainly because I keep my eyes and ears open. One word from me, and the high and mighty Hamiltons will be in the pits."

"I don't have any idea what you're talking about."

"I'm sure you don't, but if you're as smart as I think you are, you'll take my word for it. I can ruin your daddy. I promise, marrying me will be the lesser of two evils. You might even learn to like it."

Angrily Audrey disengaged herself from his grasp, ran to her horse and mounted. As she galloped away, tears of fury stung her eyes, and a despondent sense of failure and inadequacy overtook her. All of her life she had heard people tell her how fortunate she was. "You have everything, Audrey," they would say. "Looks, money, wit, intelligence."

But the one precious commodity called love, the thing that other women seemed to find so easily, had eluded her completely. Until Jesse. How could she have fallen for that kind of man? Was there some kind of flaw in her psyche? She felt embarrassed, humiliated.

At that moment Audrey was sure she would never regret anything as much as the minutes she had spent in Jesse Murdoch's arms. She had no way of knowing how much more there would be to regret.

CHAPTER ONE

Phoenix, Arizona
Five Years Later

"CAREFUL, AUDREY," Helen Drake warned as she strolled into the office and took a seat behind her desk. "The boss is in a very peculiar mood this morning."

Audrey had been deeply engrossed in the new brochures the graphics company had sent over that morning, but Helen's remark brought her head up. "Peter? I wonder what's wrong."

"Don't ask me." Helen shrugged as she whipped the cover off her typewriter. "He got a phone call a few minutes ago, and it really played heck with his sweet disposition. He didn't even finish his dictation, and he wants you to get in there right away."

"Of course," Audrey said, getting to her feet immediately and leaving the office.

"In there" was the office only a few yards down the mezzanine corridor from Audrey's own. She lightly tapped on the door marked Manager, then pushed it open and stepped inside.

Peter Sorenson was standing with his back to her, hands clasped behind him, staring out the window that overlooked the sixteenth fairway. He turned slowly and faced her with a dark, worried expression. A scowling Peter was an unusual sight. Audrey had often thought he had the most placid disposition of anyone she'd ever known.

"Yes, Peter?" She approached his desk.

"Sit down, Audrey."

Not even his customary "good morning." Puzzled, Audrey sank into one of the leather chairs facing the desk, crossed her long shapely legs and watched her employer slip into his swivel chair. He picked up a pencil and began drumming it on the desk. "I've just had a call from the Benedicts," Peter told her.

"Oh?" That got Audrey's attention. The Benedicts were the wealthy family who owned the Greenspoint, the posh resort hotel near Phoenix where Peter was manager and Audrey his assistant. She knew very little about the prominent family, but if one could believe rumors, the Benedicts owned half of Arizona.

"It seems one of them is paying us a visit this afternoon. Why, do you suppose?"

Audrey uttered a little laugh. "You're asking me? I have no idea. I've never so much as set eyes on any of the illustrious clan."

"It's been years since I have. They never stay here, or in any public place for that matter. They have a house in Paradise Valley, and that's home when they're in Phoenix. All our dealings with them are through lawyers, although I'm sure they have some of their spies check us out from time to time. But the Benedicts never show up, so why this unexpected visit?"

"I'm sorry, Peter, I don't have the foggiest idea."

"The old patriarch died last week. A shake-up maybe?"

Audrey could only shrug. How was she to know why people like the Benedicts did anything?

"You know, Audrey, scuttlebutt has it that the Melton chain has made an offer for a Phoenix hotel." Peter's tone was ominous. "So far it's all very hush-hush, but what if that hotel is the Greenspoint?"

She looked at him blankly. "What if?"

"You and I might be out of work, that's 'what if.' The Melton bunch likes to bring in their own people." He paused to let her digest that. "Now, just suppose the Benedicts have received an offer and are sending one of their own here to look us over, to decide if we're worth keeping."

Audrey did her best to appear concerned, but she couldn't understand why an impending visit from one of the owners was such a big deal. Surely Peter wasn't worried about the impression the hotel would make. The Greenspoint was the grande dame of Arizona resorts. The hotel had played host to heads of state, deposed royalty and spoiled movie queens, always to raves. The Benedicts couldn't possibly be any more particular or demanding than some of the celebrity guests they had dealt with in the past.

"Strictly conjecture, Peter," she said.

"Maybe. It just seems damned funny to me that one of 'em is showing up, out of the blue, with no warning, no explanation. Well, something's up, you can bet on it." Peter picked up a notepad and read from it. "Boyd Benedict, that's the one who'll be here. I'm not sure if he's a son, a nephew or what, but he's a Benedict, so he has clout." He looked squarely at Audrey and spoke earnestly. "Let's give him a hotel stay he won't soon forget. And if he wants the grand tour, I'll expect you to handle it with aplomb. We'll put him in the Durango Suite.''

Audrey nodded.

"Now, I want you to get up there and make sure it's ready.''

"You know it's ready, Peter.''

He went on as if she hadn't spoken. "Get in touch with housekeeping. Then spread the word among the staff. I want everyone to drown the man in contentment. I'm sure I don't have to stress the need for making his visit a perfect one.''

"Of course not. I'll get right on it.'' She stood up. "Mr. Benedict won't have any complaints, you can be sure of that. The President was lavish in his praise.''

"The President of the United States doesn't own the Greenspoint. The Benedicts do!''

"True,'' Audrey conceded.

"And you might tell everyone that if I hear any complaints from the man, some heads are going to roll!''

Audrey looked down at him, horrified. "Oh, I'll do no such thing! This is a seasoned staff, but you'll have everyone so uptight they won't be able to do their jobs. I'll simply tell them to be on their toes and to proceed in their usual efficient manner. That should impress Mr. Benedict more than anything.'' Pivoting, she left Peter's office and returned to her own.

"So, what's up?'' Helen demanded as Audrey stepped into the room.

Audrey crossed the carpet and sank into the swivel chair behind her desk. Succinctly she told her secretary about the impending arrival of one of the owners. "It's certainly gotten a rise out of Peter. Helen, what do you know about the Benedicts? I've never even seen any of them.''

"I don't think any of us have," Helen said. "I've seen some pictures in the newspapers, but that's about it. They're powerful, influential, and they keep a low profile. They've been around for...oh, I don't know...forever! If you were a native you couldn't avoid hearing about them. They're sort of Arizona's answer to the Kennedys. There are Benedict Memorial this-and-thats all over the place. I think they first made their money in ranching, but I'm sure no one really knows what all they're involved in now. They don't give out interviews, and they stay strictly to themselves.''

"Well, let's just hope Boyd Benedict turns out to be a man who appreciates class when he sees it.''

Helen uttered a little gasp, and her eyes widened. "Is it Boyd Benedict who's coming?'' she asked breathlessly.

Audrey nodded. "Why?''

"He used to cut a pretty wide swath through Arizona society. Made all the gossip columns frequently, but I haven't heard much about him lately. He's probably married and settled down by now. Ooh, I'm anxious to get a good look at him. I hear he's really something.''

Audrey smiled. She, like everyone else at the Greenspoint, was well aware of Helen's penchant for the opposite sex. "Helen, you'll think he's 'something' if he's breathing.''

"Probably,'' Helen said and laughed wickedly.

A FEW MINUTES LATER Audrey stepped out of her office into the mezzanine's carpeted corridor. Turning right, she walked toward the stairs that led to the main lobby. As she passed one of the hotel's ballrooms, she paused for a moment and watched a group of waiters putting the finishing touches on a dozen or so banquet tables. A professional organization was holding its annual awards dinner at the hotel that evening, and the ballroom glittered with crystal, silver, white linen and fresh flowers. No one, she thought, did this sort of thing quite as well as the Greenspoint.

Continuing on, she smiled and spoke to two young bellboys who were passing by, but she didn't slow her pace and was oblivious to the frankly admiring stares that followed her. What the two young men stared at was her shapely figure—slender, leggy and full-breasted. Her carriage was erect, and she moved with ease and grace. Her ash-brown hair was thick and glistened with health. When worn down it fell to her shoulders in a waving cascade and framed an oval face with delicate features that were memorably attractive. What most people remembered longest, however, were her eyes—large, expressive, straightforward and of a lovely shade of brown flecked with golden glints.

At the head of the stairs she paused, and those unusual eyes took in the scene below. There was an amazing lack of hustle and bustle in the lobby, even though the hotel was booked almost to capacity. Guests who checked into the resort expected serenity, impeccable service and a gracious atmosphere, and they received it. The lobby of the Greenspoint exuded an air of elegance and charm, of quiet opulence. The overall ambience was one of stepping back in time to a less frantic era. Audrey never tired of it.

But even if she had hated it she would have stayed. For three years the Greenspoint had been her haven of peace and protection. Here she felt safe. Here she could forget the past and not worry about the future. She still found it hard to believe that with only high school typing, some shorthand and eighteen months' experience with an advertising agency in Dallas she had fallen into such a marvellous job.

"You're a natural, Audrey," Peter had told her when he made her his assistant. "You know how to meet people, and you know how to pamper them. That's what this job is all about, and you don't learn it in a classroom."

Audrey had learned the social graces from her socialite mother, a woman of flawless good taste. She called upon the lessons learned at Constance Hamilton's knee almost every day. Whenever a guest was difficult or displeased, she always asked herself, "How would Mom expect to be treated? What would impress her?" It worked every time.

She began a slow descent of the winding stairway, her alert eyes taking in everything at once. Several middle-aged matrons sat engrossed in needlepoint and magazines. Teenagers in tennis togs crossed the lobby carrying racquets. Golfers came and went. Laughing children in swimsuits dashed through the glass doors leading to the loggia surrounding the pool.

At some tables by the tall front windows, groups of elderly men sat engaged in card games. Intently Audrey searched their faces, looking for one in particular. Not finding it, she crossed the lobby and went out onto the long covered veranda that ran the entire length of the front of the building. Most of the rocking chairs were occupied, but, again, she didn't find the face she was seeking.

Just then Craig Smith, a young college student who worked part-time at the hotel, bounded up the steps and onto the porch. Audrey halted him.

"Craig, have you seen Bert?"

"Who?"

"My friend, Bert Lincoln. You remember."

"Oh, you mean the old guy with the beard and shaggy white hair? No, come to think of it, I haven't seen him in weeks."

"Four weeks, to be exact." Audrey frowned and bit her lip. "And I didn't particularly like the way he looked last time he was here. Kind of...tired and pale. I do hope nothing's happened to him."

Craig fell in step beside her as she reversed her direction. Opening the door to the lobby for her, he said, "You've become real fond of that old gentleman, haven't you, Audrey?"

"Oh, he's such a sweet guy, and so lonesome. I guess I feel sorry for him. He must not have a family. I can't imagine a family letting him roam around alone at his age."

"How long's he been coming here?"

"I first noticed him about nine months ago. He'd show up every day and sit on the veranda, sometimes all day long. He seemed to enjoy just watching people come and go. He intrigued me, so I started talking to him, and first thing I knew we were friends. I don't have any idea where he lives or what he used to do for a living, but you're right, I've become awfully attached to him. I always worry about him when I don't see him for a while.''

Craig flashed her a boyish grin. ''Well, I wouldn't worry about him too much, Audrey. He seems to come and go like a phantom. He'll show up again one of these days.''

''I hope so, Craig. I hope so.'' She smiled sheepishly. ''I also hope I haven't been taken in by a pair of old, sad eyes. The last time he was here I loaned him fifty dollars—money I could ill afford, I might add.''

''Boy, are you easy!''

''Probably. Well, if you see him, come and get me, okay?''

''Sure.''

''See you around, Craig.''

''Take care, Audrey.''

Audrey waved a greeting to the desk clerk as she swept through the lobby, past the cocktail lounge, the gift shop and the beauty parlor, to enter the Gold Circle Room, the most opulent of the Greenspoint's three restaurants. In the gleaming stainless-steel kitchen she found the young chef, Jacky Jordan, backing out of the industrial-size refrigerator.

''Good morning, Jacky.''

''Hi, Audrey. You look like a breath of spring. What brings you down so early in the day?''

''I'm here, like Paul Revere, to sound the alarm. The Benedicts are coming.''

''The Benedicts?''

''The people who own these hallowed halls. And actually there'll only be one.''

"They're ranchers, right? He probably eats well-done prime rib and drinks black coffee with his meals." A contemptuous look crossed Jacky's face.

Audrey laughed. "Just tell everyone to be on their toes. You may have dealings with the man, and you may not."

"They're always on their toes, but I'll give them a pep talk."

"Thanks, Jacky. By the way, you know Mrs. Marsten in two-twelve, don't you? Today's her birthday."

"Gotcha. One cake, coming up."

From the dining room Audrey made her way to the lounge for a short talk with the bartender, then one by one she conversed with the desk clerk, the people in the coffee shop, the bell captain and the housekeeping staff. Once she was sure that everyone had been contacted, she stepped into the elevator and went up to the third floor and the Durango Suite.

The suite was the Greenspoint at its grandest. Consisting of a parlor, two bedrooms and two baths, it was a study in subdued elegance and supreme comfort, designed for guests who were accustomed to the finest of everything. Not a luxurious detail had been overlooked. And, as Audrey had expected, it was spotless, at the ready, although the Durango was not heavily booked. Not many people, even wealthy ones, cared to fork over the astronomical sum the suite commanded.

Audrey made a slow, painstaking inspection of the place, noting with satisfaction the thick, oversize towels in both baths, the imported castile soap, the luxurious gold fixtures, the gleaming tile on the floors and around the sunken tubs. Back in the parlor she made a mental note to have the florist deliver fresh flowers right after lunch. And, of course Mr. Benedict would receive complimentary hors d'oeuvres and a bottle of wine in late afternoon, then fruit, croissants and coffee in the morning. She checked the sideboard in the dining room to make sure it was stocked with liquor and mixes. It was ironic, she thought, that the guests who could afford anything got all the free goodies.

Satisfied that not even a Benedict could find fault with these accommodations, she left and took the elevator down to the mezzanine and Peter's office. His expression still was as dark and gloomy as an approaching desert thunderstorm.

"Everything's ready, boss," she announced brightly.

"It had better be," Peter replied tersely, without glancing up from his desk.

IT WAS MIDAFTERNOON when word reached the executive offices that Mr. Benedict had arrived and was checking in. Peter, who had been waiting anxiously in Audrey's office, jumped to his feet and hurried to the door.

"Wait here!" he commanded over his shoulder as he disappeared into the corridor.

"I don't think I've ever seen Peter so uptight," Helen commented when he was gone. "Is this really that big a deal?"

"Who knows? Peter sure seems to think it is." Audrey continued checking the inventory one of the housekeepers had given her. She fully expected Peter to be tied up with their VIP guest for some time, so she was surprised when he returned to her office in less than twenty minutes. She could see that his meeting with Mr. Benedict hadn't done anything to brighten his mood. His brow was deeply furrowed.

"Well?" she demanded impatiently when Peter merely stood in front of her desk, silent and scowling. "Is our guest satisfied with the suite?"

"I have no idea. He didn't say a word about it."

Audrey shrugged. Perhaps to a Benedict the Durango Suite wasn't all that impressive. "Did he say anything about selling the hotel?"

"No."

Why was he being so confoundedly mysterious? "Peter, why are you making me drag this out of you? Did he give you any idea why he's here?"

Peter tugged on his chin and eyed her intently. "Yes, he did. That's what's so peculiar."

"Peculiar? If you ask me, you're the one who's acting peculiar. Why is the man here?"

"He wants to see you."

Audrey's eyes widened. "M-me?"

He nodded. "You."

"Peter, is this some kind of joke?"

"No joke. As a matter of fact, I got the distinct impression that the man's chief reason for being here is to see you."

"That's absurd. Why on earth would one of the Benedicts come here to see me?"

"I can't imagine. We shook hands, introduced ourselves, then right off the bat he asked me if my assistant's name was Audrey Hamilton. When I said yes, he asked if you were here. I told him you were, and he asked me to send you up right away."

Audrey glanced at Helen, whose eyes were wide with bewilderment, then back at Peter, who was staring at her in the strangest way. "That's all? He didn't say why he wants to see me?"

Peter shook his head. "What have you been up to, Audrey?"

"Nothing!" She affected a nonchalance she certainly didn't feel. "You know there's a reasonable explanation for this. Maybe he just wants to meet all the key staff. I've done nothing to make him single me out."

"You'd better get on up there," Peter said.

"Yes, of course," she mumbled. Squaring her shoulders and trying to ignore her suddenly nervous stomach, she hurriedly left the office and took an elevator to the third floor.

CHAPTER TWO

AUDREY'S FIRST IMPRESSION of the man who answered her knock was of height. She was five-six and wearing two-inch heels, yet he still towered over her, so she had to assume he was six feet or more. Then her dark eyes met his smoky gray ones, moved downward, and her next impression was of startlingly white teeth that contrasted sharply with tanned skin. When her gaze took in the entire countenance of craggy male features, her interest quickened into something that went far beyond normal curiosity.

Somehow she found her professional welcoming voice. "Mr. Benedict?" she inquired politely.

"I'm Boyd Benedict, yes."

He fit none of her preconceived notions about him. For one thing, since Helen had told her Boyd Benedict used to cut a wide social swath, Audrey had been expecting someone a bit older, someone approaching middle age. But this man was, she guessed, no more than six or seven years older than she and was undeniably handsome in a rugged sort of way.

A shock of dark brown, almost black hair topped his head, and his skin was very tanned. It was not the sort of tan that came from long hours by the pool, but rather the tan acquired from years of being in the outdoors. That was another surprise. Considering all the Benedicts' various enterprises, she had fully expected a businessman, but this man simply didn't look the part of an executive.

Laugh lines splayed out from the corners of his mouth and eyes. His features were sharply defined—piercing eyes, prominent nose, strong mouth, a slight cleft in the chin—and his physique was admirable—broad shoulders, trim waist and hips. He was wearing a cream-colored shirt, sleeves rolled to the elbows, and dark tan slacks that hugged well-shaped thighs. Both were of Western-cut. "Vital" and "virile" were the words that immediately popped into her head. Even without money and influence, Boyd Benedict would have attracted attention, especially female attention, wherever he went.

"I hear he's really something," Helen had said. She had heard right. Suddenly Audrey was very conscious of the way she herself looked. The tailored peach blouse and the simple off-white skirt had seemed quite all right when she had dressed that morning. Her hair had been swirled into a French twist, a hairdo she felt made her appear older, less ingenuous. Neat, feminine, businesslike—the image she tried to project on the job. Only now she felt like a drab wren and was absurdly wishing she looked more alluring.

Collecting her wits, she extended her hand and flashed her brightest smile. "I'm Audrey Hamilton, the assistant manager, Mr. Benedict. Did you want to see me?"

Then the most peculiar thing happened; Audrey was at a loss to explain it. The smile on his face faded abruptly, and his expression changed from one of idle curiosity to one of startled confusion. He glanced down at her outstretched hand, then took it briefly, furtively.

Boyd Benedict's eyes raked over her in a way that made her cringe inside. Men normally weren't indifferent to her, but Audrey didn't think she had ever been so thoroughly scrutinized. Nor did she think she had ever had a man react to her in such an odd way. His eyes asked questions she couldn't interpret. Suddenly her face felt very warm, her mouth dry, and she experienced a brief wild urge to run from him. Inexplicably, she felt threatened.

But her years at the Greenspoint, dealing with the public and disguising her reactions to unpredictable human behavior, had instilled in her a poise that never completely abandoned her. "You wanted to see me, Mr. Benedict?" she inquired again.

He brought himself up to his full height. "Oh, yes, I did. Forgive my rudeness. I was staring, wasn't I? It's just that you're something of a surprise."

Audrey's heart lurched as the mystery deepened. He had known her name and her position at the hotel, but he easily could have acquired that information. The question was, why would he? And why had he, too, formed some preconceived notions? Why on earth would the prominent Mr. Benedict have given her a moment's thought?

Stepping back, Boyd made a wide sweep with his arm. "Yes, Miss Hamilton, I wanted to see you. Please come in."

Automatically, Audrey moved forward to stand in the center of the room, although some strange instinct was demanding she leave. She could feel the man's gray eyes beating through the back of her head.

Her own eyes darted about, making observations and seeking a safe place to rest.

The suite was decked out for a celebrity's arrival, and she supposed the man behind her fit into that category. The bouquet the florist had sent was extravagant, to say the least. A bottle of fine California Cabernet Sauvignon stood next to it. Inhaling deeply, Audrey slowly turned around to once again face Boyd Benedict's unsettling stare.

"What did you wish to see me about, Mr. Benedict? Are your accommodations satisfactory?"

"They're fine, just fine," he said in a way that suggested he'd barely noticed his elegant surroundings. "Please have a seat, Miss Hamilton." His voice was rich and low and carried authority.

Audrey would have preferred to remain standing, for she felt that being seated would somehow put her at a disadvantage. Nevertheless, she stiffly crossed the room and took a seat on the sofa, crossing her ankles and primly folding her hands in her lap. She swallowed rapidly several times, hating the way he made her feel. The poise she believed would never abandon her was dangerously close to doing just that.

I'm going to be fired, was her immediate thought. But that was ridiculous, and she knew it. One of the Benedicts wouldn't show up in person to fire an assistant manager. She waited with suspended breath.

Boyd walked purposefully to the dining table and opened a briefcase that was lying there. Withdrawing some papers, he propped a hip against the table and studied them for what seemed forever. The room was so quiet Audrey could hear the thump-thumping of her own heartbeat. Finally he looked up.

"How old are you, Miss Hamilton?"

"Twenty-seven."

"It is Miss, isn't it? You aren't wearing a ring, although not all women do."

"Yes, it's Miss." What on earth was all this?

"Have you ever been married?"

"No."

"How long have you been working here at the Greenspoint?"

"Three years." Audrey thought if he didn't get to the point of all this she might actually scream.

One dark eyebrow arched slightly. "And you're already the assistant manager?" His tone implied that she couldn't possibly have come by the position honestly.

Audrey clinched her teeth. "I...I have a friend who knows Peter. Three years ago he was looking for someone to fill in for his secretary, who was on maternity leave, and my friend recommended me. It was supposed to be a temporary job, but the secretary never returned, and Peter and I had discovered we worked well together. He eventually hired Helen Drake and promoted me."

Boyd digested that and seemed to accept it. 'And before that?"

Audrey's heart constricted. Dear God, was that what this was about—her past? How could Boyd Benedict know anything about that? "I spent a year and a half with an advertising agency," she said simply and prayed that would satisfy him.

Apparently it did. "All right, Miss Hamilton, now I'll tell you why I wanted to see you. I'm afraid I'm going to have to ask you a very personal question, and I expect a direct answer.''

The first bristle of indignation struck Audrey. The man was unbelievably abrasive. Being a Benedict didn't give him that right. ''Very well,'' she said stiffly and braced herself for whatever was coming.

''What exactly was your relationship with Bertram B. Benedict?''

Audrey blinked. ''Who?''

''Bertram B. Benedict. I'm sure the name is familiar to you.''

''No, Mr. Benedict, it isn't. I've never heard of the man.'' Relief engulfed her. This wasn't what she had feared at all.

''Come, come, Miss Hamilton, I was hoping you would be completely honest with me. It's vitally important that I know the exact nature of your relationship. Nothing can be served by lying to me.''

Audrey's face flushed crimson, but she forced herself to remain calm. ''I'm not lying, Mr. Benedict. I don't know anyone by that name. I would tell you if I did.''

Boyd uttered an impatient sound and slammed the papers down on the table. Glaring at her, he barked, ''Let's not play games! I'll find out the truth sooner or later.''

His tone was insufferable. Audrey didn't care who he was or how important his family was. She didn't even care that he could have her job in an instant. ''I'm not playing games!'' she exclaimed angrily. ''I don't know anyone named Bertram B. Benedict.''

''Miss Hamilton, I'm a very busy man. Coming here to see you has taken time I really couldn't afford, and I'm anxious to finish this business so I can go home. Now, please tell me what I want to know, and we can get this over and done with...."

"Get what over and done with?" Audrey's temples began to throb. "I don't have the slightest idea what you're talking about."

Boyd glowered at her. "I'm going to insist that you cooperate with me. It's imperative that I know all about your relationship with the man."

Audrey took a deep breath. There was plenty she would have liked to say to him, such as what he could do with his insistence, but yelling back and forth would accomplish nothing. He was being rude and overbearing, but she wasn't going to lose her composure. Boyd Benedict obviously had mistaken her for someone else, thank God, and she was certain they'd get the whole thing straightened out in a minute.

"You must have me confused with someone else, Mr. Benedict. Another Audrey Hamilton. It can't be an unusual name. I told you, I've never met Bertram B. Benedict. I'm sure I would remember if I had. Why would I lie to you?"

"I can't imagine," Boyd said tersely.

Audrey was becoming curious about Bertram. Who could he be? Probably a brother, cousin, nephew who'd gotten himself mixed up with a woman, a woman the lofty Benedicts didn't approve of. Seeing the grim expression on Boyd Benedict's face, she was relieved that she wasn't the Audrey Hamilton in question. She had a feeling that life could be unpleasant for anyone who got crosswise with the powerful family.

Boyd picked up the papers and brandished them at her. "Then possibly you can explain why a man you say you've never met would choose to mention you in his will."

Audrey's mouth dropped, and her eyes widened. "Will?" she asked incredulously. "Well, I...can't imagine. I'm sure there's been a mistake. It simply can't be me."

Boyd read from the paper. "Audrey Hamilton, currently employed as assistant manager, Greenspoint Hotel, Phoenix." He lifted his eyes. "Does that sound as though there's been a mistake?"

"No, I..." Audrey was certain she'd never been so confused. Her mind reeled and stumbled, but it was useless to try to sort and analyze what she had just heard. None of it made any sense. "I can't explain any of this, but you must believe me, I've never met anyone by that name. I would know, wouldn't I? Was he..." She faltered. "He must have been a relative of yours."

Boyd's eyes moved over her. Audrey clearly saw the suspicion in them and was at a loss to understand why he wouldn't believe her. Did she just look suspicious? He waited a moment before saying, "Yes, he was my grandfather."

"Oh, yes...I remember that a member of your family passed away recently. I sent flowers from the staff. There was a picture in the papers, but it certainly wasn't of anyone I've ever known."

"That photograph was taken fifteen years ago when my grandfather was still a very active, vigorous man. It bore little resemblance to the man he had become." Slowly, deliberately, Boyd placed the papers back on the table, folded his arms across his chest and leveled a look at her. Audrey stifled the urge to cringe. Instead, she met his gaze steadfastly.

"Let me tell you some things about my grandfather, Miss Hamilton. They just might jog your faulty memory." The bite of sarcasm was unmistakable. "He was eighty-one, was rather stooped and had thick white hair that he was careless about having cut. He often wore a beard. He had a gift of gab second to none, and his proudest possession was a railroad watch his father had given him—"

"Bert!" Audrey cried. The description fit her elderly friend to a T.

"So!" Boyd said with satisfaction. "You admit knowing him. Perhaps now you'll tell me the nature of the relationship."

"I...I know a man named Bert who fits that description. He comes to sit in a rocking chair on the veranda, and we talk. I've always felt sorry for him because he seems so lonely. I thought...honestly I thought he didn't have a family."

Abruptly she stopped as the full realization hit her. "Oh, if Bert's your grandfather...he's dead!" She placed her hand on her forehead. "For days now I've wondered what had happened to him. He'd stayed away so long this time."

"He'd lived with a bad heart for years."

"I...didn't know that." Her eyes grew misty. "He didn't talk about the present. He liked to reminisce about the way things were when he was young."

Boyd stared down at her bent head. "Are you asking me to believe that you didn't know who he was?"

"Yes, because it's true! How was I to know? He told me his name was Bert Lincoln, and I didn't question that any more than I question that you're Boyd Benedict.'' The man could go to hell! All Audrey could think of was her old friend, the sweet, lonely man who was dead.

"He was called Bert, all right, but Lincoln was my grandmother's maiden name.''

Boyd stepped back, shaken by the young woman's distress. Shoving his hands in his pockets, he walked to the window. None of this was working out the way he had envisioned. Audrey Hamilton had turned out to be a surprise, and that was an understatement. Ever since the reading of the will, a document that had been drafted less than a week before his grandfather's death, Boyd and his father had speculated on what the Hamilton woman would be like. Buck Benedict, in his characteristically cynical fashion, had expected a worldly sophisticate with a dollar sign for a heart. Boyd, on the other hand, had imagined an empty-headed bit of fluff whose feminine wiles had captivated the old man.

Well, they both had been wrong, and that put Boyd at a disadvantage. He thought he would have known how to deal with a gold digger or a flirt, but he wasn't prepared to deal with a lovely young woman who had genuinely cared for her friend Bert. She wasn't faking her grief. He'd never seen anyone more sincere. So now what did he do?

Sighing, Boyd took a moment to wish he weren't the one his father always sent to "put out fires." Why not Brent once in a while? His brother was all business. Brent could have dealt with Audrey Hamilton dispassionately.

He turned around to see Audrey flicking at her tears with a forefinger. From his hip pocket he removed a handkerchief, crossed the room and handed it to her.

"Th-thank you," she whispered.

Boyd cleared his throat. "How long had you known my grandfather?" he asked. Now his own curiosity was sharpened.

Audrey alertly noticed that the imperiousness had vanished from his voice, replaced by a husky, uncertain quality. "Less than a year," she said. "He simply showed up one day and sat on the veranda for hours, watching people come and go. Then the next day he was back, and the next. Finally I spoke to him, and we had a nice long chat. After that, I kept my eye out for him. Little by little we became friends. He seemed to be interested in my job, how I liked working here."

"And you never inquired about his background or his family?"

She shook her head, dabbing at her eyes. "I was content to just listen to him. He told me anecdotes about 'old' Arizona. And he liked to talk about his wife. Her name was Margaret. But, of course, you know that."

"Yes. My grandmother died two years ago. Granddad never got over it. He'd begun spending most of his time at our house in Paradise Valley, rather than at the ranch where the rest of the family lives. Too many memories, I guess."

"Weren't you worried about him, an old man living all alone like that?" Audrey asked with censure.

"Miss Hamilton, the Paradise Valley house is staffed by a full complement of servants who took care of my grandfather's every need and whim, and they included a chauffeur who was his constant companion. I'm positive that when Granddad was here at the hotel, Clarence wasn't far away. Besides, no one, I mean no one, told Bertram Benedict what he could and couldn't do. He must have taken to spending time here at the Greenspoint and, for reasons known only to him, chose not to tell anyone who he was. It wouldn't have been difficult for him to remain anonymous. It had been years since he'd appeared in public. He had lost quite a bit of weight, and that scruffy beard was an effective disguise.''

Audrey looked up at him through misty eyes. "Then you believe me? Honestly, I had no idea who he was. I thought he was just a lonely, impoverished old man."

"My grandfather was quite possibly the wealthiest man in Arizona."

Audrey shook her head, trying to equate the elderly man she had befriended with the patriarch of the state's most prominent family. But it was impossible. Bert had been such an unassuming person. "The last time I saw him I loaned him fifty dollars. I was afraid he wasn't eating right, and he never had any money on him."

Boyd had to smile at that. It sounded like the old man. His grandfather, for all his wealth, simply never had thought to tuck twenty dollars into his wallet. He hadn't even carried a wallet. In fact, there had been a standing joke among Bert's acquaintances: "If Bert asks you to lunch, be prepared to pick up the check."

"When I told him to spend it wisely because it was all I could afford to give him, he—" Audrey's voice broke with emotion ''—he said it would be returned to me tenfold. I assumed he meant in God's blessings or something like that.''

Boyd turned his head for a moment. *Great, just great!* he thought. *I really needed this.*

Silence descended. Then Audrey inquired, ''May I ask about the bequest? Did Bert happen to leave that railroad watch to me?''

''As a matter of fact, he did.''

She smiled sadly. ''I admired it once, and he said he would leave it to me someday. Imagine his actually remembering to do it.''

Then something occurred to her. If Boyd Benedict had taken the time and trouble to come to see her because of the bequest, the watch must have some family significance. ''If the watch is valuable, a family heirloom or something of that nature, I'll understand, of course. I wouldn't dream of accepting it under those circumstances.''

''No, the watch is yours.''

Audrey's shoulders rose and fell. She understood none of this. Earlier he had been so furious, so accusing. There was more to all this, she was sure of it. ''It was awfully nice of you to come here to tell me about this in person, but you're a very busy man, as you pointed out. Couldn't you have informed me of this by telephone?''

''Miss Hamilton, I'm here because my grandfather also bequeathed you something else.''

''Oh? What was it?''

Boyd inhaled deeply. He picked up the papers. Slowly his eyes skimmed over them. Then he read aloud the pertinent passages. ''To my friend, Audrey

Hamilton...I'm sure she'll know why...the sum of one hundred thousand dollars." Boyd quickly looked up at her. He wanted to monitor her reaction to the news.

CHAPTER THREE

FOR A MOMENT Audrey could only stare at him in stunned disbelief. She couldn't have heard correctly. Even if she had, it no doubt was some kind of joke, and a poor one at that. "Wh-what did you say?" she gasped.

Boyd relaxed. She had passed with flying colors. No actress, no matter how accomplished, could have played the scene with such sincerity. And he was at a loss to explain why that pleased him so much. It struck him suddenly that he must have been hoping she would turn out to be the real McCoy, and he didn't understand that, either. "You heard correctly. One hundred thousand dollars. Nice little sum, wouldn't you say?"

"You can't be serious!"

"Oh, I'm completely serious, I assure you. You'll be receiving official notification from our lawyers any day."

Audrey couldn't think. Her mind whirled with stupefaction. There was such an air of unreality to all this. "Well, I...I don't know what to say. I'm...just having such a hard time believing any of this. Why would Bert do such a thing?"

"Apparently he thought you would know why, and I was hoping you might be able to enlighten me."

Her hands nervously twisted the handkerchief. "I've told you everything I know. I felt sorry for him. He'd just sit there, like he didn't have a soul in the world."

"I'm surprised someone didn't ask him to leave. This hotel is a pretty classy place. Why let a scruffy old man loiter around?"

"Someone mentioned it to Peter once, but I intervened. After all, Bert did no harm."

"I can't help wondering why you singled him out, one old man among many."

Audrey's head jerked up, and she looked at him with cold unflinching eyes. He was still suspicious, damn him. "Not one among many, Mr. Benedict," she snapped. "The only one on the veranda who was all alone. That's why I singled him out."

To Boyd her explanation was like a slap in the face. Unnerved by her cold regard, he walked to the window, paused a moment, then turned suddenly and said, "Miss Hamilton, I have to make a phone call. I'd like you to wait right here while I go in the bedroom and place it. Will you do that for me?"

Why should I? was her first thought, but she was weary of their sparring, and there was still so much to be cleared up. "All right," she mumbled.

"Thanks. This shouldn't take but a few minutes."

Audrey stared after his retreating figure, certain she knew the reason for the call. He would be checking in with the rest of his family, waiting for further instructions. She imagined that all really prominent families operated that way. She further suspected that the Benedicts didn't like outsiders, even innocent, unwilling ones, intruding into their lives. What must they have thought when they learned that Bert had left an unknown woman such an incredible sum?

Although the bedroom door was closed, she could hear the sound of Boyd's voice. She couldn't make out any of the words, but her ears burned anyway. Oh, Lord, the last thing she wanted was trouble—she'd had enough of that, thank you—and somehow she felt that getting involved with the Benedicts would lead to trouble beyond her wildest imagination.

INSIDE THE BEDROOM, Boyd sat on the edge of the bed, phone to his ear, and listened to his father.

"What's the woman like?" Buck Benedict demanded.

"Young, pretty, intelligent. Not at all what we were expecting."

"God a'mighty, what was Dad thinking of? What was the relationship?"

"Friends. Just friends."

Buck scoffed. "The hell!"

"No, Dad, I believe her. She's the genuine article. She didn't have any idea who Granddad was, and she's thunderstruck over the inheritance."

"Just how pretty is this woman anyway?"

Boyd swallowed his irritation. "I haven't been taken in by a lovely charmer, if that's what you're thinking. The Hamilton woman thought he was just a lonely old man."

"How the hell did she meet him?"

"Get this—he used to show up here at the hotel and rock on the veranda all day."

"Dad?"

"Uh-huh. She befriended him. She—" Boyd paused to chuckle "—she once loaned him fifty dollars. You know how that would have touched Granddad."

"Damned if she didn't get a good return on her money!"

"Whatever his reason for leaving her all that money, he apparently wanted her to have it."

"It's not the money," Buck growled. "I don't give a damn about the money! Hell, Dad left ten thousand to that bellhop in Flagstaff. But a hundred grand? The newspapers are going to have a field day with this."

Boyd rubbed his chin thoughtfully. "I don't suppose there's any way of keeping it quiet."

"No, there isn't. We don't need this kind of notoriety! Lonely old man wiling away his dotage on a hotel veranda, grateful for the kind attentions of a sweet young thing, leaves her a bundle. Everyone will think we neglected him, or that Dad had become senile. Dammit, he was a force to be reckoned with in this state for half a century, and that's the way I want him to be remembered." A pause followed, then Buck spoke urgently. "Listen to me, Boyd, I don't want that woman talking to reporters or anyone else, do you hear me?"

Boyd frowned. "And just how am I supposed to prevent it?"

"Don't let her out of your sight. I mean it. Don't let her talk to anyone, not anyone. And first thing in the morning you bring her down here where we can keep an eye on her. I want her under this roof until the threat of scandal blows over."

"Come on, Dad, this isn't a good time to have to play watchdog. Roundup starts next week, and we're all going to be busy as hell."

"I don't care. I want her here."

Boyd's breath made a whistling sound through his teeth. "Dad, you're not dealing with a docile child. Audrey Hamilton is a grown woman, and I don't think she's going to take kindly to being ordered around. I can't bind and gag her and drag her to the Triple B."

"You can if that's the only way to get her here," Buck bellowed. "She'll damned well come. You might remind her that she's going to be pretty well off thanks to this family, so she owes us something. I don't care how you get her here, just do it!"

Boyd knew better than anyone how useless it was to argue with Buck Benedict. "I'll see what I can do," he said resignedly.

"Find out about her family. With our lousy luck she'll have kinfolks in every nook and cranny of the state, and they'll all show up with their hands out. Get her here, Boyd! And remember, don't let her out of your sight until you do."

"Am I supposed to sleep with her?" Boyd asked facetiously.

"If you have to." And there wasn't a trace of face-tiousness in Buck's voice.

AUDREY LOOKED UP when the door to the bedroom opened and Boyd reappeared. His mouth was set determinedly, but otherwise she couldn't read anything in his expression. During his absence she had thought and thought about the situation and had decided the money wasn't worth a big flap. That was the last thing she wanted. If it came down to a court battle... She shuddered just thinking about it. So when he stepped into the room she took the initiative.

"Mr. Benedict, I can well understand that your family wouldn't want me to have that money, and I can't really blame them. If you're worried that I'll cause trouble over it..."

Boyd silenced her with a wave of his hand. "The money was my grandfather's to do with as he pleased. Take it and have a good time."

A good time? She would have money again, be financially secure... again! But now she really was perplexed. "Then I don't understand why you're here. Couldn't your lawyers have handled all this?"

In an instant Boyd decided how he would deal with Audrey Hamilton—with the truth, not only the truth about what he wanted her to do but why he wanted her to do it. Gut instinct told him it was the best way. He was a good judge of people, and she was no fool.

He crossed the room and took a seat beside her. Gently touching her on the arm, he said, "Miss Hamilton... ah, may I call you Audrey?"

Audrey stiffened. The touch of his hand sent a sensation like an electric shock through her. He was so close she could feel warmth emanating from his body, and her nostrils were assailed by the citrus tang of his after-shave. His head bent closer to her, and she set herself on guard. "I... wish you would."

"Audrey," he began earnestly, his voice turning warm and confidential. "It's imperative that you tell no one about this inheritance."

"All right, I won't."

"So imperative, in fact, that my father wants you to come to our ranch with me and remain there until this blows over."

"What?" she cried incredulously. "That's ridiculous! I can't do it. I have my job, and—"

"I'm sure that once I explain this to Peter he'll be more than happy to give you the time off."

Oh, Audrey was sure of it, too. Peter would go along with anything the Benedicts wanted. "Aren't you making too much of this? I promise I won't say anything to anyone. I'm a very private person, and I don't do much socializing. I'd rather not go."

"Our ranch is a delightful place, Audrey, but it's remote and the one place where we can regulate who comes and goes. Actually, I'd think you would welcome the chance to get away from here. Confronting those vultures from the press can be a grueling ordeal for the uninitiated."

Audrey almost choked. "The press?" she asked, horrified.

He nodded solemnly. "Once the news of this inheritance hits the newspapers, as it will any moment, everyone will want a statement from you. Unfortunately, we Benedicts are the source of endless gossip. This bequest is going to make colorful copy. You'll be bombarded day and night."

A sinking sensation hit Audrey's stomach. Oh, God—the chaos, the notoriety, the cameras and reporters. Hopefully he was exaggerating. "Is Bert's will really that newsworthy?"

"A dozen or so years ago my grandfather was listed as one of the three most newsworthy men in Arizona.

The other two, as I recall, were the governor and Barry Goldwater."

"Just leave me alone," she implored, her voice almost a whisper. "I won't say anything to anyone."

"I'm sure you mean that, Audrey, but a skilled reporter could force you to say things you had no intention of saying."

She was such a spirited filly that Boyd was expecting a flat refusal, but he alertly noticed that his last remark had struck some kind of responsive chord, so he quickly pressed his advantage. "And it won't only be the press who'll hound you. Long-lost friends will pop out of the woodwork. Every imaginable investment scheme will be offered to you. You'll be besieged with requests for donations."

Nothing he could have said would have made a greater impact on Audrey. How on earth had she gotten involved in this? Why hadn't Bert considered all the ramifications when he wrote that will? But, of course, he hadn't known anything about her life before she'd come to the Greenspoint. Once again she felt herself being swept into a tangle of circumstances she couldn't control. "How...how long would I have to stay at your ranch?" she inquired hesitantly.

Boyd smiled. That had been incredibly easy. "It's hard to say at this point. A week or two. The public's attention span tends to be short. This won't be news long."

"But I can't leave my job for two weeks! There's a big convention coming up, and it's my responsibility."

"You might want to give some fresh thought to your job's importance in your life. Thanks to my grandfather, you'll soon be financially comfortable."

"I . . . I guess I will," she said vaguely. "It's all so unreal."

Boyd pressed on. "I dislike putting it this way, but I think you owe us one small favor. All we're asking is that you enjoy our hospitality for a short time, then you can be on your way with the means to do whatever you want."

Audrey sighed. She wanted to refuse to go along with the Benedicts and be done with it. She had become accustomed to controlling her life. For three years now she had been the one in charge, the one who had made decisions, and she cherished her independence and freedom more than anything. They had been hard-won.

On the other hand, she needed the sanctuary the Benedicts were affording her. She wanted all this to pass over as quickly and quietly as possible. She didn't want to cause the family any problems, for Bert's sake, and she certainly didn't want media attention focused on her.

Besides, in a more pragmatic vein, she had a feeling Boyd wouldn't leave the Greenspoint without her. "All right, Mr. Benedict. Provided it won't jeopardize my job here in any way, I'll go to your ranch with you."

Boyd got to his feet, rubbing his hands together with satisfaction. "Good! We'll leave first thing in the morning. It's too far to turn around and drive back now. Is there anyone who'll be worried about you if you're gone for a week or two?"

She shook her head.

"No parents?"

"No."

"Brothers, sisters, aunts, cousins?"

"No."

"Almost everyone has someone," he persisted.

"I don't." No one but Aunt Martha in Houston, and she'd prefer cuddling up with a colony of lepers to admitting she was kin to a Hamilton.

"A man then?"

"No."

"That seems unusual. A woman your age who looks like you do would reasonably be expected to have a man in her life."

Audrey accepted that as a compliment. "Naturally I date several men, but none is special. And even if one of them calls for me, he won't think it the least unusual for me not to be here. I sometimes work odd hours, and I travel around the state on occasion."

Boyd could hardly believe their good fortune. She was as unattached as it was possible for a person to be. "All right now, Audrey, I'll have to fill Peter in on all this. He'll have to know where you'll be, but he's the only one who will. Then we'll go to your place so you can pack. No need to make a production of that. If you find you want or need something you don't have with you, someone will be glad to go into town and get it for you."

Audrey was quick to note he didn't say *she* could go into town and get it. Apparently she was going to be held under close surveillance. They would be surprised to discover how cooperative she was going to be. "Can't I pack tonight, since we aren't leaving until morning?"

"No, you'll pack and come back here with me. You'll be staying here tonight."

"You mean here in the hotel?"

"I mean here in this suite with me."

Audrey gasped. "Oh, really! I can't stay here with you."

He silenced her with an inscrutable look. "You can and will. This suite has two bedrooms, Audrey. I assure you I have nothing improper in mind. My father's instructions were not to let you out of my sight until I've deposited you safely at the Triple B, and that's the way it's going to be."

"Do you always do exactly what your father wants?"

"Just about. Do you live far from here?"

Resigned to the incredible turn of events, Audrey acquiesced quietly. "No, not far at all."

"Good. Can we take your car? I flew to Phoenix and am without transportation."

"Of course. Will we be taking my car to the ranch?"

"I hadn't thought about it. Do you want to?"

"It might be a good idea. That way, when it's time for me to come back, I can just leave, without troubling anyone for a ride."

"I don't see anything wrong with that." Boyd went to the telephone and dialed an in-house number. A few seconds passed, then he said, "Peter, this is Boyd Benedict. Can you come up to my suite right away? There's something important I need to discuss with you. Yes, right away. Thanks."

He replaced the receiver and turned to Audrey with the air of a man whose mission had been accomplished. "Wipe that worried frown off your face, Audrey. Fate seems to have thrown us together for a while, so we might as well become friends and enjoy it. Won't you please call me Boyd?"

Enjoy it? Warning lights were flashing in her head. Five years ago, when her serene, comfortable life had started coming apart at the seams, she had somehow coped. Now, however, a nagging inner sensation told her that this startling involvement with the Benedicts was going to tax her ability to cope to the limit.

CHAPTER FOUR

TWO HOURS LATER Audrey was edgy and restless, ready to jump out of her skin. She often had yearned to stay in the Durango Suite, to be surrounded by its luxury and remember what it felt like to belong in such a place. Now she realized it could be just as boring as any other hotel room if you were stuck in it.

And stuck she was. Boyd didn't intend letting her out of his sight, and he had work to do. The moment they had returned from her apartment he had opened his briefcase, spread papers all over the dining table, placed a calculator beside his right hand and set the telephone nearby. And his head had been bent in concentration ever since.

Audrey had learned to enjoy solitude, and welcomed it most of the time, but this enforced confinement had her feeling jittery. She wandered from room to room, then kicked off her shoes, stretched out on the sofa and tried to lose herself in the paperback novel she had grabbed as they left her apartment. Twenty minutes later she gave up and put it aside. Settling back against the sofa cushions, she kicked off her shoes, tucked her feet under her and gave in to her thoughts.

Peter had been just as cooperative as she'd known he would be. He was stunned to hear of her inheritance but relieved that the hotel wasn't changing hands. Naturally he'd insisted that Audrey do whatever the Benedicts wanted. Sworn to secrecy, he had been instructed to tell anyone who asked for her that she was on vacation and couldn't be reached. Helen would know better, of course, and Audrey wondered if Peter would confide in the secretary. Probably not, she decided. Helen had an incurably loose tongue, and Peter was aware of it.

Her eyes strayed across the room to Boyd, seated at the dining table. Now that the day's shocks had subsided somewhat, Audrey was concentrating more of her interest on the man who had entered her life so abruptly and dramatically. Even though he had accompanied her to and from her apartment, she knew very little about him. His conversation had focused entirely on the weather and how Phoenix had grown. He was, she noticed, marvelously adept at not talking about himself.

She wondered if he was married. Probably. He was, roughly, thirty-four or -five, and most men that age were married. Of course, he might be divorced.

A woman couldn't fail to notice him. He was splendidly male and not nearly as formidable as he had seemed at first. He was also brimful of self-confidence, but she supposed that went with the territory. A member of the illustrious Benedict clan would hardly be shy and unassuming.

She wondered if he had any children.

She had made a few close-up observations of him. His eyes were very expressive and candid, without deviousness. She usually admired people whose emotions were open. Plus, Boyd Benedict was one fine-

looking man, and she was no more immune to that
than any other woman. She'd be willing to wager every
cent in her savings account that he knew exactly how
attractive he was and wasn't above using it to his advantage.

Thinking of her meager savings account brought
money to mind, which in turn reminded her of her
changed circumstances. It wasn't entirely real to her,
not yet, but little by little it was dawning on her that
life, if she so desired, could be very different from now
on. She, who for three years had existed from paycheck to paycheck, could once again buy all sorts of
luxuries. No, it wasn't real. Not yet.

She glanced at her watch, then back to Boyd, who
was still working. Didn't he know what time it was?
Her stomach was reminding her that it had been a long
time since lunch, and the salad she had eaten. Slipping on her shoes, she got to her feet, walked to the
window and looked down. Waiters were setting up
trestle tables on the loggia beside the pool, and some
delicious aromas were beginning to waft upward as
trays of food were brought out. Audrey swallowed and
ran her tongue across her lips.

Just then Boyd laid down his pencil, rubbed his eyes
tiredly and stretched his arms high above his head,
flexing his shoulder muscles. Audrey turned at the
sound of rustling movements. "All finished?" she
asked hopefully.

He swiveled his head. "Um-hmm. Sorry it took so
long."

"What are you doing?"

"Paperwork. There's an astonishing amount of it associated with running a ranch the size of the Triple B."

"Triple B," she mused. "I have to assume that has something to do with the family name."

"Right. The first Benedict to move out to public lands was Bernard B. Benedict of Pennsylvania. The offspring have had triple-B names hung on them ever since. Corny as hell, right?"

"I guess most family traditions are sort of corny, in a nice way. So, you're Boyd B. Benedict."

"Yep."

"What does the B stand for?"

"Nothing. None of the middle B's stands for anything."

She indicated all the papers spread out on the table. "Why don't you get a computer?"

"Oh, we have several of them, but I don't happen to have one with me." He looked at his watch. "I had no idea it was so late. Bored?"

"A little," she admitted.

"I haven't been very good company."

"I didn't expect you to keep me entertained. As you pointed out, you had to take time you could ill afford."

Boyd winced. "I guess I said that. Pompous ass, huh? Tell you what, Audrey. I'll clear away this mess, take a shower, then we'll have a few drinks, and I'll have dinner sent up. How does that sound?"

"Must we stay cooped up in here? There's a Polynesian buffet on the loggia tonight. Can't we go down to it?"

He gave it some consideration. "Nope," he finally said. "Better not. Dad wants you kept under lock and key."

On second thought, Audrey decided that being kept under lock and key was safer.

"If it's the buffet you want, I'll call downstairs and have them send up enough for two," Boyd offered. "How's that?"

Audrey turned from the window, shrugging nonchalantly. "If it eases your mind, have dinner sent up. I'm going to take a bath."

Boyd wrapped an arm around the back of the chair, propped his chin on it and watched her leave the room. With masculine approval, he noticed the movement of her trim hips beneath the off-white skirt, the scissoring motions of her shapely legs. He liked the proud, erect way she held her head. In fact, he admitted there was a great deal about Audrey he liked.

Yet there was something about her, something he couldn't quite put his finger on. She'd seemed nervous from the beginning, which wasn't surprising, but her nervousness had intensified when he'd begun asking questions about her past. He'd dropped the questioning, since what she'd done before coming to the Greenspoint wasn't pertinent. Still, it made him wonder.

And she'd been totally against going to the ranch with him until he'd mentioned newspapers, reporters, the media. Then she'd grabbed the idea like a lifeline. But there wasn't anything particularly suspicious about that. Media attention scared the dickens out of most people, and Audrey had described herself as a private person.

His mind exploded with questions about her, and he hoped they would be answered before the evening was over. Normally he was pretty good at gleaning a lot of information from a person's face and mannerisms, but he hadn't figured out Audrey. Nor had he figured out why she unsettled him so. From the moment she'd first stepped into the suite, his equilibrium had been in a curiously unbalanced state, and he was filled with a knifelike awareness of her every second she was near. He was quite certain nothing remotely like this had ever happened to him before.

It was strange. He'd been every bit as annoyed as the others over his grandfather's will, a fact that had nothing to do with the money. Rather, it was a disturbance, and the Benedicts didn't kindly tolerate disturbances in their lives.

He had been even more annoyed when his father had summoned him into his august presence and ordered him to "get to Phoenix, find that Hamilton woman and get to the bottom of this." It had seemed to Boyd that the platoon of fancy lawyers they kept on the payroll should have handled it. There were dozens of things he would have preferred doing.

But now he was glad he had come. Audrey bothered him, but she intrigued him more. He didn't entirely trust her, though she had passed all the tests. There was an air of mystery about her, and he usually didn't like mysterious women. Still, he was filled with the sure knowledge that meeting Audrey Hamilton wasn't something he soon would forget.

AUDREY SANK DEEPER into the warm comfort of the perfumed bathwater and reflected on how easily one could adapt to luxury. It was adapting to a lower standard of living that tested a person's mettle.

She could hear the sound of the shower in the bathroom next door and Boyd's slightly off-key baritone rising above it. That created an air of intimacy that she found nerve-racking, though she smiled as she listened. He was no great shakes as a singer, but his voice was strong, lusty and confident, like the man himself. What was there about the sound of rushing water that made a man want to burst into song? She recalled that all her father had to do was step under a shower's spray to turn into a poor man's Pavarotti.

She gave herself a shake. She wanted no memories of her father.

The shower next door stopped and so did the singing. Audrey envisioned Boyd reaching for a towel, pulling it back and forth over those admirable shoulders, then down his back to his attractive male derriere. His chest, she decided, would be smooth and as bronze as his arms. There might be a few tufts of dark chest hair that would taper in a thin line down to his waist and below.

Warmth diffused Audrey's face. She reached for a washcloth, soaped it and scrubbed vigorously. The action effectively dispelled the appalling stirrings inside her. How could she spend even a minute thinking of Boyd Benedict as a desirable man? Their paths were destined to cross only briefly, and she suspected that any woman who had the bad sense to get emotional about him would live to regret it.

Good Lord, I don't even know if he's single!

She stayed in the tub until the water cooled. After drying, she wrapped the towel around her sarong-fashion, applied her makeup and went into the bathroom to dress. She reached for a rose-colored sundress. It was an exquisite garment with a halter top, obi sash and full skirt, a dress she hadn't worn in years. Swirling her hair up again, she slipped her feet into low-heeled sandals and gave her reflection in the mirror a cursory glance. Then she left the bedroom and returned to the parlor.

During her absence one of the night staff had brought a tray of fruit and cheese and placed it on the dining table. She was nibbling on a slice of kiwi when she became aware of the heady masculine aroma she was beginning to associate with Boyd. Turning, she discovered she was staring at the broad expanse of his chest. The two-inch heels she had worn earlier made quite a difference; now she felt dwarfed by him.

"Don't you look nice," he said. "That color's great on you."

"Thanks."

"Shall we have a drink?"

"I guess so. Some of the wine would be nice."

"Only wine? Wouldn't you like something stronger? There's an impressive array of complimentary booze in the sideboard."

"No, thanks. Wine is fine. I'm not accustomed to much alcohol."

While Boyd poured their drinks, Audrey took a seat on the sofa and studied him at leisure. He was wearing a pearl-gray shirt, open at the throat and tucked into the waistband of darker gray slacks. He wore his clothes well, she noted, and the color of the clothing emphasized the smoky hue of his eyes. His hair was still damp from the shower, its curl more pronounced, especially at the back of his neck. In all her life Audrey didn't think she had seen a more attractive man.

He brought their drinks and took a seat beside her on the sofa. "Do you have medical or moral objections to alcohol?" he asked.

"Not at all. Wine is also alcohol. I guess I drank my share of liquor in college, beer busts and all. But frankly, it's expensive, and we working women have to watch those hard-earned dollars."

Boyd sipped his drink and tried to study her without being too obvious. She somehow didn't fit his image of a penny-pinching working woman. The dress she was wearing, for instance. It looked expensive, and it didn't seem to him that a working woman who wouldn't spend money on alcohol would fork over eighty or ninety dollars for a dress like that. Working women bought sensible clothes that could do double duty, didn't they?

You're a suspicious bastard, Benedict, he thought. That dress would look perfect at a Polynesian buffet on the loggia. Maybe she needed things like that to wear to some of the hotel's activities. Her clothing requirements probably differed from those of a secretary or accountant.

"Well, you're probably fortunate not to get tied up with the stuff," he said. "During my late teens and early twenties, alcohol was far too closely associated with recreation."

"How's that?"

"During those years I worked on the ranch when I wasn't in school, and more than anything I wanted to be accepted by the real cowboys, the pros. So that meant going into town on weekends, getting tanked up on beer and winding up in . . . er, altercations."

"Fistfights? Good heavens, why?"

"Beats me," he said with a lazy chuckle. "I guess we thought we were supposed to, that it was expected of us. It was part of the mystique of being a cowboy. It also was exhausting."

"But . . . who did you fight?"

He grinned charmingly. "Anybody we didn't know."

Audrey laughed. Boyd took a hefty swallow of his drink while she sipped daintily at her wine. Then he turned and lavished a smile on her that could have melted an igloo. "I don't want to talk about me. Let's talk about you. I don't know much about your background. You're twenty-seven, never been married, have no family. Where's home originally?"

"Texas," she said.

He noticed she averted her eyes briefly. "That takes in a lot of territory. Where in Texas?"

"Dallas."

Maybe, he thought. Maybe not. Dallas was a convenient answer. But she had come up with it quickly, so it probably was true. Why did suspicions persist that had nothing whatsoever to do with his grandfather? Audrey was one of the loveliest women he had ever met. Why not enjoy that, come on to her strong and see what happened? "Nice place. Ever go to the Astrodome?"

She leveled a tolerant look on him. "The Astrodome's in Houston, as I'm sure you know. Yes, I've been there many times, but more frequently to places like Texas Stadium, Reunion Tower and the State Fairgrounds, which are in Dallas.''

Again she had given him an answer that made him feel apologetic. "Sorry, Audrey, I get Dallas and Houston confused. And I have this affliction: I'm terribly curious about people, so I ask a lot of questions. Sometimes I come across like an investigative reporter.''

"Or a district attorney," she added and immediately wanted to bite her tongue. Her insides churned with agitation. That dumb question about the Astrodome—why? Why was he testing her? He didn't seem to have any qualms about the inheritance; that and their employer-employee relationship were their only common denominators. He was looking at her in the strangest way, peering deeply inside her—too deeply.

"What brought you to Phoenix in the first place?''

"An invitation from a friend, the friend who knows Peter. Once the job here came along, I stayed.''

"You never went back to Dallas?''

"No.''

"That seems odd.''

"Does it? There simply was nothing left for me in Dallas, that's all.''

"Is your friend still here in Phoenix?''

"No, her husband was transferred. They live in Seattle now.'' *So there's no one here in Phoenix who can tell you a thing about my past,* she thought with relieved satisfaction. It was time to get off the subject. "Tell me about your family, Boyd," she urged. "They're into things other than ranching, right?''

He took the hint. The lady didn't like talking about the past. But she had no family, so perhaps there was some tragedy in her background, something too painful to recall. "Yes," he said, "and sometimes all those other things overshadow the ranching. My dad considers himself first and foremost a businessman, and he's been chiefly responsible for our diversification. Granddad, on the other hand, called himself a cowboy and professed to have no interest in the other things. My brother Brent is a businessman, too. He runs the office in Tucson."

"And what are you?" she probed. "Cowboy or businessman?"

"A little of both, I guess. But given the choice, both Betty and I would ranch exclusively."

"Betty?"

"My sister, the best cowhand the Triple B has. She majored in animal science at Arizona State, and she knows those cows inside and out."

Audrey raised her glass to her lips, took a sip of wine and then asked the question she'd been itching to ask. "Are you married?"

"No."

"Ever been married?"

"No. And that probably was the only real disappointment in Granddad's life. He thought I should have married years ago. I suffered through several of his clumsy attempts at matchmaking before he gave up on me."

"He was a darling man," Audrey mused.

"He was a firebrand in his heyday. But, of course, you wouldn't have seen that side of him. I was terrified of him when I was a kid. Later, he became my hero."

They sipped their drinks in silence for a moment, then Audrey asked, "Why haven't you been to the Greenspoint before?"

"As long as things are running smoothly, why interfere? We have plenty of problem spots that require constant attention."

"Peter does a good job."

"I admire loyalty to the boss."

"I'm completely sincere."

"I'm sure you are. Do you enjoy your work?"

"Yes, I do. Every day."

"Why?"

She gave some thought to her answer. "For one thing, this hotel feels aristocratic. Staying here is rather like visiting a wealthy relative who, for one reason or another, wants to pamper you outrageously. I don't mean just in this suite, but in every one of the rooms. We like to give our guests little extras...like turning down their beds at night, setting out candy and fresh flowers. Things like that pay off in return visits."

"Whose idea was that...the 'little extras'?"

"Peter's. Well...maybe one or two were mine. Like I said, we work well together."

Boyd drained his glass and got to his feet. "More wine?"

"No, thanks."

"Then I'll order dinner." He sauntered to the phone and placed the order, then walked to the sideboard and mixed himself another drink. "What are your plans now?"

"Plans?"

"You'll soon have enough money to do anything you want. What are you going to do?"

"I don't know. I really haven't had time to think about it. I might not 'do' anything, just stay here and enjoy my job."

She heard the plop-plop of ice cubes, then he was walking toward her, sitting down beside her, again too close. The scent of him was wonderful. "Now, that surprises me. It seems to me that anyone who'd just received an unexpected windfall would have dozens of things to spend it on—travel, a new car, something."

Audrey stared down into the almost empty goblet. Funny, last week she'd been fretting because her Datsun needed new tires. Now she could buy a new car, but why do that when the Datsun only had twenty thousand miles on it? She'd pay it off and live a payment-free life for a couple of years. She could get a larger apartment or make a down payment on a small condo, but she loved her little apartment. She'd simply fix it up. She could take a trip to someplace she'd never been, but there were few appealing places she hadn't been. She'd become so sensible and frugal in three years, and that pleased her. Learning to make ends meet had given her more self-confidence than anything she'd done in her life. "Oh," she said lightly, "I'm sure I'll find something to do with it."

"Yeah, money's easy to get rid of."

"I don't intend getting rid of it, not at all."

"Investments?"

"I'm too conservative for that. I'll put it in the bank and draw the interest."

"There are better returns on your money. You could build a hundred thousand into a tidy sum."

"I don't want a lot of money."

"You really are a different one, then. How do you know you don't want a lot of money?"

Audrey ignored her stomach's flip-flop. She mustered a smile. "I just know, that's all. I don't want anything that will complicate my life."

"And you think money would complicate it?"

"It might. You've seen my car and my apartment. Why would I want more than that?"

Boyd recalled her apartment—small, impeccably neat, very feminine and furnished with an eye for detail, though nothing in it looked expensive. While she packed he'd wandered around the living room and kitchen, looking for anything—photographs or something—that would give him further insight into the woman. There was nothing, not even a magazine addressed to her. "Then Granddad seems to have wasted the bequest."

She looked at him askance. "I beg your pardon."

"I'll bet he expected you to take the money and have a ball with it."

"I don't think so. I'll bet he wanted that money to take me into my old age."

"Why would a twenty-seven-year-old woman even think of her old age?"

A knock on the door heralded the arrival of their dinner and effectively terminated the conversation, much to Audrey's relief. He was trying so hard to get her to open up and tell him the story of her life. He wouldn't succeed. There wasn't a soul left on the face of the earth who really knew Audrey Hamilton. She allowed no one to get close to her.

Boyd got to his feet, started for the door, then stopped and looked back at Audrey. "Maybe you'd better go powder your nose or something."

Cocking her head, Audrey quizzed him with her eyes. "Our waiter might know you," he said, explaining his request. "Probably no harm in that, but we might as well play it safe. I'd prefer that no one sees us together."

"You don't overlook details, do you?"

"Hopefully, never."

Audrey rolled her eyes toward the ceiling, but nevertheless she went into her bedroom and stayed there until she heard Boyd call her name. When she returned to the parlor, he was inspecting the food-laden cart.

"You may have to help me with some of this stuff. My idea of food is beef and more beef."

Audrey would have bet on it. "Let's see...roast pork, yams, fried shrimp. And this is salmon marinated in lime juice, these are scallops, and those little crispy things are curry puffs. Everything's delicious, I promise." And in the end, she noticed, he sampled a little bit of everything.

Boyd was easy to talk to, so dinner passed pleasantly. She listened to him and watched him intently throughout the meal, putting in a word now and then and wondering what it was about him that inspired her usual interest. Oh, there was an attraction, all right, and it was based on more than his good looks. She'd met dozens of attractive men since coming to Arizona. The Greenspoint drew them like flies, all those suntanned Greek gods who played golf and tennis and lazed around the pool. Not one of them had aroused more than a brief flurry of interest in her. There was something distinctive about Boyd. The moment she'd laid eyes on him, before he'd given her that incredible news, she'd felt some sort of inner stirring, and she simply didn't react to strangers that way. It alarmed her that she had this time.

Boyd was asking her a question. "Pardon? I'm sorry, Boyd, what did you say?"

"I asked if you wanted more of the pork or shrimp or anything. They sent up enough food for six people."

Audrey glanced down at her plate. She had cleaned it but could scarcely remember actually eating. "Oh, no, thanks. I'm stuffed. Did you enjoy it?"

"Yes, I did. It was a nice change of pace."

"Jacky, he's our chef, does wonderfully authentic Polynesian dishes."

"Well, I'll take your word for tnat, since I wouldn't know the authentic from the bogus." Boyd pushed his plate away and got to his feet. "I'll just wheel all this out into the hall, and then we can get some fresh air on the terrace."

The suite's small terrace overlooked the pool below. It was later than Audrey had realized. The pool's lights had been extinguished, and the waiters were stripping the buffet tables. The hotel's grounds were as quiet as they ever got. From the terrace, they could look on beyond to the lights of nighttime Phoenix, a city that was growing, spreading, splitting its seams.

"I liked her better when I was a kid, some twenty years ago, before the snowbirds discovered her," Boyd commented.

"Then you've spent a lot of time in Phoenix?"

He nodded. "And in Flagstaff, and in Tucson, and in Prescott. We have interests all over."

This was said without a trace of conceit, nor was it said to impress her, Audrey instinctively knew. He'd merely made a statement of fact. Considering who he was, who his family was, Boyd was surprisingly unpretentious. She stood at the railing and felt him behind her. He casually placed a hand at the small of her back as he moved to stand beside her. It was a simple gesture that meant nothing, but some queer trick of nature was playing havoc with her erotic senses. Her pulses were pounding.

Then, in a surprising move, Boyd's hand moved from her waist to her nape. "Your hair's coming down," he drawled.

Audrey's fingers flew to her neck to touch the wayward tendrils. "Oh, when it's this clean I can never do anything with it." She could feel the hairdo slipping, so she reached up and deftly removed all the pins, and her hair fell to her shoulders.

"You should never wear it up," Boyd said huskily. "Hair like that should never be confined." He experienced an absurd urge to tell her she was the most beautiful woman he'd ever seen.

"I'm going to take that as a compliment."

"Good, because it was meant to be one."

"Thanks, then."

"You're welcome."

Somewhere in the back of Audrey's sensible mind lay the thought that the entire day had been a wonder. The man standing beside her—a man she hadn't known when she'd crawled out of bed that morning—was gazing at her in a most seductive way, with an air of familiarity that certainly didn't exist. A little thrill of excitement raced through her, and she had to look away.

This couldn't be. She wouldn't allow herself to be drawn to Boyd in any romantic sense. He was probably only having a little flirtatious fun with her anyway, or putting on an act designed to weaken her defenses and let him inside her head. It wouldn't work. There was a time in her life when she had taken people at face value, but her father and Jesse Murdoch had cured her of that. Now she was cautious, and she was going to put an end to this mood of near intimacy Boyd was trying to create.

She stepped back from the railing, away from him slightly, and clasped her hands in front of her. "I think I'll say good-night now, Boyd. It's been a long day."

An odd little half smile crossed his face. "So soon?"

"Yes, I...I've been up since six, and I'm really very tired."

"All right, Audrey. I don't see any need for an early departure tomorrow. It might be nice to sleep in for a change. Let's plan to make it to Tucson in time for lunch. That'll get us to the ranch by early afternoon. Are you sure you don't mind taking your car?"

"Not at all. See you in the morning."

"I'll have breakfast sent up. Good night, Audrey."

"Good night."

Boyd watched her leave and shook his head in bafflement. He, too, had sensed the intimate mood, but it was nothing he'd deliberately created. It was just there, an almost tangible presence between them.

By now he should have known far more about her than he did. He knew nothing, and he obviously wasn't going to get anywhere with Audrey by calling upon his well-practised masculine charm. She intrigued him, she worried him, she fascinated him. And he was going to find out what made her tick. Sooner or later he would find out all there was to know about Audrey Hamilton.

CHAPTER FIVE

AN HOUR OR SO down the highway that stretched from Tucson to the Mexican border, the Santa Cruz Valley dozed in the afternoon sun. Audrey had expected desert; instead she discovered a lovely grassy valley some four thousand feet above sea level. The brilliant sun splashed pink and purple shadows over the jagged mountains that rimmed the horizon. The heady fragrance of mesquite wood fires perfumed the air. The space and silence were awesome. She felt worlds removed from the bustling sunbelt cities to the north. Here roadrunners and deer darted undisturbed, cattle ambled lazily and horses grazed peacefully. The valley, she decided, would be the perfect place to hold the world at bay until Bert's will became stale news.

Audrey stole a sidelong glance at her traveling companion. Boyd had insisted on doing the driving, which had suited her fine. The trip had passed uneventfully, broken only by their stop for lunch in Tucson. She had spent more uninterrupted time with him during the past twenty-four hours than she had with anyone else in the past five years. Yet still he baffled her.

Yesterday he had been full of curiosity about her, but today he had been casual, disinterested, even remote. Not once during the trip had the conversation strayed toward the personal. She thought about last night's mood of intimacy and decided it had been a product of her imagination. The mood today had been anything but intimate. She was relieved, of course, but it was unexpected.

She studied him covertly. That morning when she'd emerged from her room, the sight of him had taken her by surprise. His expensive tailored clothes had been replaced by a faded blue shirt, scuffed boots and the most disreputable pair of jeans she had ever seen. They were worn almost white at the knees. When she had commented on the clothes, he had grinned and said, "This is the real me. Yesterday I was traveling incognito." Now he had added a battered straw cowboy hat that was in almost as bad condition as the jeans. He could have passed for any fifty-dollar-a-day cowboy she had ever known. Except Boyd was undeniably more attractive than most, and the scruffy clothes only enhanced his rugged good looks. She forcibly tore her gaze away from him and returned it to the landscape whizzing past the window.

Abruptly Boyd braked, slowed and turned off the highway onto a country road. A few miles down the deserted stretch he made another turn, driving over a cattle guard and under an iron arch whose lettering announced that this was the Triple B Land and Cattle Company. Audrey's attention was drawn to the sights ahead of her. The ranch headquarters was a cluster of buildings on the west side of the road. There were barns and corrals and sheds and all the other trappings of a modern cattle operation. The ranch house itself was a sprawling whitewashed adobe hacienda situated in a grove of trees.

"Why, it's absolutely beautiful!" she exclaimed.

"Thanks," Boyd said, "but you sound surprised."

"Not all ranches are pretty." Then, remembering that she wasn't supposed to be knowledgeable about ranches, she added, "I used to visit a dude ranch when I was a kid. It was beautiful, too, but that was all for show."

"Not here. This is a hardworking ranch, no frills. We like to do things the old-fashioned way: cowboys on horseback herding cows. I keep hearing that cattle raising is all specialized now, that the old traditions are gone and cowboying is a dying art. But the Triple B has been running cattle for a hundred years, and I can't see that changing anytime soon. The altitude, the climate, the soil—everything makes this part of the state ideal for cattle. And as for cowhands, there still are a few left, and some of them find their way here every year at roundup or branding time. Some of the same faces show up year after year."

"How big is the ranch?"

"Not as big as it used to be, but it's still respectable. About forty thousand acres—the biggest privately owned spread in these parts. The government owns about eighty-five percent of Arizona, you know, but my family has managed to hang onto this land since Geronimo's last stand. There's an Apache graveyard in the southern quadrant of the ranch."

Boyd swung the car into the circular driveway fronting the house. In the center of the yard a fountain bubbled cheerfully; beneath it stood huge pots filled with red and white geraniums. A pair of barking dogs heralded their arrival. Boyd parked alongside a tan pickup, just as a man in soiled khakis appeared and called to him in Spanish. Boyd answered in the same language, and Audrey noticed that his accent sounded perfect. "Jorge will see to your luggage," he said, turning to her. "Let's go inside and find Mom."

The interior of the Benedict house was a surprise. Audrey didn't know what she had expected, perhaps something more like the old ranch house in Texas—sturdy masculine furniture, steer heads and gun racks on the walls. This place was entirely different, as elegant in its way as the Greenspoint. There were arches and curved wood doors that emphasized the hacienda look, but Audrey took note of the magnificent Baccarat chandelier in the dining room to her left. And the living room on her right was furnished with splendid antiques.

Boyd motioned her to follow as he led the way down a hall to a capacious, sun-drenched room with floor-to-ceiling windows and chintz-covered furniture. Here the colors were bold and vivid; plants of every description abounded. Unlike the front rooms, the sun room had a beckoning warmth that proclaimed, "This is home!"

A woman was seated on the sofa in front of one of the windows, and she stood when they entered the room. Slender and silver-haired, she exuded an air of ultrafemininity, although she was dressed in tailored slacks and a plain white shirt. In some ways she reminded Audrey of her patrician mother. Without a doubt, this woman was responsible for the elegant decor. "Hello, darling, I'm glad you're back," she greeted Boyd.

"Mom, I'd like you to meet Audrey Hamilton. Audrey, this is my mother, Elizabeth Benedict."

"How do you do, Audrey. Welcome to our home."

"Thank you, Mrs. Benedict. It's such a lovely place."

"How nice of you to say so, my dear." Elizabeth then turned to her son. "Your father is at the Summerfield camp and left instructions for you to join him the minute you arrived."

Boyd nodded. "Just let me get Audrey settled in."

"Perhaps you should go now," Elizabeth said firmly. "You know how your father is. I can see Audrey settled into the guest room."

"Well...maybe you're right." Boyd glanced at Audrey apologetically. "I hate like the devil to run off and leave you."

"It doesn't matter," she said, though it did. "You just go do whatever it is you have to do."

"Have you had lunch?" Elizabeth inquired.

"Um-hmm. We stopped in Tucson. I'd best get moving if Dad wants me." He touched Audrey on the arm. "See you later."

He left the room. The heels of his boots beat out a staccato rhythm as he walked back down the hall, across the foyer and out the door. Foolishly, Audrey felt abandoned. Facing Boyd's mother, she managed a credible smile.

"Come, Audrey," Elizabeth said. "I'll show you to the guest room." And Audrey fell into step behind her.

The house was large and built in a U-shape around a central brick courtyard. All of the bedrooms opened onto it. As she followed Elizabeth down a long hall, Audrey paused to admire a group of portraits hanging on the wall. Seeing her interest, Elizabeth stopped to explain. "This is my husband, this is Bert, and the other is Bert's father. Pity we don't have one of the original Arizona Benedict. Someday Brent's and Boyd's portraits will hang here. Traditionally, the Benedict men have their portraits painted on their fiftieth birthday."

Audrey wondered why there were no portraits of the Benedict women but didn't ask. "Bert was such a distinguished-looking man," she commented, studying the picture of her friend. It bore little resemblance to the man she had known.

"Yes, he was in younger years. Formidable, too. I was frightened to death of him when I first came here as a bride. How long had you known him?"

"A little less than a year."

"Strange," Elizabeth murmured obscurely. "But then, Bert had become very unpredictable. We never knew what to expect from him. He changed a lot after Margaret died."

"I wish I could have known her. Bert talked about her constantly."

"She was a lovely woman, so gentle and refined. She and Bert presented quite a contrast. This way, Audrey."

She led the way to a room two doors down the hall. A four-poster bed dominated the guest room; over it hung a distinctive Navaho tapestry. A large brass urn holding a dried flower arrangement stood on the floor beside an upholstered wing chair, and several pieces of Native American pottery sat on top of the polished walnut dresser. The room, above all, looked comfortable and inviting.

"How charming!" Audrey exclaimed.

"I think you'll be comfortable in it," Elizabeth said. "There's a private bath over there."

"It's very nice. I hope I won't be imposing on your hospitality for long, Mrs. Benedict."

Elizabeth faced her squarely. "I suppose the length of your stay will depend on Buck. He's very adamant about this. We've all been instructed to say nothing to anyone about Bert's will. Sara and I thought it best to cancel several upcoming social engagements in order to avoid a barrage of questions."

"Sara?"

"My daughter-in-law, Brent's wife. You'll meet everyone tonight."

Audrey was acutely conscious of her awkward position in the household and felt she should apologize. "I'm awfully sorry for any inconvenience I've caused you."

Elizabeth brushed her comment aside with a wave of her delicate hand. "Don't fret over that, my dear. The important thing is to let Buck handle it as he sees fit. He'll take care of everything; he always does. Now, I'm afraid I'm going to have to leave you. I have an appointment at the hairdresser's in Agua Linda, and I'll have to rush to make it. I'm sure Betty will be along the minute she hears you've arrived. It's going to be nice for her to have a woman to talk to. She and Sara have so little in common." Boyd's mother then gave Audrey an appraising glance. "I wonder why my daughter doesn't look as feminine in jeans as you do. Betty's really an attractive girl and has a nice figure, but she always manages to look like she just slid off a horse. I suppose that's because she usually has. Well,

Audrey, please make yourself at home. Maria and Tina are always around, so if there's anything you want, feel free to ask one of them for it."

Audrey assumed that Maria and Tina were household domestics. "I'll be fine, Mrs. Benedict. Thank you for being so kind."

Elizabeth cast her eyes around the room before leaving and closing the door behind her. Audrey stared at the door a minute, then sank into the wing chair by the window. *Well, here I am,* she thought. What now? Elizabeth's gracious welcome hadn't eased her sense of discomfort. She felt like an intruder and fully expected the Benedicts to consider her one. There was no way she would feel at home in this house, and she prayed her stay would be of short duration. What in the world was she going to do for the remainder of the day? What about tomorrow and the day after that? The entire situation was ludicrous.

As she sat pondering her preposterous exile, there was a knock at the door. "Come in," Audrey called, and the door opened to admit two people. One was the man in khakis whom Boyd had referred to as Jorge. He carried her luggage. Setting the suitcases on the floor at the foot of the bed, he gave her a shy smile, mumbled something in Spanish, then hurried out of the room. The other was a young woman whom Audrey guessed to be in her early twenties. She was tanned, wholesomely pretty and wore her jeans and cowboy boots as though born to them.

"Hi, Audrey, I'm Betty Benedict."

Audrey brightened. "Boyd's sister."

"Ah, yes. Boyd's sister, Brent's sister, Buck's daughter. The story of my life." She crossed the room and sat on the edge of the bed, facing Audrey. "Mom's afraid you might be shy about asking for what you want at first. Don't be. This is a very informal household."

"Thanks, but I feel strange about being here, considering the circumstances."

"Yeah, I can imagine, but you'll get over that, I hope." Betty leaned back and propped herself on one elbow. Audrey noticed how much she favored Boyd. She was tall and slender and shared her brother's dark hair and smoke-colored eyes. And, also like Boyd, she had that easy friendliness that seemed inherent in people who live in open spaces and sunny climates. So far, the Benedicts she had met had been amazingly unpretentious, and she wondered if the rest of the clan would prove to be the same. If so, this stay might turn out to be a pleasant one.

"Frankly," Betty went on, "this whole business has been the most exciting thing that's happened around here in ages. How did you meet Granddad?"

Audrey's succinct account of her friendship with Bert amused Betty, who chortled delightedly. "Oh, can you beat that? I'll bet he got the biggest kick out of not letting anyone know who he was. There was a fey side to his sense of humor. He was my favorite person on earth. Granddad sometimes worked hard on that gruff exterior of his, but his heart was made of marshmallows." She looked at Audrey thoughtfully. "What did you think of Boyd?"

"Well...he's...nice."

"Really? If that's true, I'm glad. Sometimes he tends to come on like barbed wire, but that's because he has to work so hard at being a Benedict. And sometimes it is work, believe me. If the truth were known, Boyd would be happy spending the rest of his life right here and leaving all the other stuff to Dad and Brent, who seem to like the business and high finance end of it.'' Betty paused to chuckle. ''Boyd was mad as the devil when Dad sent him to Phoenix to find you and 'get to the bottom of this!' I'll bet he changed his mind fast when he saw you, though. Both of my brothers have always had an eye for pretty women.''

Audrey smiled, not only at the compliment but at Betty's frankness. ''Is Sara pretty?''

''Yeah, in a cool sort of way. She's from one of Tucson's toniest families, but, dear God, she loves being a Benedict! You'll see what I mean when you meet her. Sara's nice enough, but she's so upper crust she always makes me feel like a peasant. More my fault than hers, though. Well, Audrey, I can imagine you're not exactly thrilled over being here, so I guess it's up to me to see that you aren't bored to death. The Triple B is pretty much a man's world, so there's not a whole lot to do if you aren't involved with the cattle. That's one reason Mom and Sara are such social butterflies. Let's see . . . I could give you a tour of the ranch. That ought to kill some time.''

''That sounds great. But I don't want to keep you from anything you have to do.''

''You won't. There's nothing that absolutely, positively has to be done this afternoon. Do you ride?''

''I do, but I haven't in some time.''

Betty glanced at her watch. ''Well, maybe we ought to drive. We can cover more territory in less time.''

''My car's here. You're welcome to use it.''

However, when Betty saw the Datsun she frowned and said, "Some of these roads are pretty rough. We'd better take something a little sturdier."

The chosen vehicle was a midnight-blue Cadillac that Betty drove at a heart-stopping rate of speed. Audrey was thankful that her little car had been spared such punishing treatment. The ranch was crisscrossed by a network of roads, some hard-surfaced, some little more than dirt paths. To Audrey's horror, there was no perceptible difference in Betty's speed, regardless of the condition of the road.

The sights, sounds and smells of the ranch brought back both painful and happy memories. Though the Texas ranch had been mostly a hobby for her father, Audrey had loved it there. It was the aspect of her former life that she missed most of all. And the Triple B was no ordinary ranch; its sheer size was unbelievable. The Hamilton ranch had been perhaps a third as big, small enough that there had been landmarks everywhere. To Audrey's eyes, everything here looked like more and more of the same. "Do you ever get lost?" she asked.

"Shoot, no!" Betty replied. "I know every square foot of this ranch. I've never lived anywhere else, unless you count the dorm in college. Even then, I came home most weekends. I've just never been able to stay away for long."

"Is that why you're still here? I mean, most women your age would have left home by now, to get married, to get a job in the city or something."

"Ranching's the only thing I've ever done or wanted to do," Betty said simply. "I studied animal science at Arizona State."

"I know. Boyd told me."

"Did he now? What else did my brother tell you about me?"

"He said you're the best cowhand the Triple B has."

Betty looked enormously pleased, leading Audrey to suspect that what Boyd thought of her was important to the young woman. "Well, I'll be! He'd cut out his tongue before he'd tell me that. But he's right. I can work circles around any man on this place, and most of 'em know it. I can't imagine living any way but the way I live, and I can't stand a city for more than a day or two. I start feeling all closed in."

"Do you intend staying here forever? I thought you said the Triple B is pretty much a man's world."

"That's okay. I can handle myself in a man's world. At least I can in this man's world. I don't know what I'll do, Audrey. Most of the time I don't think about it one way or another. I've been mildly content since leaving college, and I just take it one day at a time."

Mildly content? Audrey tried to remember the last time she had met someone who was satisfied with being mildly content. Everyone these days, it seemed to her, was searching for absolute, complete happiness. She and Betty had that in common—she, too, chose to take life one day at a time and not make too many plans for the future.

The road they were traveling on ended abruptly. Instead of turning around, Betty stopped the car and switched off the engine. Audrey glanced around, thinking perhaps Betty wanted to show her something, but she couldn't imagine what it would be. For as far as the eye could see there was nothing but grass and sky and the mountains in the background. She quizzically glanced at the woman behind the wheel.

"Do you mind?" Betty asked. "I'm supposed to meet someone here."

Audrey shrugged. "Fine with me," she said, thinking that the far-out spot was an unlikely place for a meeting.

Betty gestured with one hand. "Here he comes now."

Audrey looked in the direction Betty indicated. Over a rise of ground a lone rider appeared. For a moment she watched absently, but as the rider drew nearer, she froze with shock. Surely her mind was playing tricks on her. She couldn't be seeing what she thought she was. It was impossible!

Then another minute passed, and she knew what she saw was no trick of the mind, no apparition. She wasn't going to need an introduction to the man on horseback; she recognized him immediately. If the black cowboy hat shaped into a Montana peak hadn't been enough of a giveaway, the way he sat in the saddle would have been. Jesse Murdoch!

Audrey's stomach twisted into a tight knot. Years ago she had fled her past, put it firmly behind her. Through great force of will she had reached the point where she rarely thought about it. Now, out of the blue, a very big part of that past rode toward her on a bay stallion. What cruel twist of fate had placed them in the same place at the same time?

This can't be happening, she thought wildly. *The past can't resurrect itself without warning.*

Then Jesse was upon them and she knew it could. A moment or two passed before he saw her, and Audrey took advantage of that to scrutinize him carefully. He hadn't changed much; maybe he seemed a little older, but that was about it. He still was a devilishly, dangerously handsome man. What a shame that such an unprincipled bastard was so physically attractive.

Jesse finally saw her. His eyes widened in disbelief as the color drained from his face. Reigning in his horse, he stared at her, absolutely thunderstruck. Audrey was sure the only thing that got her through the startling encounter was seeing Jesse's stupefied expression. He looked as though he had been kicked in the stomach. *He must think he is the unluckiest so-and-so on the face of the earth,* she thought with malicious satisfaction.

Betty had opened the door and gotten out of the car. "Come on, Audrey," she called over her shoulder. Jesse slowly dismounted, but his eyes remained riveted on Audrey, who also was getting out of the car.

The strange tension that filled the air went unnoticed by Betty. The young woman's eyes shone as she slipped a possessive arm around Jesse's waist and stared up at him adoringly. "Jesse, I want you to meet my new friend. She's going to be staying with us awhile, so I want you two to be friends, too. This is Audrey Hamilton. Audrey, this is Jesse Murdoch."

Audrey stopped some distance from Betty and Jesse, and a contemptuous smile curved her mouth. "How do you do," she said stiffly.

Jesse managed to lift his hand and touch the brim of his hat with a forefinger. "Hello." His voice was none too steady.

"Audrey's from Phoenix," Betty explained. "She works at the hotel the family has there. She's here because . . . well, it's a long story. I'll tell you about it later. Like I said, she's going to be here awhile, so I guess it'll be up to you and me to see she has a good time."

"Of course," Jesse muttered, finally tearing his stunned gaze away from Audrey to attempt a smile at Betty. "Been here long?"

"No, we just got here. I've been showing Audrey around. How was your day?"

"Busy, as usual. Listen, Betts, I hate running off, but a couple of the boys found some calves that need some doctoring. They've taken 'em down to the infirmary, and I'd better go supervise. I'm not sure those boys know what they're doing."

"Do you want me to meet you there? I'm the best amateur vet on the ranch."

"Oh, I don't think that's necessary. I wouldn't want you to leave your . . . friend."

Betty stepped back. She looked terribly disappointed. "Well, I guess Audrey and I really should be getting back to the house anyway. We'll be expected to put in an appearance at the cocktail hour. Will I see you tonight?"

"I'll do my best."

"Ten-ish?"

"Fine." Jesse glanced in Audrey's direction without making eye contact. "Nice . . . er, meeting you. Be seein' you around."

She nodded curtly but said nothing. She hadn't recovered from the startling encounter as nicely as Jesse had, but, then, she wasn't as adept at deceit as he was.

Giving Betty an affectionate pat on the shoulder, Jesse mounted and rode away swiftly. Sighing, Betty turned to Audrey apologetically. "I did so want you to get to know him. Any other time I'm sure he would have stuck around to visit with us, but he's very busy. I'm afraid everyone around here has come to depend on him. Boyd says Jesse's the best cowhand he's come across in years. You just don't run into his kind much anymore."

Fortunately, Audrey thought caustically. So charming, handsome, dangerous Jesse was up to his old tricks! How she wanted to warn Betty about the clever, devious fortune hunter, but she couldn't very well do that without revealing things about her past that were no one else's business. And, too, if the starry-eyed expression on Betty's face was any indication, the woman was already totally smitten. She probably wouldn't have believed anything Audrey had to say. How did that man so easily ingratiate himself? Then she recalled her own starry-eyed self five years ago and had her answer.

In spite of herself, Audrey was curious about the circumstances that had brought Jesse to the Triple B. As she and Betty returned to the car she questioned the young woman. "If his kind are so hard to come by, how did you find him?"

"We didn't. He found us. Jesse used to work on a spread in Texas, but its owner got into some kind of trouble with the government, and the operation shut down. So, in tried-and-true cowboy tradition, Jesse started moving west, working here and there, searching for a ranch that still did things the old-fashioned way."

No, he was searching for a ranch whose owner had an eligible daughter, Audrey reflected. Jesse was a clever one, but not clever enough to change his method of operation. Dismayed, she slid into the passenger seat and closed the door. Another ranch, another daughter, another love-struck female. She hadn't known Betty but a few hours, yet she already liked her. Betty didn't deserve Jesse; no woman did. Audrey wouldn't have wished Jesse on her worst enemy.

But there was nothing she could do about it. Whatever happened to any of the Benedicts wasn't her concern, and Betty, after all, was a grown woman who could take care of herself. Audrey was somewhat consoled by the knowledge that Jesse would have to be one worried man about now, wondering if she was going to blow the whistle on him, the way Sam Graves had all those years ago. The thought of him "stewing" in his own caldron was so pleasant that Audrey almost smiled.

"Is it serious between you and Jesse?" she asked offhandedly.

Betty started the car and reversed direction. "Not as serious as I hope it's going to be," she said with a grin. "Of course, there are a few problems. A certain caste system exists on a ranch, so that puts Jesse and me at opposite ends of the social structure. And, as Benedicts, Boyd and I are supposed to marry well, the way Brent did. But I'm hoping the fact that everyone thinks so highly of Jesse will count for something."

"What does Boyd think of him?"

"Boyd? Well . . . I doubt he thinks of him at all, except as an unusually good cowhand. In time I'm hoping to enlist Boyd as an ally in this, though. Dad listens to my brothers more than he lets on.'' Betty sobered and cast an anxious glance Audrey's way. "I don't know why I'm trusting you with all this. You see, no one knows about me and Jesse—not yet. I'd like to keep it that way.''

Audrey stared vacantly through the windshield. Betty had no way of knowing what a trustworthy confidante she had chosen. "Don't worry, Betty. You can count on me. I wouldn't dream of saying a word to anyone.''

CHAPTER SIX

THE OUTING had taken up more of the afternoon than either woman realized. When they returned to the house Betty glanced at her watch. "It's later than I thought. We're going to have to get a move on, friend. Dad expects everyone to gather in the sun room at six-thirty sharp."

What would happen if someone was late, Audrey wondered, recalling how Boyd had hopped to earlier that afternoon. Apparently no one kept Buck Benedict waiting. "No problem. I'll be ready."

"I don't envy you, Audrey. You're going to be on display tonight, no getting around it."

Audrey smiled nervously. "I hope I don't disappoint them."

"I'll tap on your door when I'm ready, and we'll go in together. Now, don't let Dad intimidate you. He's really a nice person, but he plays the role of head of the family to the hilt. He's like a traffic cop when we all get together—you come here, you go there, you stay here. Even men who've worked for him twenty years or more stand a little in awe of him. Granddad was the only person who ever had any real influence with Dad, and those two used to have some arguments that rocked these walls."

Wonderful, Audrey thought as she ducked into the guest room. Just wonderful! She was beginning to wish she could forgo the "pleasure" of meeting Buck B. Benedict. Frankly, she was tired of adjusting to one startling development after another.

Someone had considerately unpacked her suitcase and put everything away. The few dresses she had brought had been pressed and hung in the closet. After a moment's deliberation, she decided on the sundress she had worn the night before. She took fresh underwear and panty hose out of the dresser, then laid it all across the bed. In the bathroom she took a quick shower and shampooed her hair. Towelling dry, she slipped on a knee-length terry cloth robe, cinched it around her waist and stepped back into the bedroom just as a knock sounded at the door.

It would have to be Betty or one of the servants. "Come in," she called, and the door opened. Boyd entered the room. He was freshly showered and had changed from jeans and boots to dark blue slacks and a white shirt. He looked, in a word, marvelous.

"Oh, I . . . I thought you were Betty."

"I just stopped by to see how you're getting along, if you need anything. I can come back later." But he made no attempt to leave, and his eyes boldly moved over her damp, tousled hair, her scrubbed face, her shapely legs beneath the robe's hem.

"No . . . that's all right. Have a seat. It will just take me a minute to get dressed." She scooped her clothes off the bed and carried them into the bathroom. Once there, however, she couldn't find her bra. She would have sworn she had gotten one out of the dresser, but it wasn't there. With a disgusted sigh, she opened the door and saw Boyd sitting on the edge of the bed. One strap of the wispy undergarment was draped over his forefinger, and he was studying the bra as though it were the most fascinating thing he'd ever seen. When the door opened he glanced up.

"You dropped something," he said with a grin.

"So...I did." Flushing slightly, she walked to the bed, all but snatched the bra out of his hand and returned to the bathroom. She was almost certain she heard him chuckling as she closed the door.

While Boyd waited, he recalled his afternoon with his father. Naturally, Buck had been curious about Audrey and wanted a full report. Boyd had given a lot of thought to what he said. "There's not much I can tell you about her, Dad, since she's not one for talking about herself. She used to live in Texas. Her parents are gone, and she seems to have no other family. She came to Arizona to visit a friend about four years ago and ended up staying when a part-time job at the hotel came along. She's...I guess 'reserved' is the word I'm looking for. She's obviously intelligent, poised, attractive. From what I've been able to gather, her job demands it. I'm convinced she had no idea who Granddad was. She thought he was 'sweet.' That's about it."

"How does she feel about being brought here?" Buck had wanted to know.

"She seems to realize it's best for everyone concerned. No one likes dealing with the press."

Boyd had been relieved that his father accepted the report without more questions. For reasons he didn't fully understand he'd decided not to voice any of his reservations or suspicions about Audrey. Maybe he hoped they would prove to be unfounded.

The door to the bathroom opened, and she emerged, looking fresh, energetic and very beautiful. The dress she was wearing was the same one she'd had on last night. Boyd was aware of a peculiar stirring in the region of his heart, and it appalled him. There was no place in his life for an attraction to a woman he had doubts about. His eyes remained on her as she walked to the dressing table, sat down and flipped open her makeup case.

"So, how was your afternoon?" he asked.

"Enjoyable," Audrey replied. "I spent it with Betty. I really like her."

"That's good. I think Betty could use a woman friend. She works almost exclusively with men, and she and Sara are too different to be really close. What did the two of you do?"

"Oh, she showed me around the ranch, and . . . she introduced me to a man named Jesse."

Boyd nodded. "Jesse Murdoch. Good man. We're thinking of making him foreman. I guess Betty can keep you busy while you're here. God knows, she always seems to find something to do. Maybe you won't be too bored."

"I doubt I'll be bored at all," she lied. "And I'll try to stay out of the way."

"You won't be in anyone's way." He watched as, stroke by practiced stroke, she applied her makeup, then brushed her hair. His reflection in the mirror seemed to be making her nervous—he could tell by her somewhat jerky movements—but he didn't want to take his eyes off her. When she finished, she stood up and turned to face him. Boyd shoved himself off the bed and went to stand in front of her. "Lovely," he said matter-of-factly, but his gaze was like a physical caress. "A true work of art."

"Well...thank you." The compliment came as a surprise. Audrey's breath caught somewhere between her lungs and her throat. He was standing very close, and she loved the smell of that after-shave. She would have liked to tell him how nice he looked, too. But she was sure he knew how handsome he was, just as she was sure she was reading more into his expression than he intended.

There was a chameleon-like quality to him. Earlier that day, during the drive from Phoenix, he had been thoroughly remote. Now potent, sensuous energy seemed to radiate from him. Unwillingly, she stared up at him, her mouth slightly parted in fascination.

Boyd frowned slightly. He didn't recall that either of them had said or done a thing out of the ordinary, yet the atmosphere in the room had changed dramatically. He experienced an absurd urge to reach out and finger a few strands of her silky hair.

At that moment Betty rushed into the room. "Hey, Audrey, you ready? Ooops..."

Audrey could visualize the picture she and Boyd must have presented, standing so close and gazing deeply into each other's eyes. Giving herself an imperceptible shake, she quickly stepped back to put some distance between them.

Betty looked at Audrey, then at her brother, a mixture of surprise and amusement on her face. "When did you say you two met each other?" she asked, stifling a bubble of laughter.

Boyd collected himself, took both women by the arm and propelled them out the door. "Come on," he said gruffly. "Let's not keep the others waiting."

WHEN THE THREE OF THEM entered the sun room, four pairs of eyes turned toward them. For a moment, Audrey had the distinct sensation of being under a microscope. Then Elizabeth rose and rushed forward.

"Audrey, dear, how nice you look."

"Thank you, Mrs. Benedict. How was your afternoon?"

"Rather hectic. I barely made my appointment. I do hope you were able to amuse yourself."

"Yes, I had a delightful time. Betty took me on a tour of the ranch. It's impressive, I must say."

"Good. Boyd, why don't you introduce Audrey around."

"Of course." Placing a hand on the small of her back, he guided Audrey toward a blond woman who was stylishly dressed in a soft shade of blue. "Audrey, this is my sister-in-law, Sara."

"How do you do, Sara."

"It's nice to meet you, Audrey." Sara's lips barely moved when she spoke, and she had the iciest blue eyes Audrey had ever seen. Her beauty was of the Dresden-doll type, and she projected the image of the quintessential socialite. Not an easy person to get to know was Audrey's immediate impression.

Boyd then turned to the tall, slender man at Sara's side. Audrey would have known the man was related to Boyd no matter where she had encountered him. The physical resemblance was remarkable, though the rugged handsomeness she associated with Boyd was less pronounced in his brother, possibly because of his more pallid complexion.

"Audrey, this is my brother, Brent," Boyd intoned.

"How do you do, Brent."

"Welcome to the Triple B, Audrey."

Boyd applied a bit of firm pressure on Audrey's waist as he guided her toward a man who had been standing aloof from the rest of them. "And, Audrey, I'd like you to meet my father. Dad, this is Audrey Hamilton."

Buck B. Benedict was bigger-boned than either of his sons. The Arizona sun had burned a permanent layer of bronze in his skin, and his hair was more salt than pepper. Tall and straight-shouldered, only slightly soft in the middle, he was distinguished and maturely attractive. He greatly resembled the portrait of Bert that hung in the hall.

But it wasn't Buck Benedict's looks that arrested Audrey's attention as much as the aura surrounding him. He was a commanding presence, a figure of authority. Here was a man of importance, his manner said, a man in charge of himself and all he surveyed. He was so unlike Bert, who had been such a simple man. But then Audrey was reminded that she had known Bert in the twilight of his life. Apparently her old friend had been just as authoritarian as his son in earlier days.

Would Boyd be the same fifteen or twenty years down the road? She wondered why that question had even crossed her mind.

She studied the man who now was the patriarch of the family. She found Buck more interesting than intimidating, but, after all, she had been raised in a household where prominent people had often been guests, and during her years at the Greenspoint she had shaken hands with presidents, prime ministers and princes. It would take more than Buck Benedict to intimidate her.

"How do you do, Mr. Benedict," she said politely, extending her hand.

Buck took it and shook it firmly. "Welcome to my home, Audrey. I trust you are being looked after properly."

"Yes, I am. Your wife and daughter have been most gracious."

"Good, good. I apologize for any inconvenience we might have caused you, but it was necessary. Now, please sit down and have a drink with us."

The male hand at her waist dropped, and Boyd said, "I'll get it. Audrey prefers to drink wine. What'll you have, Betty?"

"Get me a beer," his sister said and motioned for Audrey to join her on the sofa.

Elizabeth, Brent and Sara took seats around the room, while Buck moved to the far end to sit in a huge high-backed rattan chair behind a long table that served as a desk. This had the immediate effect of directing all eyes to him, something Audrey suspected the desk's location was meant to do.

Boyd brought drinks to Audrey and his sister, then went to stand in front of the big windows, slightly apart from the mainstream. He sipped absently on his drink and focused his attention on his father, who, as usual, was "holding court." Buck, he noticed, was playing it low-keyed tonight. Normally these predinner gatherings took on the air of a business meeting, with everyone reporting on the day's events. Tonight, however, his father kept the mood more amiable and social.

Within minutes Boyd's attention strayed to Audrey. His dad didn't seem to faze her a bit, and that was unusual, since Buck intimidated just about everyone at first. She was as calm and collected as if she had known the family her entire life. What kind of background had instilled such poise in her? Somehow he didn't think it came solely from greeting the famous and near-famous at the Greenspoint for three years.

Alertly, he listened to the conversation flowing around the room. Everyone was bombarding Audrey with questions, but Boyd noticed how adroitly she evaded any that were personal. Instead she launched into a series of anecdotes about some of the celebrities who had stayed at the Greenspoint, which made for amusing entertainment but wasn't very enlightening. Why he was obsessed with knowing more about her he couldn't imagine—yet he was.

She's such a lovely charmer, he thought with a sigh. *I just wish she rang true.*

Audrey wasn't accustomed to being the center of attention, and she was uncomfortable having all eyes trained on her. Moreover, she was acutely aware of Boyd standing off to the side, studying her intently. She could feel his eyes beating down on her, so she carefully avoided looking directly at him. A strange feeling persisted—that he was just waiting for her to make a slip of the tongue. Damn him. The others seemed to have no trouble accepting her at face value. Why was he so suspicious?

She more or less had braced herself for the first questions concerning her relationship with Bert, but no one said a word. In fact, everyone was exceedingly courteous. The reason for her impromptu "visit" to the Triple B was not mentioned. Still, Audrey was on edge, and she felt a great surge of relief when the plump woman named Maria appeared to announce dinner.

The evening meal in the Benedict house, Audrey was soon to learn, was an unhurried affair meant to last an hour or more, and nothing was allowed to interfere with it. The food, which was served in courses by Maria and Tina, was hearty and laden with calories. First came a spicy soup. It was followed by a rice dish laden with chili peppers and onions. The main course was steak strips rolled in flour tortillas and accompanied by beans, avocado slices and the Mexican tomato relish curiously named *pico de gallo*, or "rooster's beak." Just in case anyone still had room, the meal was topped off with sherbet, almond cookies and strong coffee laced with chocolate.

Audrey's appetite was completely satisfied after the rice, but as a guest she felt obligated to eat a respectable amount of everything. She noticed that none of the Benedicts had the slightest trouble putting away the food. She wondered if the altitude had something to do with their robust appetites, since she herself had consumed more at this one meal than she normally did during an entire day. She also wondered how the women kept their svelte figures if this was their typical fare.

Buck and Elizabeth sat at opposite ends of the table, with Boyd and Audrey on one side, Betty, Brent and Sara across from them. Conversation throughout the meal was dominated by the men, whose interests were many and varied. Buck and his sons hopped from the weather and pasture conditions to state and national politics, Wall Street and the cattle market. The family, Audrey soon surmised, was very active politically. Elizabeth's and Sara's lone contribution to the talk concerned a luncheon they were planning for the wife of a state senator. Betty kept silent except when the conversation turned to cattle. As for Audrey, she said virtually nothing at all.

Dinner finally ended, and Buck got to his feet. As if on signal, the others also stood and began filing out of the dining room. Betty lingered to speak to Audrey. "Everyone else will watch TV for a while, but I'm in the middle of a great book, so if you don't mind, I think I'll go to my room."

"Of course I don't mind, Betty. Please don't think you have to stay by my side every minute. I want to turn in early, too."

"Okay, see you in the morning. We'll find something to do tomorrow."

Audrey smiled. "Good night. Thanks for everything."

Betty left, and Audrey turned to push her chair into place. She discovered Boyd standing behind her. He took the chair and slid it up to the table. "Did you enjoy your dinner?" he asked.

"Very much. It was delicious."

"You didn't eat much."

"I ate far more than I usually do."

"Were you serious about turning in early?"

"I thought I would."

"Then I'd better warn you of something. Dad has it on good authority that the terms of Granddad's will are going to break in the morning papers. He wants all of us to stay fairly close to home for the next few days."

"Where else would I go?" Audrey inquired sensibly.

"Where else indeed?"

At that moment Maria and Tina appeared to clear the table. Boyd fell into step beside Audrey, and they went into the foyer. "Of course," he said, "I'm beginning to think we could have let you talk to the press all you wanted, and there'd be no harm done."

She stopped and eyed him quizzically. "I beg your pardon?"

"You're amazingly adept at talking without saying anything. You've been with us all evening, and still we know almost nothing about you."

Audrey tensed slightly. "You know everything that's important."

"Really? I wonder."

"Tell me, Boyd, are you always this vastly curious about people you've just met?"

"Only when they make me so. Only when they withhold the most basic information about themselves. Where were you born?"

An amused glint came into her eyes. "Guthrie, Oklahoma."

"I thought you were a Texan."

"I was born in Guthrie because my folks were returning from a trip to Kansas when I put in an unexpected appearance. You see, I was premature...almost six weeks premature, to be exact. My mother had to remain in Guthrie a month before they'd let her take me home. Isn't that fascinating?"

Her sarcasm didn't dissuade him. "What did your dad do for a living?"

"He owned his own business."

"Were you very young when he died?"

Audrey's mouth set in a tight line. "He died five years ago. My mother died a few weeks earlier."

Boyd felt a rush of color diffuse his face. "Good Lord, Audrey...I'm sorry. I..."

Audrey stepped back from him. "Now, if you'll excuse me, I must tell everyone good-night."

Boyd watched her walk away and chastised himself severely. He'd come across like an insensitive clod. Why couldn't he have left well enough alone? She was being cooperative as hell, and the rest of the family seemed to harbor no suspicions. Why did he? Why was he so damned interested in her past? It had no bearing on anything.

He was still standing in the foyer, lost in his thoughts, when he heard Audrey return from the sun room. She paused a moment, and he searched his brain for something to say. Before he could, however, she turned and disappeared down the hallway. He heard the door to the guest room open and close behind her. He felt terrible. Had it been physically possible, he would have kicked his own butt.

I HOPE HE'S damned well satisfied, Audrey thought as she closed the door. She had rather enjoyed that embarrassed look on Boyd's face. Maybe now he would leave her alone. Everything she had told him was the unvarnished truth, yet it had revealed nothing important.

The room was completely dark. She reached for the light switch on the wall, then saw that the door to the veranda was standing slightly ajar. Not wanting to lure a swarm of insects with the light, she crossed the room to close the door. As her hand closed around the knob, however, she caught a whiff of the clean, fresh scent of night air. It was irresistible. Stepping out onto the veranda, she gazed up. With no nearby city lights to obscure its beauty, the sky was like black velvet studded with a million diamonds. At this elevation, the stars seemed close enough to reach out and touch. Drawn by nature's spectacle, she crossed the veranda and walked out onto the lawn. There, not even the few lights from the house detracted from the breathtaking view. How long had it been since she'd really seen a night sky? It was back on the ranch in Texas, and that seemed a lifetime ago.

Mesmerized by the night, Audrey at first didn't see the shadowy outline of a man's shape moving toward her. He was almost upon her before some movement caught her eye. Startled, she opened her mouth, but a rough hand closed over it, silencing her. Wide-eyed, she looked up into the face of Jesse Murdoch.

"Hush," he growled. "Don't make a sound. Understand?"

Mutely she nodded. Jesse studied her uncertainly for a moment. Then, apparently satisfied she wouldn't cry out, he dropped his hand and clutched her upper arm. "Small world, isn't it, Audrey?"

Angrily, she flung his hand away. "What are you doing here?"

"I work here, and I'm simply taking my customary nightly stroll. I might ask you the same question."

"I'm getting some fresh air, and I want to be alone."

"I don't mean what are you doing outside," Jesse said. "I mean, what are you doing here at the Triple B? I damned near fell dead when I saw you this afternoon."

"I can imagine," Audrey countered acidly. "Knowing that made my day."

"Repeat, what are you doing here?"

"I don't consider that any of your business."

An unpleasant smile crossed Jesse's face. "Still sore after all these years, huh? I only did my civic duty, Audrey. Your daddy was a crook."

"Oh, come off it, Jesse! I know you, remember? My father did a dreadful thing, and he deserved to pay for it, but I question your motives for turning state's evidence. I don't think your 'civic duty' came into play for an instant."

"You do me an injustice. I've always been a law-abiding citizen."

"That's right. There's no law against what you do, not one on the books, anyway. And since you have the moral fiber of a mountain goat—"

"Betty said you work for the Benedicts?" Jesse interrupted brusquely. "How well do you know them?"

"Again, that's none of your business." Audrey took a deep breath. "Leave Betty alone."

"Hey, the woman's crazy about me. I'd break her heart if I left her alone. I'm not going to do anything to hurt Betty. I'll make her happy. If I feather my own nest into the bargain, what's the harm in that?"

"You know something... the awful part is, I think you really believe that. Do something decent for once in your life, Jesse, and leave her alone."

He grabbed her arm again, this time clutching it with painful tightness. "Now you listen to me. When I saw you this afternoon, my first thought was that you'd throw a monkey wrench in all my plans. But the more I thought about it, the more I realized you weren't going to say a word, not one damned word. If you were going to say something to the Benedicts about me, you'd have done it by now, and I'd know about it."

His grip on her arm relaxed, and his ugly smile returned. "I don't know what your business with the Benedicts is, and I don't care, as long as you don't interfere. If you know them at all, then you know what upstanding citizens they are. Hell, they practically own this state, and they have some pretty high-and-mighty friends. I don't think they'd want to have much to do with a gal whose daddy was sentenced to a federal pen. So you keep your mouth shut about me, and I'll keep mine shut about your daddy's shenanigans. Everybody will live happily ever after, and that includes your friend, Betty. Deal?"

Uttering a sound of contempt, Audrey shoved him away. "I don't deal with scum!" she hissed. She turned on her heel and marched back across the patio and into her room. But before she could close the door, she heard another one open. That was followed by the sound of footsteps hurrying across the patio. Turning, she peered into the darkness in time to see Betty step out onto the lawn. Going to meet Jesse, Audrey guessed. Obviously he'd been waiting for her when he'd seen Audrey.

Closing the door, she leaned against it a moment, her chest heaving in agitation. *Oh, Audrey,* her inner voice said in despair, *you know you should blow the whistle on Jesse! Betty's such a nice person.*

I know, I know, she responded tiredly, *but I can't. It would require spilling too many things that I've kept bottled up for years. Why should I chance throwing my own life into turmoil again? Betty isn't my responsibility.*

Jesse infuriated her to the point of making her sick to her stomach, but he'd been very right about her. If she had been going to say anything about him to the Benedicts, or at least to Betty, she would have done so by now. And that was the worst of it. Knowing she probably could send Jesse out of Betty's life with only a few words, and having no intention of doing so . . . well, that really made her sick!

CHAPTER SEVEN

THE SUN HAD BARELY PEEPED over the horizon the following morning when Buck and his three offspring gathered for breakfast in the dining room. They helped themselves to the food from several chafing dishes on the sideboard, then took their customary places. In the center of the table was the usual pile of newspapers that were delivered to the ranch every morning from the nearby town of Agua Linda. The pile contained the morning editions of the major state papers, along with a day-late *Wall Street Journal*. This morning the *Journal* was neglected. The Benedicts were interested in only one story.

They ate in silence until Buck, having thumbed through most of the newspapers, murmured, "Well, it's not too bad. Just straight news stories so far. But there's a lot of human interest stuff here, so I fully expect the phone to start ringing off the wall any minute. May I remind all of you that I'll be the one to handle all calls." He folded a paper, placed it beside his plate and looked at Brent. "Are you sure you want to go to the office today?"

Brent nodded. "Might as well. I'll just pass the word that I'm not seeing anyone or taking any calls. No problem."

Buck shifted his attention to Boyd. "What about you, son?"

"I'll spend most of the day hiring the extra hands we need for roundup. A couple showed up yesterday, so the word's gotten around. I expect more today."

Buck nodded. "You know, this isolation is hard on your mother and Sara, so they've decided to go to Los Angeles for a few days of shopping." He turned to his daughter. "Guess looking after our guest will be up to you, Betty."

"Suits me. I really like Audrey." Betty's eyes darted to Boyd. "That doesn't mean I have to miss roundup, does it?"

"Sorry, love," Boyd said sympathetically. "We can't very well go off and leave Audrey alone. That wouldn't be fair."

"I know, but I haven't missed a roundup in five years." Then Betty had an idea. "Boyd, Audrey says she can ride a horse. I thought I'd take her on my rounds today. If she proves she can handle herself..."

"Oh, hey, come on." Boyd chuckled. "Surely you're not thinking of asking a greenhorn to tag along. You know how the men feel about women on roundup. It goes against the grain."

"I'm a woman, or hadn't you noticed?"

"That's different."

"Give me a little credit, brother dear. I wouldn't dream of bringing her along if I didn't think she could handle it."

"It's not a good idea," he said stubbornly.

"Think about it," Betty persisted just as stubbornly.

"Talk to me tonight, but I'm afraid the answer is going to have to be no."

AUDREY AWAKENED EARLY, disturbed by some unfamiliar sounds. Then she realized it was the lack of sounds that disturbed her. Her apartment in Phoenix was in a large complex located just off a busy thoroughfare. The area began teeming with activity and noise at a very early hour. Now she turned her head on the pillow and listened. Muted voices came from somewhere. The kitchen, she guessed, for she could smell the delicious aroma of freshly brewed coffee. And from outside, in the far, far distance, came the lowing of cows and the bawling of calves. Otherwise, all was quiet.

Sitting up, Audrey hugged her knees to her breasts and yawned. She had slept fairly well once she'd finally fallen asleep, but the combination of the strange house, strange bed, Boyd's questioning and the disturbing encounter with Jesse had kept her awake an hour or more after she'd gone to bed.

At some point before succumbing to sleep she had conveniently absolved herself of any responsibility for warning Betty about the unscrupulous man. Now, in the light of morning, her damnable conscience began nagging her again. She liked Betty a lot. Given the time, Audrey thought the two of them could become close friends. And the Benedicts, after all, were Bert's family. She certainly owed her old friend plenty.

A moment later, however, she successfully shook off her guilt feelings. Whatever happened in this house was not her concern. Once she went back to the Greenspoint, she more than likely would never see any of them again. And since no one seemed to begrudge her the inheritance, none of them would ever again give her another thought.

Besides, she thought confidently, something might happen to thwart Jesse's big plans. Betty was no dummy; she might see through him eventually.

You were no dummy either, Audrey, that nagging inner voice reminded her, *but what if Sam Graves hadn't happened along when he did?* She shuddered just thinking about it.

She suddenly realized that she was hungry, and she wondered if breakfast was being served. After last night's gigantic dinner she had planned to forgo breakfast altogether, but coffee, juice and perhaps some toast wouldn't play too much havoc with her weight. Flinging aside the covers, she padded into the bathroom, took care of her morning routine, then dressed hurriedly and followed her nose to the dining room.

Betty, her father and both brothers were seated around the table. "Good morning," Audrey said brightly, and every head turned in her direction. She had the distinct feeling she had interrupted a conversation that had concerned her. When she noticed all the newspapers spread out on the table she was sure of it.

"Hi," Betty replied cheerfully. "Sleep well?"

"Yes, thanks."

The Benedict men mumbled greetings and started to rise, but Audrey raised her hand in a staying gesture. "Please, don't get up."

Buck and Brent paused and sat back down, but Boyd got to his feet. "Let me get you some breakfast," he offered, pulling out the chair next to his.

"I can get it," Audrey protested.

"Please, let me."

She slid into the chair. "Thanks. Just juice and coffee."

"Oh, you'd better eat more than that," Betty advised. "I thought I'd take you on my rounds, and that means a lot of riding. Lunch will be whatever we can carry in our saddlebags."

Audrey hungrily eyed the sausage, eggs and hash browns on Betty's plate. "Well, maybe a little food, but very little, please."

"I'll fix you up," Boyd said, moving toward the sideboard where several covered chafing dishes stood, along with the coffeepot and a decanter of juice. "How do you like your coffee?"

"With a touch of cream." She watched him as he took a plate and heaped it with too much food. He certainly was playing the part of the solicitous host this morning. Atoning for his previous sins, she thought with some satisfaction.

Boyd placed her food in front of her and took his seat again just as Buck got to his feet. "Have a good day, all of you. I'll see you tonight." With that he left the room.

Brent wasn't far behind. Standing up, he said, "I'll be off to the mill. Keep the home fires burning." He nodded politely to Audrey and walked out.

Boyd got up and carried his coffee cup to the sideboard for a refill. "Either of you two ladies need more coffee?" he asked. When both Audrey and Betty shook their heads, he filled his cup, downed the contents in a few gulps and set it on the sideboard. "Guess I'd better get rolling," he announced and made for the door.

But as he passed Audrey's chair, in a surprising move, he reached out and gave her shoulder a reassuring pat. The gesture, performed casually, and so quickly he barely broke stride, brought her head up with a jerk. He seemed to be trying to make her feel better. Better about what? Then her eyes fell on the newspapers, and she thought she had her answer.

Now that they were alone, Audrey turned to Betty. "The papers . . . is it bad?"

"No. I don't see what all the commotion is about," Betty said. "Granddad left a bunch of money to a bunch of people. So what?"

"Did he leave anyone else a hundred thousand dollars?"

"Well, no, but . . . Forget it, Audrey. You just had the bad luck to get tangled up with a family that seems to fascinate the media. Damned if I know why. Frankly, I think we're a pretty uninteresting lot."

Audrey sighed. "I wouldn't blame any of you for feeling resentful. No one likes having a complete stranger show up and throw everything out of kilter." She reached across the table and picked up the newspaper Buck had been reading. She saw it was the state edition of a Phoenix paper. Scanning the page, she noticed a headline in the lower right-hand corner: Phoenix Woman Beneficiary of Benedict Estate. She set the paper down, deciding she didn't want to read the article. "How do you manage to get these papers so early when you live way out here?" she asked.

"Some newsdealer in Agua Linda gets them from a dealer in Tucson who carries a big selection of out-of-town papers. Dad reads most of the state papers and the *Wall Street Journal* every day. I'm sure he pays handsomely for them, but he can't do without his papers. Listen, Audrey, the whole business will blow over in a few days."

"I hope so."

"You and I are going to be busy, so the time will pass like that." Betty snapped her fingers.

"Betty, please...I told you, I don't want you to feel you have to keep me entertained."

"I don't. You're going to keep me entertained. I'm riding fence today, and I could use the company. You'll enjoy your stay here so much more if you ride, because a lot of the ranch can only be reached on horseback. I'll pick your mount for you."

Audrey knew exactly what riding fence entailed, and the thought of riding again appealed to her. Once, she had been completely at home in the saddle. "If you don't mind riding herd on a greenhorn, I'd love to go along."

"Do you have boots?"

"No, sorry."

"What size do you wear?"

"Seven, seven-and-a-half, depends on the shoe."

"I have a pair that are a bit small for me. You can wear those. And you'll need a hat or that sun will kill you. No problem. I have plenty of hats." Betty pushed herself away from the table and stood up. "It's time for my weekly business conference with Dad, so I'll give you a holler when I'm ready. Okay?"

"Fine. Betty, do you suppose anyone would mind if I call my office? I'll make it collect, of course."

Betty thought about it, then shrugged. "Has Dad told you not to make any calls?"

"No, it hasn't been mentioned."

"Then I don't see anything wrong with it. The phones in the bedrooms are a different number from the one in Dad's study, so you won't be interfering with business calls."

"Thanks. See you later." Audrey left her half-eaten breakfast and went back to her room to place a call to the Greenspoint. It seemed much longer than twenty-four hours ago that she had left Phoenix.

Helen screeched when she discovered who was on the line. "Audrey!"

"Hi, Helen. What's going on?"

"Are you kidding? I'll tell you what's going on. It's hit the fan, that's what's going on! Where are you?"

"In exile."

"Jeez, you wouldn't believe this place. Our nice laid-back little office is about as laid-back as Mission Control at T-minus-ten-and-counting."

Audrey's stomach made a sickening revolution. "Can I talk to Peter?"

"Yeah, guess so. Every light on this phone is lit up. Hold on."

Peter came on the line almost immediately. "Audrey?"

"Helen tells me confusion reigns. I'm sorry, Peter. Wish I were there."

"No, you don't. I've spent the past hour with the phone stuck in my ear. And some guy got past the security people downstairs and found his way up here. I thought I was going to have to throw him out bodily. He wanted to talk to you about some land in Colorado. So far three insurance salesmen have called, to say nothing of every newspaper in the state. Seems everyone wants to know the real story behind your relationship with Bertram B. Benedict.''

Audrey groaned. ''And to think I had hoped all this would pass quickly and I could come home.''

''If you're smart you'll stay right where you are. If these people can't find you, they'll lose interest after a while. Be grateful that the Benedicts were thoughtful enough to protect you from all this. You'd hate it.''

He was right. Dear God, that she of all people had gotten involved in something like this! Wasn't once in anyone's lifetime enough?

BOYD CAME out of the stables just as Betty and Audrey were preparing to ride off for the day. He approached them, his eyes all for Audrey, who looked downright fetching in boots and a cowboy hat. He took note of the mount Betty had chosen for her—a gentle cutting horse named Ranger—and he approved. You could turn a child loose on Ranger.

''You don't need to worry,'' he said, coming up to her. ''Ranger's as gentle as they come.''

''I'm not worried.''

''Betty tells me you've ridden before.''

''Yes, but it's been years.''

''Was that back in Texas?''

''Um-hmm.''

In a fluid motion, Betty swung up on her own horse. ''Ready?'' she asked Audrey.

''Yes.''

Boyd stepped forward to give Audrey a leg up, but she didn't seem to need his help. Effortlessly, she swung herself up in the saddle, gently nudged Ranger and trotted off beside Betty. Boyd hooked his thumbs in the pocket of his jeans and stared after them. In particular he noticed the easy way Audrey sat in the saddle. Most true greenhorns approached a horse, even a gentle one, timidly. She didn't. To his knowledge she was a city slicker, yet she sat a horse as though born to it. That was one more interesting piece of information about a woman who intrigued him in ways he didn't fully understand. He was still trying to come to grips with his strong attraction to her.

AUDREY THOROUGHLY enjoyed the day out on the open range. She and Betty rode the entire length of the fence on the western boundary of the ranch, stopping often for Betty to dismount and repair breaks in the barbed wire. At midday they sat beneath the shade of an ancient tree and ate the lunch Maria had provided for them. Audrey listened while Betty gossiped about her family, something she loved to do.

"Boyd once commented that the Benedict clan is organized along military lines, and I guess he's right. Dad's definitely the colonel of the regiment, and Granddad was sort of a commanding general. We all have jobs to do, and it's been that way as long as I can remember. Brent oversees the banking and real estate from the Tucson office. Boyd's the troubleshooter and PR man. He runs around smoothing ruffled feathers. He also sets overall policy for the ranch, and I carry it out."

"What about your mother and Sara?" Audrey asked. So far it seemed to her that Elizabeth and Sara's main task was to look beautiful at all times.

"They spend most of their time entertaining and being entertained by wives of people Dad considers important. They're pretty good at it, too. And they spare me from having to do much of it, thank God."

"How long have Sara and Brent been married?"

"Seven years. And no kids. They were supposed to have kids. All of us are supposed to have kids, but you gotta figure Brent and Sara might never have them, not after seven years. Sad, really. I know Sara feels...inadequate. Now, since any kids I have won't carry the name, I guess it's up to Boyd to give the world a new generation of Benedicts."

Audrey strove for casualness as she asked, "Any prime candidates for a wife?"

"Nope, not one. Sometimes Dad acts like that's a personal affront. Boyd was supposed to marry a woman named Linda Ames, but it never happened."

"Supposed to?"

Betty nodded. "Yeah, Linda's father was a state senator and a drinking buddy of Dad's. The two of them thought that marriage would be perfect. It was really funny the way they tried to throw Boyd and Linda together. Trouble is, neither of them cooperated. Shoot, they'd known each other since they were in grade school. Oh, they went through the motions of dating for a while, but then Linda went off to college and married some starving medical student. Now the man's a big-shot radiologist in Los Angeles, and Linda has three kids, all boys. Dad all but cries when he thinks about it." Betty paused to chuckle. "I feel sorry for the woman who finally snares my younger brother. I'm afraid Dad will look on her as a brood mare. He might insist she have a gynecological checkup before the wedding, like Princess Di.''

"What about you, Betty? I believe you said you're expected to marry well, too."

Betty's face clouded. "Yeah, and that presents problems, real problems. I've had plenty of 'suitable' men paraded by me. Dad's about as subtle as a meat cleaver when it comes to matchmaking. But ever since I was old enough to think about such things, I've dreamed of a man exactly like Jesse, a cowboy who loves this life the way I do and doesn't yearn for more.''

Oh, Betty, Audrey wanted to wail, *Jesse isn't what he appears to be at all. His real yearnings would stagger you.* "Could you defy your father?" she asked.

"I don't know. I've never had to. None of us have. I wonder if either Boyd or I could just dig in our heels, stick out our chins and say, 'No, that's not what I want.' I wonder.''

Audrey's heart sank, but then, almost immediately, a ray of hope stirred inside her. Buck B. Benedict might belong in another century, but that could prove to be a blessing in disguise for Betty, though she wouldn't think so at the time. Buck just might thwart Betty's romance with Jesse for good. It was a comforting thought.

Off and on for the remainder of the afternoon she pondered the things Betty had told her about the family structure. It was a bit archaic, to say the least. Peculiar that a dynamic man like Boyd would go along with all that dynasty nonsense. But then she was reminded of how little she actually knew about him . . . and how little his private life meant to her.

BY DINNERTIME that evening, Audrey was beginning to be painfully aware of every minute she had spent on Ranger. There wasn't a muscle in her body that didn't ache. She and Betty returned to the house late, so there was only time for a hasty shower instead of the hot bath she wanted. Audrey would have liked nothing better than to miss the dinner hour completely, but she was ravenously hungry after all the fresh air and exercise. So she suffered through another sumptuous, leisurely meal and excused herself as soon as she decently could.

"I hope you don't mind," she said as the family began filing out of the dining room, "but I seem to have overdone it today. I think I'll soak in a hot bath and fall into bed."

Betty looked at her apologetically. "I should have known better than to keep you out so long."

"I'm sure I'll feel better in the morning."

Actually, Audrey suspected the others were relieved to see her go. They would have plenty to talk about but couldn't, or wouldn't, as long as she was around. She said good-night and went to her bedroom. Once there, she filled the tub with steaming water, shed her clothes and climbed in, stretching out full length. The liquid heat worked wonders, soothing the soreness. She stayed in the tub until the water cooled, then briskly rubbed herself dry. Now she thought she could sleep.

Slipping into the knee-length terry cloth robe, she walked into the bedroom and turned down the bed covers. A bed had never looked so inviting. But before she could take off the robe and put on her gown there was a knock at the door. Opening it, she was astonished to see Boyd standing in the hall.

"You weren't already in bed, were you?"

"No, I just got out of the tub." Audrey then noticed he held a bottle in each hand. One he thrust toward her.

"Aspirin," he said.

"Thanks. That might help."

He held up the other bottle. "Liniment. Tonight you looked as though every step was an effort."

She smiled ruefully. "I'm afraid it was."

"Tomorrow will be worse if you don't use this stuff." Over her shoulder he glanced at the bed. "A good rubdown will work miracles. I'm something of an expert, since I've rubbed down many a sore horse in my day. If you want to go over there and lie on your stomach, I'll see what I can do for those legs of yours."

"Well, I..." She had the worst feeling that her cheeks had just turned a flaming vermilion.

"You'll thank me for it in the morning, I promise."

"I, ah..." She opened the door wider and stepped back to allow him to enter. "I guess... you'll probably do a better job than I can."

"On your tummy, please."

Self-consciously, Audrey complied, stretching out across the bed and pillowing her head on her arms. She tried to relax but felt herself tense as the mattress sagged when Boyd sat down. Beginning at her feet, he slowly worked the liniment into her legs. The sensation was indescribably pleasant, and Audrey found it impossible to remain tense under the onslaught of his soothing touch. She swore she could feel the soreness abating, though her mind was focused more on Boyd's strong, sure fingers than on her sore muscles.

"Was today very bad?" she finally asked, feeling the need for some conversation. "I mean, with the newspapers and all."

"Not really."

"Were there a lot of calls?"

"Quite a few, but nothing Dad couldn't handle."

"What did he tell them?"

"The party line is that the family isn't personally acquainted with any of these people mentioned in Granddad's will. If we don't know them, we can't very well give out any information about them, right?"

"And they buy that?" From her experience Audrey knew that a reporter would stop at nothing to get a story he or she really wanted.

"Probably not, but what can they do? Dad did get a little steamed over one call, though. Ever hear of Jerome Jordan?"

Audrey frowned in thought. "Seems I have, but I can't remember who he is."

"Gossip columnist. Arizona's self-appointed chronicler of the rich and famous."

"Oh, yes. The man who uses all the exclamation points. I've read his column a few times and always felt sorry for the people he writes about. I wonder how he gets by with all that stuff."

"You've read him, all right. He loves taking pot-shots at any Benedict. He called Dad this morning and suggested—I'm not making this up—that you might have been Granddad's illegitimate daughter.''

Audrey raised up on her elbows and looked over her shoulder in wide-eyed disbelief. "That's despicable!"

"But very like Jerome Jordan. Lie down and relax. Anyway, that was about the worst of it. Dad handled it with aplomb, and not even Jerome would dare print such nonsense. But that should tell you the kind of thing you would have had to deal with if you'd stayed at the hotel."

Audrey settled her head back on her arm. "I... guess I should thank you, all of you, for asking me to stay here."

"You're welcome," he murmured dryly. Discreetly, he inched the hem of her robe to midthigh as his practiced hands continued their soothing ministrations. Audrey felt her face growing warmer. His tactile touch elicited a sharp sensation in the pit of her stomach.

Boyd worked slowly, kneading and stroking, until his fingers encountered the hem of her robe and decency demanded he stop. Abruptly he pulled the garment down to its original length, screwed the cap on the liniment bottle and set it on the bedside table. Getting to his feet, he said, "Your bottom will be sorest, but I guess I'll let you take care of that."

Audrey shoved herself to a sitting position. "Th-thanks."

"Don't mention it," he replied with a grin. "My pleasure. Feel better?"

"I... think so."

"Good. Now, take a couple of those aspirin, and you'll feel almost brand-new in the morning."

"All right."

"Night. Sleep well."

"Good night."

Boyd walked to the door, then turned back to look at her. "Don't go to sleep without taking care of the derriere, or you'll be sorry tomorrow." And he left, closing the door behind him.

Audrey's heart was beating so rapidly she thought it would jump out of her chest. With some difficulty, she got up and reached for the bottle of liniment. Shrugging off the robe, she poured the liquid into her hands and massaged it into her buttocks, imitating Boyd's sure strokes. Then she gulped down two aspirin before putting on her gown and sliding between the cool sheets.

Plumping her pillow viciously, she made a conscious effort to empty her mind. She wasn't going to think about Boyd. He was nothing to her, nothing! In a week or so she would be back at the Greenspoint, back to the life she had so painstakingly made for herself, and the Benedicts once again would be nothing more than the wealthy family who owned the hotel where she worked.

Still, just before succumbing to her weariness, she thought of his strong, sure hands kneading and coaxing the soreness out of her legs. She hadn't wanted him to stop. A delicious tingling sensation spiraled up her spine. She fell asleep with a smile on her lips.

SLEEP DID NOT COME so easily for Boyd. He prowled his room restlessly before undressing and sliding into bed nude. Then he rested his head on his folded arms and stared at the ceiling.

He recalled his conversation with Betty after Audrey had gone to her room. His sister seemed to think Audrey could handle a horse and herself and would be no problem on roundup. Still, he'd refused, though he hated making Betty miss the adventure. Fall roundup was the high point of a ranch's year, the final accounting. Betty, of all people, deserved to be in on it since she worked as hard as anyone on the Triple B.

His sister had been disappointed by his refusal but magnanimous about it. Betty agreed that leaving Audrey at the ranch, especially with Elizabeth and Sara gone, not only would be unfair but would border on rudeness. After all, Audrey hadn't asked to come here. So that was that, the end of the matter.

What Boyd didn't understand was his lingering regret. Being honest with himself, he admitted he wanted Audrey along, and that wasn't sensible. Traditionally, the men disliked having women on roundup. They tolerated Betty because she had proved herself, but Audrey was a different matter entirely. Still, he wished she could go, and that didn't make any sense.

He sighed. A mixture of resignation and self-disgust overtook him. He had a problem, and his problem was lying in bed in the guest room. Try as he might, he couldn't be indifferent to Audrey. He had told himself time and time again to stay away from her, yet he gravitated to her like a fly to honey. And when he was alone with her she made him feel vulnerable, a feeling he despised above all others. Still he found excuses to seek her out.

From the beginning he had suspected that falling head over heels for her would be the easiest thing in the world. He didn't want to think it might already have happened.

CHAPTER EIGHT

AUDREY STROLLED from the house in the general direction of the stables, searching for Boyd. She was very upset over the conversation she'd had with Betty at breakfast, and though she doubted talking to Boyd would do any good, she had to try.

The ranch grounds teemed with activity and with more people than Audrey had previously seen milling about. She knew that the ranch had hired on extra men to help with the roundup, and she spotted three of the newcomers perched on the top railing of the corral fence. All three of the men were young, lean, wore black cowboy hats and sported facial hair. Looking at them, one was reminded of a Wanted poster. She was familiar with the type—itinerant drifters who followed the flow, hiring on wherever and whenever a ranch needed extra help, willing to sacrifice anything for this archaic way of life. Her father once had referred to them as "the infatuated few."

Audrey had almost reached the stables when Boyd came riding up on the beautiful horse he called Rocky. She saw that he had a young calf draped across his saddle. The poor animal had a bleeding tear in his cinnamon-colored hide, and his small white face was as frightened as a hurt child's.

"Oh!" she cried in dismay. "What happened?"

"The little guy strayed from his mama and got tangled up with a barbed-wire fence." Boyd dismounted and gently removed his hog-tied passenger, cradling him in his arms like a baby. "He needs some attention."

"Do you want help?" Audrey asked, falling in step beside him as he headed for the barn.

"I don't think you want to watch this, Audrey."

"I guess you'll have to cauterize the wound, right?"

"Right. He's gonna bawl his head off."

"You might need someone to help you hold him."

"All right. If you're sure you want to, come along."

One section of the barn had been partitioned off and was used as an emergency first-aid station for the ranch animals. A long stainless steel table stood in the center of the area, and a glass-fronted cabinet contained medical supplies. The place was as clean and sanitary as was possible under the circumstances. Boyd nodded toward the cabinet. "There's a blue spray bottle and some gauze pads in there. Would you mind swabbing down the table? I seem to have my hands full at the moment."

Audrey quickly performed the chore, then Boyd placed the calf on the disinfected table where it lay helplessly bawling for its mother. Audrey did the best she could to comfort the animal, soothing and petting it while Boyd cleaned and disinfected the wound. All went well until he applied the caustic solution. The calf thrashed and bellowed in protest, forcing Audrey to tighten her hold on him. "Come on, darling," she cooed, "it's going to be all right. Just calm down. You're going to feel lots better in a few minutes."

The pain did subside gradually, and Boyd released the rope binding the calf. Setting the animal on its feet, he pushed open a door that led to an isolation pen outside. "Sure sorry you had to learn about barbed wire the hard way, little feller." Smiling, he turned to Audrey. "They're curious as little kids. Thanks for your help."

"You're welcome, but I didn't do much."

"That's not true. You were a big help. It's hard to hold an animal and doctor it at the same time. The veterinary work didn't seem to bother you."

"No."

"Unusual."

"Guess I'm tougher than I look."

"Guess so. You don't look tough at all." They left the barn and walked as far as a Jeep parked at the side of the house. "How are the muscles this morning?" Boyd asked.

"Pretty good. Just a little sore."

"Didn't I tell you? Missed you at breakfast. I thought you might still be suffering some."

"No, but I'm afraid I overslept. Betty was the only one left in the dining room when I got there." Audrey stared at the ground a minute, then lifted her eyes. "Boyd, she tells me she asked if I could go along on roundup but you refused."

"Not a good idea," he remarked tersely. "The men don't like it."

"But if I weren't here, Betty would be going."

"Right, but Betty's a cowhand. You aren't."

"I can handle myself. I wouldn't be in the way. No one would have cause to complain. I promise. I wish you'd let me go."

"'Fraid not."

"Then I insist that you let Betty go. I can tell she wants to very badly."

Boyd shook his head. "Mom and Sara left for L.A. this morning. You'd be alone."

"I don't need a keeper." Audrey fought to keep the exasperation out of her voice. "Are you worried I'll run away? I promise I'll stay here like a good girl until I'm officially released."

"I'd hate to think you feel imprisoned," he said with a frown.

"Oh, of course I don't, but I wish you would try to understand how awful I feel about keeping Betty from something she obviously wants to do."

"She'll survive and live to see another roundup."

Audrey could see she was getting nowhere fast. Boyd, she was discovering, could be a maddeningly stubborn man. She decided to drop the subject for the time being, though she certainly planned to mention it again . . . and again.

Glancing around, she spied a pile of supplies on the ground beside the Jeep. There were cans of motor oil and large containers of gasoline. Boyd began loading them into the back of the Jeep. "What are you doing?" she asked.

"Gotta hook up a couple of windmills to gasoline engines. Summer rainy season's over and the wind's died."

"Why on earth would you do a job like that?"

"I wouldn't ask any man on this ranch to do something I don't do myself." Then impulsively, he added, "Want to come along? You seem to want a taste of ranch life."

"I really don't mind spending the day alone," she hedged.

"Are you sure? There's not much for you to do around here. Look at that gorgeous sky and tell me you want to spend the day thumbing through magazines. Windmilling's not my favorite chore, but at least it keeps me outside, and I sure could use some company."

Audrey hesitated. Common sense told her to steer clear of Boyd. He was far too curious about her, and keeping her guard up constantly was tiring. Besides, she seriously doubted he really wanted her company. It occurred to her that, save for the hours she'd spent sleeping, she hadn't been out of the sight of a Benedict since she had arrived at the Triple B. She wondered if that was a coincidence or by design. Perhaps Buck wanted someone to keep an eye on her at all times. Perhaps that was why Boyd insisted Betty miss roundup. If that was true, it rankled.

Still, there was something enormously appealing about the prospect of spending the day with Boyd. A perverse part of Audrey's nature was curious about him, too. "Well, if you really want some company..."

Boyd grinned. "I'll ask Maria to pack a lunch for two. Meet me here in about twenty minutes."

AN HOUR LATER, somewhere out in the vast grasslands of the ranch, Audrey perched on the hood of the parked Jeep and watched Boyd as he wrestled with a contrary pump jack. This engine apparently was giving him some trouble, and his mouth worked as busily as his hands. A muttered "goddammit" reached her ears.

She thought it unusual that Boyd, who easily could have been a rich man's spoiled son, seemed to enjoy the physical labor as much as he did. He worked efficiently, with economy of movement. He actually wasn't at all like the impeccable gentleman she had first encountered in the Durango Suite.

Minutes passed, then he returned to the Jeep. Hopping down from her perch, Audrey climbed back into the vehicle. "Did you get it fixed?" she asked.

"Sure," he replied. "I know all the right cuss words. Are you bored?"

"Not at all. This is nice."

He chuckled. "If windmilling appeals to you, you'll like anything."

"Oh, it's not that. It's everything...the weather, the wide open spaces..."

"The company?" he prodded playfully.

"Of course," she said with a smile. "That, too."

Boyd shifted into gear. With a lurch the Jeep moved forward, and they drove to the next windmill. By the time he'd finished with that one it was one o'clock, so he suggested they stop for lunch. He knew the perfect place, a grassy meadow at the foot of the Santa Rita Mountains. He parked near a spot where water tumbled down from the crags and crevices to form a slow-moving stream. "There's a blanket in back," he told Audrey. "Spread it out and I'll get the food."

Maria had packed cold fried chicken, bread, butter, a plastic container filled with raw vegetables, another with fruit, and a thermos of iced tea. They sat cross-legged on the blanket, and while they ate they talked.

"Have you always lived here, Boyd?" Audrey asked.

"Yep, I was born here. So was Dad. So was Grand-dad. When my great-great-grandfather left Pennsylvania, he went to Texas, bought two hundred head of longhorns and moved them onto the public domain in 1879, though he didn't get a clear title to the place until the Apaches were routed. The original deed is hanging in Dad's study. It was signed by President Grover Cleveland in 1895. The Benedicts have been here ever since."

Audrey shook her head in wonder. "That kind of family continuity is almost unbelievable. What was it like, growing up surrounded by all that tradition?"

It was a simple question but hard to answer. Boyd found it almost impossible to explain what it was like growing up as a Benedict in the valley, the source of the local citizens' pride and gossip, with so much to live up to. "Oh, not so bad, I guess," he said offhandedly. "But I'll confess something to you—when I was younger I hated seeing my name in the newspapers. I think that was the worst of it, knowing I couldn't indulge in normal teenage mischief for fear of landing on the front page. There have been many times when I wished my last name was Smith."

Audrey could understand that. To a lesser degree, bearing the name Hamilton in Dallas had sometimes been a burden. She guided her questioning along another path. "I think you said the ranch used to be bigger. How much bigger?"

"About a hundred thousand acres at one time, but as the family's business interests grew, we sold off some. Dad and Granddad used to argue about that a lot, along with other things."

Betty had mentioned Bert and Buck's arguments. Audrey slowly was piecing together a new picture of her elderly friend. More and more in her mind, Bert was becoming the "firebrand" Boyd had described that night at the hotel. "Betty told me that Bert and your father used to argue a lot. What did they argue about, other than selling your land."

"Politics, mainly. Granddad had the old-time cowman's inherent distrust of anything done or said in Washington, D.C. Occasionally he would tolerate 'interference' from Phoenix but never from the federal boys. Dad, on the other hand, is fascinated by politics and politicians. He always wanted Brent to run for office, but my brother just doesn't have the charisma for it. Don't get me wrong—Brent's a good guy and has a great head for business, but..." He shrugged and let the sentence die.

He didn't need to explain. Audrey had noticed how reserved Boyd's brother was. On a scale of one to ten, she felt Brent's personality rated a four or five, at best. She couldn't imagine the man hitting the campaign trail, pumping hands and hugging babies. And Sara wasn't much in the warmth department, either. Brent's wife was beautiful and gracious but terribly aloof. "What interests you, Boyd?" she asked. "Over and above work, I mean. I really don't know much about you."

He gave it some thought. "Oh, ordinary things. I like country music, football, baseball. Guess I'm Joe Average."

"No hobbies, no passions? Does anything unusual fascinate you?"

He regarded her over a drumstick. "Yep. You fascinate me."

It was, to say the least, an unexpected answer. "I do?"

"You do."

"In what way?"

"In many ways. You say you don't know much about me, but I know even less about you."

Audrey tensed, a reflex action. Every time she began to feel comfortable and at ease around him, his inquisitiveness reared its head. It was a shame that she had to keep so much of herself locked inside. That tended to place boundaries to her life and make attachments difficult to form. Boyd was the first man in years who had interested her beyond idle curiosity. *If things were different,* she reflected, *I believe I could feel some honest emotion for him.*

The thought alone was exciting. For some time now Audrey had been aware of a vague restlessness growing inside her. Basically she had been alone for five years, and an intrinsic part of her longed to savor romantic love. Occasionally she had reevaluated her priorities. Was it really so vital to keep her past a secret? After all, she'd done nothing wrong, and any man worthy of her time and interest surely would realize that. But always she would quickly recall those awful days after her father's trial when she'd been a victim of "guilt by association." No one would ever know how difficult it had been to start a new life. So everything would be locked away again.

Boyd saw her troubled expression and thought of all the questions he wanted to ask. *Where did you learn to ride a horse? How come you weren't the least bit squeamish about handling a wounded animal? What makes you think you'd last fifteen minutes on a roundup?* They would have to remain unasked. He'd never find out anything about her if he kept her wary. The last thing he wanted was an aloof Audrey. He enjoyed being with her too much. "The chicken's good, isn't it?" he commented casually.

Audrey released her pent-up breath. Maybe she'd been wrong; maybe he hadn't been going to pry, after all. She had become too touchy, and that, she realized, only added to her air of mystery. "It was delicious."

"Are you finished?"

"Lord, yes. I'm stuffed. I'm going to have to do something about this voracious appetite I seem to have acquired. When I get back home I'll have to go on a diet, and I despise dieting. It makes me crotchety."

"Surely you don't have weight problems." Boyd thought she was as trim and sleek as a colt.

"I do if I don't watch it." Audrey wiped her hands and mouth with a napkin, then waited for him to finish eating. When he did, she began clearing away the debris. Repacking everything in the hamper, she brushed aside Boyd's offers of help. "You've been working hard, and I need to move around. Just relax and digest your food. I'll do this."

She smoothed out the blanket, then carried the hamper and thermos to the Jeep. When she returned

to their picnic spot, she found Boyd stretched out full
length on his back, eyes closed, as blissfully relaxed as
a baby. A soft smile curved her mouth. She stood over
him for a moment. He was, she decided, the picture of
masculine perfection, and she marveled at the pleasure she derived merely from looking at him. In re-
pose his face was very somber. Audrey rubbed her
hands on her jeans, dismayed at the crazy emotions
and unmanageable thoughts he aroused in her.

Apparently he was asleep; his chest rose and fell in
even, shallow breathing. She sank to her knees beside
him, thinking she might get in a nap herself. The
combination of sun and food had made her drowsy.
She raised her face to the sun and closed her eyes.
Then she reopened them and glanced down to find
Boyd staring at her.

It seemed to Audrey that he was focused squarely on
her mouth. His gaze lingered there before moving
down to her breasts, and he made no effort to pretend
he was looking elsewhere. The expression on his face
sent her heart knocking against her ribs.

"I'm... sorry," she stammered. "Did I awaken
you?"

"No, I wasn't asleep. I was watching you watch
me."

"You just looked so peaceful. What were you
thinking?"

"Oh, nothing much." Boyd pushed himself to a
sitting position, brought his knees up and folded his
arms across them. "No, that's not true. I was thinking how nice this is. Like you said earlier, the sun, the
sky, the wide-open spaces. The company, of course.
Just the two of us. Not another soul around." He

smiled lazily. "If I had come out here alone I would have hurried through and gotten back home as soon as possible, but I wouldn't mind if this afternoon went on and on, would you?"

Audrey studied him quizzically. Some sort of change had come over him, something she couldn't give a name to at first. His eyelids drooped slightly, sensuously, and his lazy smile altered. Something told her he hadn't been thinking about the sun and sky at all. "That might be nice, but we, or rather you still have work to do."

"Yes. Duty calls, but who says I have to answer immediately? I don't suppose the world would stop if the other windmill had to wait until tomorrow." Boyd reached out and took her hand in his, encasing it warmly.

Suddenly, and without too much surprise, Audrey realized what the change in him signified. He was slipping into the role of desirable male. Some men did it so effortlessly, and apparently Boyd was one of them. Now, what brought this on, she wondered. Does he think I expect it?

Fascinated, she watched like a detached spectator as he inched closer to her and cupped her face with his free hand. "You have the most beautiful eyes I've ever seen," he said huskily.

The trite line didn't seem so trite when he said it. "Thanks."

"What color are they?"

"Brown."

"Come on, Audrey, that sounds ordinary, and your eyes are far from ordinary. They have funny little gold glints in them."

"Then I guess they're brown with funny little gold glints in them." Her voice sounded odd, curiously tremulous.

Boyd's hand dropped to her waist. There was a good solid feel to Audrey, he noticed. The sun had heated her skin, and its fragrance enticed him. He hadn't planned this romantic overture; it had just happened naturally. All of a sudden it had occurred to him that she was the most interesting woman who'd ever come into his life. Then one thing had led to another.

He intended moving cautiously, however. If she rebuffed him—and the chances were pretty good she would—they still would have to see a lot of each other in the coming days. He didn't want her suffering any embarrassment or bitterness. Slowly he brought his face closer to hers.

Audrey was as still as a statue. She couldn't have moved if her life had depended on it. Her heartbeat accelerated dramatically. She thought she was pretty well insulated against this sort of thing, but within seconds she learned how vulnerable she was to this very effective act of his. She knew she could jump to her feet, break the spell, and Boyd probably wouldn't persist. What she didn't know was why she didn't do just that. Maybe because this was fun, an exciting part of an age-old game. Basically it was harmless as long as she was aware of what was going on and kept it in proper perspective.

As Boyd's face came closer, she instinctively closed her eyes and parted her lips. His mouth touched hers tentatively, with scarcely any pressure at first, as though he was testing her reaction before proceeding further. She liked that. Meeting no resistance, he increased the pressure. Tilting her head slightly, Audrey leaned into the kiss. Thus encouraged, Boyd delicately penetrated her mouth with his tongue.

The slow spreading warmth was delightfully languorous as it crept into her pores. Audrey simply gave in to the sensation of being female and desired. A number of years had passed since she last had experienced such a thrilling kiss, and she wasn't a bit shy about thoroughly enjoying this one.

Boyd wrapped his arms around her, and hers crawled up his chest to lock behind his neck. Finally breaking the kiss, he nuzzled the gentle curve of her shoulder, then gathered her close and laid his cheek on top of her head. Audrey realized she had all but forgotten the sensation of being close to a man. It felt good. She pressed her face against his chest, heard the steady thump-thumping of his heartbeat and wondered what it would be like to make love with him. She imagined he would be a magnificent lover. Perhaps it was because Boyd seemed the type who would take time to please a woman.

One of his hands began stroking her back. It was hypnotizing, eliciting a spontaneous sigh from Audrey. There they were, out in the middle of nowhere without another person for miles. A few more minutes of kissing and stroking, then he would start murmuring all the erotic nonsense designed to lull her into a state of well-being. A knot formed in the pit of her stomach. It might be nice . . .

Perhaps, but thinking about it was ridiculous. She didn't know Boyd well enough for making love to even cross her mind. On top of that, this entire episode might be nothing but a ploy on his part, something he hoped would break down her defenses and cause her to tell him more than she wanted him to know.

Moving away from him slightly, she let her arms fall to her sides. "We really should be going, or we'll never get back to the house before dark."

Boyd's hand stopped its sensuous maneuvers. He raised his head and looked at her, puzzled. What had happened? One minute she had been so pliant in his arms, soft and warm; the next minute she was pulling away. He'd thought everything had been going just fine. Naturally he hadn't expected to go much beyond a kiss, but it had seemed the start of something wonderful. What had happened?

Oh, what the hell! What difference did it make? He told himself he wasn't really disappointed. The pass probably had been a dumb move to begin with. Wrong time, wrong place, wrong woman.

"Yeah, I guess you're right," he muttered and rolled away from her. Standing up, he brushed at the seat of his pants. Then he turned to give her a hand, but she was already on her feet and moving toward the Jeep.

BOYD STUCK STRICTLY to business the rest of the afternoon. He and Audrey were friendly but impersonal, though occasionally he caught himself stealing quick glances in her direction. Each time he was aware of a catch in the region of his heart. It was easy to say that one little kiss had meant nothing; believing it was something else.

The last windmill was located some distance from ranch headquarters, so the sun was quite low in the western sky by the time they returned to the house. Audrey carried the hamper and thermos inside, while Boyd unloaded the Jeep. That done, he walked toward the bunkhouse, which stood just beyond the corrals. The long wooden building was almost deserted, but he found two of the hands seated at a card table in a far corner, playing gin rummy. They looked up when he entered.

"Hi 'ya, Boyd," one of the cowboys greeted him. "What can we do for you?"

"Have either of you seen Skeet?"

The other man jerked his head toward a side door. "Saw him go outside a few minutes ago."

"Thanks," Boyd said and walked through the door the cowboy had indicated.

The object of his search was standing at the corral fence, one booted foot propped on the first rail, puffing on a cigarette. Skeet Drummond was sixty-five, weather-worn, gray-haired and something of a fixture around the Triple B. He'd been "out to pasture" for a number of years, the victim of age and arthritis. Now he was reduced to doing odd jobs around the ranch and taking charge of the chuck wagon during roundup, but in his heyday he had worked most of the big ranches throughout the West. A cowboy for forty-seven years, Skeet considered himself a historian of sorts. He either personally knew or knew of everyone who was anyone in the ranching business, and it was the man's vast storehouse of knowledge that sent Boyd in search of him now.

"'Evenin', Boyd," Skeet drawled. "How's it goin'?"

"Pretty good, Skeet. How's it with you?"

"Can't complain." Skeet pushed his battered Stetson farther back on his head. "Ain't this weather somethin'?"

"That it is."

"Hear it's s'posed to hold clear through roundup. Good omen if you believe in omens."

Boyd draped one arm over the fence and watched as the ranch's newest filly guzzled dinner from her mother's underbelly. "Pretty one, isn't she?" he commented idly.

"Sure is," Skeet agreed. "You folks jus' might have yourselves a cham-peen in that one."

The two men contemplated mother and daughter for a few wordless minutes. Then Boyd got to business. "Tell me, Skeet, have you ever heard of anyone named Hamilton who ranched in Texas, probably somewhere within a reasonable distance of Dallas?"

Skeet squinted his eyes in thought. "Hamilton. Let's see.... Now, myself, I never worked that far east, but I did hire on at the J.A. for a while. That's in West Texas, though. Hamilton. You know, that name sounds familiar, but I can't rightly recall where I heard it."

"Sure would appreciate anything you come up with. It's pretty important."

"Oh, I'll remember directly. Almost always do. Jus' give me a few days of ponderin'."

"If you come up with something, don't mention it to anyone else, okay? Come and see me personally. Like I said, it's pretty important, and I'd just as soon no one knows I asked questions."

Skeet shrugged. "Whatever you say, Boyd."

"Much obliged, Skeet. Be talking to you."

"Sure. Take care."

Boyd walked back to the house, deep in thought. He realized he was clutching at straws. It was highly unlikely that Skeet would know anything about Audrey's family, since they might not have been ranchers at all. Still, Boyd couldn't shake the belief that the Triple B wasn't the first ranch Audrey had been on, and he was obsessed with the need to know why she chose to keep that a secret.

He had no conscionable right to pry into her past. Normally he wouldn't dream of doing such a thing, but this was no normal situation. He had to own up to the fact that Audrey was special to him. He might not want her to be, but she was. He wanted to get inside her head and heart and find out what made her tick.

His thoughts were still whirling when he opened the front door and crossed the foyer. Tomorrow he, the regulars, and the extra hands would ride out to set up camp; the next day roundup would begin. He might be gone three days or he might be gone a week. He couldn't be sure Audrey would still be at the ranch when he returned. One word from his father and she'd hop in her Datsun and be gone like a shot. Of course, the Greenspoint wasn't that far away, but his work didn't require his being in Phoenix all that often. The opportunity to really get to know her might escape him altogether.

Then, for some unfathomable reason, his mind took a different turn. If his suspicions about Audrey's background were right, she was probably no stranger to the outdoor life. She seemed damned confident she could take care of herself on the open range, and he thought a real tenderfoot would have some doubts.

But then again, she just might not have any idea what roundup entailed.

The last thing a man needed during roundup was someone who required a nursemaid. Why was he even considering taking her along? Giving himself a shake, he turned down the hall and headed for his room. When he passed Audrey's door, however, he stopped and tugged on his chin thoughtfully.

Well, what the hell? If she couldn't hack it, the world wouldn't come to an end. He could just dispatch one of the hands to see her safely back to the house. No harm done to anything but Audrey's pride. Raising a hand, he hesitated. When his dad heard about this, he was probably going to think his younger son had lost his mind. Boyd wasn't too sure he wouldn't be right. He knocked twice.

The door opened and she stood before him, dressed in a bright yellow jumpsuit. A towel was wrapped turban-style around her head. A sweet, clean scent overpowered his senses. She obviously was just out of the shower. "Hi," she said, cocking her head and eyeing him questioningly.

"Hi. I, ah...you know, it can get damned cold out on the range at night this time of year."

She stared at him blankly. "Oh?"

"Yeah. It's the altitude."

"Well, I..." She didn't have any idea what he was getting at. "I imagine so."

Boyd shoved his hands into his pockets. "Then it can turn around and be hotter'n hell the next afternoon. What I'm trying to tell you is, life on the range isn't comfortable. You sleep in a bedroll on the ground. If it rains, your only shelter is a tent, and I've yet to see one that didn't leak.''

Audrey's eyes lit up. Suddenly it dawned on her what he was offering. ''Discomfort doesn't throw me, Boyd. I'm not a hothouse plant.''

''You won't receive any special concessions or privileges because of your sex.''

''I expect none. I don't want any.'' Did she really seem that fragile and delicate to him?

''Then if you're damned sure you want to come along, I'll have Betty outfit you. But I want you to promise me something in return.''

''What is it?''

''No suffering in silence. If you don't feel well, I want you to let me know.''

Audrey smiled radiantly. ''Agreed, but I think I'll surprise you. Betty will be so pleased. Thank you.''

''Yeah, you're welcome. Well, see you at dinner.''

He ambled away, leaving Audrey to stare after him. He certainly didn't seem overjoyed by the prospect of having her along, so why had he acquiesced? What in the world had happened to change his mind? She guessed she could add ''complicated'' and ''unpredictable'' to the growing list of adjectives that came to mind when she thought of Boyd.

A feeling of accomplishment and anticipation overcame her, and it had nothing to do with the pleasure of knowing she wouldn't make Betty miss roundup. Rather, she was excited by the prospect of spending days in Boyd's company. She didn't particularly want the excitement, but it existed nevertheless.

CHAPTER NINE

THE MOOD around the dinner table that night was lighthearted, almost festive. Betty, especially, was in unusually high spirits as a result of Boyd's decision to allow Audrey to join the roundup crew. Buck looked slightly askance when the announcement was made, but after a minute's consideration he said, "Good idea." Audrey supposed it would be a relief for him to have her safely unreachable for a few days. She had no idea if he was still having to field phone calls from the press, since that was never discussed in front of her, but she hardly expected the notoriety to have died down so soon.

Once the meal was over, the three Benedict men headed for Buck's study, and Betty turned to Audrey with shining eyes. "How in the world did you ever convince my brother to let you come along?"

"I don't have the slightest idea. I would have sworn it was a closed issue, but he changed his mind for some reason."

"Strange. Once Boyd makes up his mind about something, it usually stays made. Well, whatever you did, I thank you for it. Lord, it's going to be fun having another woman along. After four or five days, that all-male atmosphere begins to get on my nerves. Come on, let's get our stuff together. You'll need a bedroll and the right kind of clothes.''

Betty led the way to a part of the house Audrey hadn't seen before, a large storage room beyond the kitchen. There she gathered up two bedrolls, a duffel bag, a couple of canteens and a first-aid kit. ''The men won't carry canteens or medical supplies,'' she told Audrey. ''They claim they're sissy, but you and I, thank God, don't have to prove how tough we are.''

They carried the gear to Betty's bedroom, where she began rummaging around in dresser drawers. ''I'll take every pair of warm socks I own, and you'll need a heavy jacket. You never know what the weather will do this time of year. For sure you'll need a jacket when you crawl out of that warm bedroll every morning. I hope you realize you'll be living in and sleeping in the same clothes for days. Fastidiousness falls by the wayside on roundup, but when we move the herd to Summerfield camp, there's a permanent bunkhouse where we'll be able to clean up and change. It always feels like heaven.''

For the next ten minutes or so the two women concentrated on the task of packing what little clothing and toiletries they would take with them into a small duffel bag. The bag and their bedrolls, Betty explained, would be carried in one of the two trucks that would accompany the crew. The trucks were the lone concession to modern civilization. Otherwise, the annual roundup ritual had not significantly changed since the 1890s.

Just as they finished packing, Brent appeared in the doorway. ''Betty, Dad wants to see you as soon as you can get free.''

Betty nodded in acknowledgment, and Brent walked away. The young woman glanced at her watch. "Damn," she muttered under her breath.

"Something wrong?" Audrey asked.

Betty cast an anxious glance toward the open door and lowered her voice. "I'm supposed to meet Jesse out back in a few minutes. Audrey, do me a favor. Go find him and tell him I'll be late."

The last thing Audrey wanted to do was talk to Jesse. She couldn't very well refuse, however; Betty would think that awfully strange. "Sure," she agreed.

"I think we're finished here," Betty said. "I'll put our bedrolls and the bag out in the hall, and Boyd will get them in the morning. Remember to set your alarm tonight. Now, I guess I'd better go see what Dad wants. Good night."

"Good night, Betty."

In her own room, Audrey opened the veranda door and stepped outside. There was a definite chill in the air. At this altitude the temperature difference between day and night could be dramatic, and she knew it would seem even more marked out on the open range. Hugging herself and rubbing her arms briskly, she hurried across the patio and onto the lawn. She assumed Jesse would be out there somewhere watching the house.

He was. He emerged from the shadows, looking somewhat surprised. "Well, well, if it isn't the heiress."

The mere sound of his voice irritated Audrey. Stiffening as he approached her, she said, "Betty's father wanted to see her. She'll be out as soon as she can get away." With that she reversed direction and started back to the house.

"Whoa!" Jesse ordered, quickly moving in front of her. "Aren't you going to stay here and keep me company until Betty comes?"

"No," she replied icily. "I told Betty I would deliver her message. It's delivered. Good night."

"Come on, Audrey, stay and talk to me. I'm itching to find out all about your inheritance, all about you and the old man. I'll bet it's an interesting story."

"Get out of my way, Jesse."

"Talk about feathering your nest! Must be nice to have money again. How'd you butter up the old codger?"

Audrey seethed inside. "Assuming I intended discussing it with anyone, which I don't, it certainly wouldn't be with the likes of you. Now get out of my way!"

Grinning sardonically, Jesse stepped aside, and Audrey brushed past him. As she crossed the patio and headed for her room, something unpleasant crossed her mind. So far she had successfully managed to stay away from Jesse, but now she would be seeing him every day. He galled her to the point of fury, and she wasn't a very good actress. She just prayed she'd be able to hold her tongue in check and keep her real feelings hidden. No one would be able to understand why she despised someone she wasn't supposed to know.

THE ALARM next to Audrey's bed went off at five o'clock the next morning. Groaning, she reached out to silence it and scrunch back under the covers. Then she remembered what day it was. For a moment the idea of going on roundup wasn't quite as appealing as it had been. In fact, it sounded downright grim. But having Boyd allow her to go was a big concession on his part and a victory of sorts for her. Flinging off her misgivings, she crawled out of bed and went into the bathroom to splash cold water on her face and brush her teeth.

Back in the bedroom she dressed in the sturdiest pair of jeans she owned and a long-sleeved shirt, heavy socks and the borrowed boots. From force of habit she walked to the dressing table to begin putting on makeup. But she realized she would be going without makeup for quite some time, so she made do with lotion and a swipe of lip balm, then brushed her hair and secured it at the nape of her neck with a scarf. She knew it probably was a bit chilly outside, so she slipped on the jacket and set a hat on her head. Her reflection in the mirror was anything but the loveliest sight she'd ever seen, but she'd look a lot worse before she set foot in this room again. Psyching herself for the adventure, she turned off the light and went into the hall.

The house was absolutely quiet. Betty's door was open, but the room was dark and empty. As Audrey walked toward the front of the house she saw that Boyd's room was the same. It couldn't possibly be much past five-thirty, but apparently she was the straggler.

The dining room was deserted, and no sounds came from the kitchen. Surely they weren't going to ride out without breakfast. Moving quietly, Audrey let herself out the front door, crossed the long porch and went around the side of the house. Lights shone from the bunkhouse in the distance, and a large group of people were gathered around one of the pickups. The smell of coffee and food permeated the fresh morning air.

Audrey suddenly was overcome by a feeling of shyness, of being someplace she shouldn't be, and she was hesitant about joining the gathering. This was an all-male inner sanctum, save for Betty, and she was about to invade it. Not only was she a female, she was a rank outsider without credentials, and she knew with certainty there were plenty of men in the group who were going to resent her presence. Not openly, of course, since she was here by Boyd's invitation, and cowboys never questioned the boss. The resentment would be there, nevertheless, and she found that hard to take.

Then a figure moved away from the crowd and walked in her direction. It was Betty, though at first Audrey didn't recognize her. Betty blended in with the group as she herself never could. "Good morning," her friend said brightly. "I was afraid you might miss breakfast."

"Am I that late?"

"Actually you're right on time. I guess the rest of us are early. Everyone's itching to go. Come on and get some coffee. There are biscuits and sausage, too. Eat as much as you can. It'll be a long time before you'll eat again."

As if on signal, the men clustered around the truck moved back to make a path for her. Audrey imagined all eyes were disapproving, but in truth, the men accepted her with equanimity. A few even touched the brims of their hats in silent greeting.

Skeet Drummond was serving chuck off the truck's tailgate. Once breakfast was over, the elderly cowboy would drive the truck containing his equipment and supplies to the campsite. There he would prepare all the meals for nineteen hungry people for as many days as it took to gather the herd, and he would do it superbly. The food served by the Triple B was one of the things that brought the same cowboys back to the ranch year after year at roundup time.

"'Mornin', ma'am," Skeet said cheerfully. "Coffee?"

"Yes, please."

The cook poured the strong black brew into a heavy mug and handed it to her. Then from a large pan he scooped up the biggest biscuit Audrey had ever seen, deftly pulled it apart and shoved a thick sausage patty between the halves. "Eat hearty. There's more where that came from."

The biscuit was almost too hot to hold, but napkins apparently weren't standard chuck wagon niceties. Audrey was certain nothing had ever tasted as good as that crude breakfast served in the morning air just as the first sign of daybreak crept over the horizon. Leaning against the side of the truck, she drank and ate and surveyed the busy scene before her.

Most of the men had finished eating and had gone to their horses to check saddles and gear. There wasn't much conversation since they weren't a talkative bunch. They never used words when a grunt or a nod of the head would do. To a man they were the sort who could spend a winter alone in a line shack with only a horse for company and think it was the greatest life on earth.

As Audrey ate she found herself searching the crowd for Boyd. Finally she spotted him standing away from the mainstream, studying something on a clipboard he was holding. Pettishly she wondered why he didn't come over and say good-morning or something. She finished the biscuit, drained the coffee cup and declined Skeet's offers of more. She would regret that before the day was over, but for the moment she felt completely satisfied and fortified.

The tempo of activity around the corrals picked up, but there didn't seem to be anything for her to do. Wanting to stay out of everyone's way as much as possible, she strolled to the spot where Ranger was tethered and checked the saddle rigging.

"I saddled him myself, so everything's perfect." Boyd's voice came from behind her.

She turned. "Thanks, but I could have done it."

"Really? I wasn't sure." His eyes raked her from head to toe. "You look dressed properly. We ride in ten minutes. Are you ready?"

"Yes."

"Stick close to Betty or me on the way. It's hard enough to find a lost calf out on the range, much less a person."

His attitude made her bristle. "Do you think I'm completely stupid? I don't intend getting lost."

"No one ever does." He walked away, the clipboard under his arm.

Since most of the others were mounting, Audrey did likewise. Ranger took a few sideways steps as his burden settled in the saddle. Almost immediately Betty rode up beside her and slung something over her saddle horn. Audrey saw it was one of the canteens.

Nudging her horse, Betty motioned for her to follow. "We might as well ride out. No need to wait for the others. I could find Number Five camp blindfolded."

The sun had cleared the horizon and was playing hide-and-seek with streaky gray clouds that would burn off by midmorning. Audrey turned in her saddle in time to see the two trucks veer off to the east, following a ranch road. Then the rest of the riders began heading their way. It was a spectacular sight. The scene reminded her of an old John Wayne movie and was something she was sure she wouldn't soon forget. Nobody was in a hurry; today would be an easy one, when all they had to do was set up camp. Tomorrow was what would test her mettle.

Still, they spent long hours in the saddle, and once they'd reached camp—which proved to be nothing more than some pens out in the middle of nowhere— there was work to do. Horses had to be unsaddled, rubbed down, fed, watered and corralled. By the time that was finished it was nearing four o'clock. The day had turned warm, so Audrey shed her jacket and tossed it aside, knowing she would need it again once the sun got low in the sky. It occurred to her that none of them had had anything to eat for ten hours. Furthermore, it looked as if it might be some time before food was forthcoming. Skeet and the truck containing the chuck wagon, having had to take a round-about route, hadn't yet reached camp. But she seemed to be the only one who found that a dismal prospect. Sighing wearily, she sat on the ground, propped an elbow on a knee, rested her chin in her hand and tried to ignore her weary bones and empty stomach.

If the others were tired or hungry, they showed no signs of it. Now that they had reached camp, the cowboys seemed to come alive. They stood around laughing and swapping stories. A few practiced rope tricks. Betty strolled away to find Jesse. Audrey was too tired and too hungry to move. When she saw Boyd walking her way, she barely managed a wan smile.

He squatted on the ground beside her. "A far cry from the Greenspoint, isn't it?" he said with a lazy smile.

She shrugged. "A bit."

"You must be tired."

"Oh . . . a little."

"Liar."

"I'll get used to it."

"Yeah, reckon you will, but you can always go back to the house if it gets to be too much for you."

Audrey gave him an implacable look. "It's not going to be too much for me, Boyd. Why don't you wait and see how I handle myself before assuming I'm going to fold?" The only way she would leave camp, she decided, was on a stretcher . . . and at the moment that didn't seem too remote a possibility. However, she'd die before she let Boyd know that.

"I just don't want you getting sick."

Audrey was sensitive to every nuance of his voice, maybe too sensitive. He sounded sincerely concerned about her welfare. On the other hand, his manner indicated that he expected her to be nothing but trouble. "I have to get my sea legs, that's all. I'll be fine. You don't need to worry about me."

Boyd stared at her a minute. He was worried about her, dammit, because he cared for her far more than he wanted to. He knew he'd never forgive himself if she got hurt or sick or whatever. He couldn't imagine what had possessed him to ask her along.

That wasn't exactly the truth, and he knew it. He'd simply wanted her close by, so if anything happened to her the blame would rest squarely with him. Getting to his feet, he said, "All right, but you promised me you wouldn't suffer in silence. I'm holding you to it." With that, he walked away, although he wanted to stay, to sit beside Audrey, talk to her, be with her. But he didn't want to give the men something to speculate on. As it was, a couple of the younger cowboys were watching him with knowing looks.

At that moment Skeet and the chuck wagon came lumbering into camp, eliciting whoops and shouts from the crew. Not far behind came the other truck carrying the tents and bedrolls. While the cook went about setting up his "kitchen" and beginning dinner, some of the hands put up their tents, though most elected to sleep under the stars. Audrey and Betty put theirs some distance from the main gathering, near a thick stand of trees, scrub bushes and knee-high grass that would serve as their bathroom, as much privacy as the two women would have for some time.

As the sun slipped lower in the western sky, everyone once again bundled up in their jackets. When Skeet bellowed "Chuck!" a beeline was made to the camp fire. Audrey's plate was piled high with steak, fried potatoes, bread and cherry cobbler. Vegetables were nonexistent; the cowboys on roundup ate carbohydrates and protein and lots of both. She ate like a starving field hand and so, she noticed, did Betty. Since mealtimes in the great outdoors were serious affairs, talk was held to a minimum, but once stomachs were full, the conversation picked up. Surprisingly, the men seldom used profanity, and that had nothing to do with women being present. They hardly ever used it. There was a certain courtliness to their style that a lot of swearing would have spoiled. An occasional "damn" or "hell" was about as lurid as it got. In fact, "dadblamed" seemed to be the favorite expletive.

And they were unfailingly polite to each other. There was a respect among them that Audrey rarely had seen displayed in the business world. They joked back and forth, and while their jokes were sexist, they weren't sexual. The homespun humor concerned women drivers, lazy wives and that sort of thing. A few of the cornier ones caused Audrey and Betty to exchange wryly amused glances, but nothing was said around the camp fire that night that couldn't safely and without embarrassment have been said in front of an eighty-year-old woman or an eight-year-old child.

Once everyone had finished eating, the cowboys went back to their amusements, practicing roping and pitching horseshoes. When it got too dark for horseshoes, some gathered around the fire to play cards, others just sat drinking coffee and telling anecdotes about other roundups. Audrey lasted as long as she could, but it had been dark less than an hour when she slipped into the tent and crawled into her bedroll. The subdued horseplay around the fire went on for some time, and just before everyone retired, one of the men brought out a harmonica and led a spirited sing-along. Audrey didn't hear a sound.

SHE AWOKE BEFORE DAWN, scooted out of the tent feet first and made for the thick brush. Returning to camp, she saw that Skeet was the only other person stirring. Audrey had feared she would be in agony after all that riding the day before, but the stiffness lasted only a few minutes. This morning she was imbued with a strange kind of energy, almost uncontainable. She went to the chuck wagon, where she and Skeet conversed in whispers while he put on the coffee and made pancake batter. She stood huddled in her jacket, watching the sun come up and marveling at the cook's efficiency with a minimum of equipment. Breakfast was pancakes, bacon, eggs and, of course, gallons of scalding black coffee, all cooked over an open fire.

An hour later all of them had saddled, mounted and sat astride their horses in a semicircle facing Boyd. He was dividing the riders into four groups, each headed by a Triple B regular. Audrey noticed that Betty didn't wait for instructions from her brother; instead she joined Jesse's group, and Boyd didn't protest.

When everyone but Audrey had been assigned to a group, Boyd rode up to her. "You'll ride with me. Stay close."

The groups fanned out in separate directions, making a wide circle through the easternmost quadrant of the ranch, gathering cattle where they found them. Following orders, Audrey stayed close to Boyd as they rode slowly through heavy brush and across endless meadows. Though they could see for miles in all directions, they didn't spot a single cow for almost an hour. Suddenly one of the riders in their group spurred his horse forward to chase seven or eight calves that had seemingly appeared from nowhere.

"I'm going down to help head them off and turn 'em toward camp," Boyd said. "You stay right here and look for strays."

Audrey interpreted that to mean "Stay the hell out of the way," so she did. She sat there for more than an hour, watching as Boyd and two other cowboys worked the brush, dredging up cattle the way a magician pulls rabbits out of his hat. Finally, having gathered a hundred head or so, the cowboys expertly turned the herd toward camp, and Boyd motioned to Audrey to follow.

The cattle formed a long tight oval and lumbered across the grasslands, stirring up a cloud of dust. One cowboy rode point in front; Boyd rode left flank, another cowboy rode right. Whether by accident or design, Audrey found herself riding drag. Occasionally one of the men would encounter a stray, and with sure, easy motions he would soon have the animal moving with the herd. It was an amazing ritual, fascinating in its repetition.

Audrey was congratulating herself on having come this far without committing one goof or getting in anyone's way when a slobbering old bull with a mind of his own suddenly turned from the herd and reversed his direction. Immediately Ranger wheeled around and started after him.

Had anyone warned her that Ranger had been trained as a cutting horse, she wouldn't have been startled. As it was, she experienced a horrifying moment of panic, fearing her mount had been spooked, and she frantically tried to rein him in. It took her only a second or two, however, to realize the kind of horse Ranger was. The summer she was sixteen she had won first place in the junior division of a cutting horse competition. Instinctively she loosened her grip on the reins and relaxed in the saddle, giving the horse his head. Almost before she knew what had happened, Ranger had overtaken the bull and nudged him back into the herd. Audrey hoped her grin didn't look as foolish as it felt.

Boyd rode up to her; the expression on his face was that of a man recovering from shock. "You all right?" he asked anxiously.

"Sure," she said matter-of-factly.

"You handled that pretty well."

"Ranger did it all."

"I know, but I'm wondering how you knew he would." His eyes still speculative, he retook his position on the left flank.

There was no stopping for lunch. As they slowly moved toward the camp they, one by one, were joined by the other groups, and the size of the herd doubled, tripled, quadrupled. Audrey continued to ride drag, partly because she now knew she and Ranger could take care of any stragglers, mostly because no one had told her to do otherwise. At one point during the long monotonous drive, a young cowboy rode up beside her and shyly handed her a strip of beef jerky. "Sure helps to stave off the hunger pangs, ma'am," he drawled.

"Thanks," Audrey said. It had been years since she'd chewed on a piece of the hard, salty stuff. She wished she could remember the young man's name, but with their black hats and handlebar mustaches so many of the cowboys looked alike.

"Joel Garrett. Idaho," he offered.

"Thanks, Joel. This is going to taste wonderful."

Touching the brim of his hat with a forefinger, he rode off.

At a spot near a water tank, the hands circled and held the herd while Boyd, Jesse Murdoch and another cowboy cut out the steer calves and their mothers, separating them from the cows with heifer calves and the young calves that had been born since last spring's branding. The heifers and young calves and most of the mothers would be turned out to pasture to rebuild the herd. The steer calves would be shipped to feedlots for further fattening before going to market. In the grisly cycle of the cattle business, the mothers of the steers would lead their babies to the cattle trucks, then go back to pasture to breed again. When the mothers reached the bovine menopause, they too would go to slaughter to be turned into "cheap cuts."

It was late afternoon before the riders returned to camp and drove the cattle into the waiting pens. Audrey calculated she had ridden maybe twelve to fifteen miles that day, but with all the scurrying to and fro chasing cattle, the others had ridden perhaps twice that far. She was covered with dust, but so was everyone else. She was tired, but tonight the fatigue felt good. The worst was over; she had earned a stripe, maybe two. From now on, as her confidence grew, each day would get easier.

After tending to Ranger, she squatted on the ground in front of the tent, removed the big hat, untied the scarf at her nape and let her hair fall free. She shook her head, massaged her scalp a couple of times, then retied the scarf. At that moment Skeet bellowed "Chuck!" Audrey was beginning to think that was the sweetest word in the English language.

She ate two bowls of the chili Colorado that Skeet dished out so lavishly, and lost track of how many flour tortillas she dipped into the spicy stuff. Afterward, using her saddle as a backrest, she stretched out her legs, sipped coffee and contemplated the Arizona sky. Out here she could see the Milky Way as clearly as she could see the ceiling in her apartment. Lost in a lazy languor, she vaguely wondered how things were going at the Greenspoint...but only vaguely. This was light-years removed from that elegance, but oddly, at the moment she didn't want to be anywhere else on earth.

Her eyes roamed over the camp scene. Boyd didn't do much sitting. He moved through camp constantly, keeping an eye on everything. Like a dorm housemother, Audrey thought in amusement. She caught sight of Betty and Jesse, sitting apart from the mainstream, and thought it strange that no one seemed to notice how close the two of them were. But then everyone treated Betty like one of the boys. Audrey herself was shown a little more deference, something that didn't particularly please her.

Lost in a private reverie, she didn't see Boyd coming toward her until he sat on the ground next to her. "Not quite as glamorous as you thought it would be, right?"

"I didn't think for a minute it would be glamorous. But there's a kind of grandeur to it."

"I know."

"Out here you get an insight into why some people love this life so much. And it's easy to see why the valley itself holds such appeal."

"Yeah. Granddad loved it in a way that's hard to describe. He liked talking about the old days, the 'old days' being the forties and fifties. The place was known as the 'Santa Booze Valley' then, because a bunch of rich New Yorkers moved in and threw round-the-clock parties. Then Hollywood started making movies here. John Wayne was an old drinking buddy of Granddad's. Guess it was pretty wild for a while. Things have quietened down, though."

Glancing toward the cowboys near the camp fire, Audrey remarked, "They're all peas out of the same pod."

"Mostly. Better educated than the old-time cowboys but cut of the same cloth."

"Are any of them married?"

"A few of the regulars are. Their wives and kids live in Agua Linda. Most of the drifters were married at one time, too, but cowboying takes its toll on a marriage. Now they just roam from place to place, carrying everything they own with 'em."

Audrey twisted her head to look at him. "Did you ever yearn for that kind of life?"

"Yeah, when I was a kid. But I also wanted to be an astronaut and to play shortstop for the Dodgers. Hard to work those three careers into one lifetime." He grinned, and she grinned back. "You impressed me today, Audrey, you really did."

"Hate to say I told you so," she said smugly and took a sip of coffee.

"I damned near had a heart attack when I saw Ranger take off," he confessed. "If you could have seen the look on your face..."

"It just took me a minute to figure out what was happening, that's all. No one told me Ranger was a cutter. I thought he'd been spooked."

Boyd sipped from his own cup and thought about what she'd said. Not only did she know what a cutting horse was, she'd instinctively known to relax, almost go limp and turn the job over to her mount. That wasn't something a person learned in a day or two. She'd been trained; he'd bet on it. If so, he could stop worrying about her. She wouldn't be a hindrance. In fact, she and Ranger could earn their keep, if Audrey was willing to admit she was no novice. Damn, he wished she would talk to him.

The cowboy with the harmonica had struck up a tune, which drew most of the others around the camp fire and left Audrey and Boyd alone on the periphery. Someone burst into song; everyone else soon joined in. "More coffee?" Boyd asked.

"No thanks. I wouldn't want it to keep me awake." Audrey laughed lightly. Nothing short of an earthquake would keep her awake tonight.

Boyd took her empty cup out of her hand. "I'll give these to Skeet." Getting to his feet, he walked over to the chuck wagon. Audrey saw him exchange a few words with Skeet. She assumed he would join the group around the camp fire. However, when he turned away from the chuck wagon he came back to sit beside her, this time very close. He stretched his long legs beside hers and slid an arm around her shoulders. Audrey felt her pulse quicken; with some effort she kept her eyes straight ahead. She pretended to be watching the music makers around the fire, but she saw nothing. All her senses were attuned to Boyd's closeness. She thought of what she must look like and was glad there was no mirror handy to confirm her suspicions. Surely she was at her unlovely worst. Of course, Boyd's clothes were as rumpled and dust-covered as her own, but none of that detracted from his attractiveness. Whenever she was near him she was reminded of the vital something missing from her life.

There were rustling sounds around the camp fire as some of the cowboys got up and made for their bed-rolls. As bone-tired as she was, Audrey wished the day didn't have to end. The soft, sensuous beauty of the night and the comforting feel of Boyd's arm around her seduced her. The hand that had been resting lightly on her shoulder moved to the nape of her neck, and he untied the scarf that held her hair. She felt it fall to her shoulders.

"I told you . . . hair like that should never be con-fined," he murmured softly.

"It's a mess," she objected shakily. "It's filthy."

"Looks beautiful to me." His fingers played with a few strands. She was covered from throat to feet in plain, unfeminine clothes, yet that seemed to make him even more aware of the feminine body beneath the masculine clothes. A stirring began in his loins. Of all the times for a man's thoughts to turn to sex, tonight was the least likely, but that was exactly what he was thinking about. She drove him crazy. He couldn't re-call a single woman who'd had such a stunning effect on him, and he wondered what he should or could do about it.

The tension that had formed between them was like a third presence. Audrey shivered. Slowly she turned her head and met his gaze. In that instant it was as though a camera had been clicked, a picture taken, one that would be around forever. Audrey finally recognized him for who he was, the other part of herself. She felt the chemistry, a hackneyed word but the only one that described the profound physical attraction between them. She felt it, and if she could trust what she thought she read in his eyes, he felt it, too.

She watched in fascination as his head bent toward hers. Like the last time, she simply gave in to the kiss and returned it, nestling into the curve of his arm, mildly surprised that his beard didn't scratch any more than it did.

Just then there was a burst of laughter around the camp fire. Audrey broke the kiss quickly and straightened, remembering where they were. Her heart was racing at breakneck speed. She felt as foolish and as furtive as a teenager smooching in the back seat of a car. Then, thankfully, she saw that no one was looking in their direction. Apparently someone in the group had botched the words to a song or told a joke.

Beside her, Boyd shifted restlessly, and she heard him sigh. "I doubt that anyone would be scandalized if we were caught kissing," he muttered.

"I don't think you want a lot of camp gossip floating around any more than I do."

She was right, though he didn't tell her that. The others were beginning to accept Audrey to a degree he wouldn't have dared hope for, but if they suspected she was important to the boss in a personal way, resentment might flare up. So romance would have to wait for a place more conducive to privacy. But he wanted her to know how he felt. Maybe then she'd tell him how she felt. Two measly kisses did not a romance make. "If I were better with words, I could keep you here an hour telling you all the things I do want." His voice was low, husky and confidential.

Audrey swallowed hard. He was taking her breath away. "Do you realize how long we've known each other?"

He pretended to give it serious thought. "Well, let's see now. We spent the first night together in the hotel suite...."

"Oh, good grief! Keep your voice down."

"Then we came to the ranch. The next night I gave you the rubdown in your bedroom. There was our picnic, and we've been on the drive two days. Gosh, Audrey, I've known you almost a week!"

"Exactly. Almost a week."

"Seems longer."

"What's that supposed to mean?"

"Just that I've thought about you for a long time. Now that you've finally shown up...it just seems I've known you a lot longer than a week, that's all."

Audrey placed her hand on her forehead and uttered a light laugh. "Do you have any idea how much it astonishes me to hear you say something like that?"

"Really? Why?"

"Well, it's brash for one thing, and I never figured you for brashness."

"This is more like it. Give me a peek at the thoughts inside your head. How did you have me figured?"

Audrey was spared having to answer that one. The crowd around the camp fire was dispersing, and Betty was heading their way. "Hi," she called. "How come you didn't join us? What have you been so deep in conversation about?"

"Oh, the nature of life and love and the mysteries of the universe," Boyd said blithely.

"All that, huh?" Betty yawned. "Sounds fascinating. If you come up with any sound conclusions, clue me in, will you? Night." Lifting the tent flap, she ducked inside.

"Good night," Audrey and Boyd chorused. A long wordless moment passed before Audrey said, "I guess I'd better turn in, too."

"Yeah," Boyd agreed resignedly. "I guess so." He got to his feet and held his hand down toward her. She took it. With one strong tug he pulled her to her feet directly in front of him. They were standing so close Audrey could feel his breath fanning the hair at her temple. For a moment they simply stared at each other, recognizing the currents of sensuality passing between them.

"You're cold," Boyd said finally.

"Not really."

"Yes, you are. You're shivering."

"Well, maybe, a little."

"You'd better... get to bed."

She nodded. "Good night, Boyd."

"Good night, Audrey. Sweet dreams."

Lifting the flap, she disappeared inside the tent, leaving him overwhelmed by the sensation of being on the verge of something wonderful, the something he had been so sure would elude him forever.

Good Lord! Could it be, was it even possible that he was, at long last, in love?

CHAPTER TEN

BY NINE O'CLOCK the camp had quietened considerably. The few who weren't already asleep were bedding down. Boyd and Skeet Drummond squatted by the dying camp fire, talking in hushed tones. "You said you remembered something, Skeet?"

"I think so. There was a fella named Hamilton...Jack, I think it was...who had a spread in North Texas. He was a big businessman in Dallas and ranched as a hobby. Does that sound like the man you're looking for?"

"Might be." Boyd's interest was piqued. "To tell you the truth, I'm not sure what I'm looking for. What happened to Hamilton?"

Skeet scratched the stubble on his chin. "My head's hit the pillow a lotta times since I heard the story, so I'm kinda fuzzy on the details. Hamilton got in some kind of trouble with the federal government, and his operation shut down."

"You don't remember the nature of the trouble?"

"Damned if I can. I do remember one thing, though. It was one of his own men who turned him in to the feds. That always stuck with me. It's one sorry so-and-so who ain't loyal to his boss. Either stick by him or quit him, I always say."

"Agreed, Skeet. Now go on."

"Hamilton stood trial and was convicted, but for the life of me I can't remember what the charge was."

"Is Hamilton in prison now?"

"Nope. Now this part I remember good. He died before he served a day."

"Did he have a family?"

"Seems like there was one, but then again I might have this mixed up with someone else."

"When did all this happen?"

"Well . . . must'a been about five years ago. I heard about it when that drifter from Texas hired on at roundup four years ago, and it was all over by then."

Boyd digested what Skeet had told him. Audrey had said her father died five years ago, but that was pretty thin evidence. He reminded himself that she might not have been even remotely connected with Jack Hamilton, but if she was, his heart went out to her. A father who was a convicted felon wasn't something anyone would find easy to live with, much less someone like Audrey. That would explain so much about her—the reluctance to discuss her past and her decision to stay in Phoenix. If her father had been a big Dallas businessman, she probably had been to the manor born, so that would explain her poise and obvious class. And if he'd owned a ranch, she might have grown up on horseback. Plus, the time frame fit. The indictment, a trial, Audrey's decision to leave Dallas and her stay with the friend in Phoenix easily could have consumed the lion's share of two years, and she'd been at the Greenspoint three.

"Thanks, Skeet."

"Hope it helped. Say...isn't the little lady's name Hamilton?" The cook inclined his head toward the tent where Audrey and Betty slept.

"Remember, Skeet, this is just between you and me," Boyd cautioned.

"Mum's the word, boss. You can count on it."

Preoccupied, Boyd restlessly prowled the outskirts of the campsite for half an hour or so before bedding down. The information wasn't something he could quiz Audrey about; it was much too sensitive. He wondered if she would ever trust him enough to tell him the story herself.

As tired as Boyd was, sleep was some time coming. He couldn't get his mind off Audrey. He was irresistibly drawn to her, and he no longer considered that a disturbing weakness. Rather, he welcomed the new dimension to his life. He'd waited a long while to find a woman like her. And she was attracted to him, too, or would be if she'd let herself.

How could he make her believe he didn't care about her past without saying it in so many words? What had gone before meant nothing...unless it jeopardized the future. Just before dropping off to sleep, for reasons that escaped him completely, he thought of his father.

THE FOLLOWING DAY was a repeat of the previous one, except they worked the northern pastures and rounded up more than five hundred head. Audrey was beginning to feel like a veteran hand, and she thought she could sense a subtle change in the cowboys' attitude toward her. When Boyd asked her to spell him during the cutting process, she and Ranger performed admirably.

Boyd rode up beside her as they drove the herd back to camp. "This job pays fifty dollars a day, plus chuck and all the tobacco you want," he said with a grin.

She laughed. "Even for a greenhorn?"

"Yeah, if the greenhorn works as hard as you do."

"So you're not sorry you brought me along?"

"I've never been sorry about that, Audrey. Never."

"Liar."

"Concerned for a while, maybe, but never sorry. And I'm not concerned anymore."

That moment of acceptance was memorable and created a kind of euphoria in Audrey. She felt wonderful. On top of everything, tomorrow they would be taking the herd to a place called Summerfield camp, where everyone who wanted to would be able to clean up and change clothes. That was something she really was looking forward to. The lack of bathing facilities was the only truly uncomfortable thing about this adventure. Once they reached the camp, two of the hands were dispatched ahead to get Summerfield ready for habitation.

Much to Audrey's regret, she and Boyd weren't alone for even a few minutes that night. The next morning the crew broke camp at dawn and moved the herd to higher ground nearer headquarters. Audrey wasn't sure what she had expected Summerfield camp to be like, but after three days at Number Five, the place was a real touch of civilization.

Situated by a clear stream, the camp consisted of a large weather-beaten bunkhouse, some horse corrals, a maze of holding pens and a windmill and water tank.

Once, when the Triple B had been much larger, Summerfield had served as year-round quarters for six cowboys, so some basic modern amenities had been added—a septic tank, water well and electric generator.

The roundup crew reached the camp around four o'clock that afternoon. After the cattle had been herded into the pens and the horses taken care of, the hands began setting up camp while Boyd, Betty and Audrey went inside to inspect the building.

There was one room austerely furnished with bunks, a long table, some chairs and a potbellied stove. A lone light bulb hung from a crudely wired socket in the ceiling. They actually would have electric light! But the camp's most welcome feature was an honest-to-goodness bathroom with a shower stall. When Audrey spied the water heater standing in the corner she realized they also would have hot water. At the moment, that seemed an almost sybaritic luxury.

"We'll be working out of here until we move the herd to headquarters," Boyd explained for her benefit. "So you two ladies can bunk in here."

"No concessions to sex, remember," Audrey admonished.

"Well, maybe one or two."

"Don't knock it, Audrey," Betty said with a grin as she stretched out on one of the bunks. "Besides, the guys would rather be outside. Sleeping on the ground is part of the mystique."

"If the weather turns bad you might have a lot of company in here," Boyd added. "But I see no signs of that, so you should have all the privacy in the world." He clomped across the bare plank floor, heading toward the door. But as he reached for the knob, he paused. "To tell you the truth, I wouldn't mind shaving and washing off some of this grime. When you two are finished with the bathroom, how about giving me a holler."

"Sure," his sister agreed, stretching languidly.

He shot Audrey a faintly mysterious half smile, then left. She crossed the room and flopped down on one of the other bunks. "Oh, I hate admitting how good this feels!"

"Yeah, I know." Betty chuckled. "The hardest thing about being a woman on roundup is pretending you don't miss the comforts of home."

"I thought you loved it."

"I love the work. I don't love being without a bathroom. I'll arm-wrestle you to see who gets to shower first."

"Be my guest. That'll give me more time to lie here thinking about how wonderful it's going to feel."

Rolling over, Betty propped herself on one elbow. "Audrey, will you do me a favor?"

"Of course."

"Do you think you can make yourself scarce for a little while tonight? I'd like to entertain a gentleman caller."

Audrey faced the wall to hide her look of disgust from the other woman. If only she could think of a way to dilute Betty's infatuation with Jesse, short of coming right out and telling her he wasn't the man she thought he was. "Aren't you afraid there'll be talk that will get back to your father?"

"Naw, as far as everyone's concerned, Jesse and I are just buddies. And none of the men would go to

Buck Benedict with the time of day unless Dad asked
for it.''

"What about Boyd?"

"If Boyd had questions, he'd ask them of me."
Betty paused, then said. "He likes you…a lot. I know
my brother. He looks at you like he's starving to death
and you're a hot fudge sundae."

Audrey thought a minute before saying, "I like him,
too."

"Well, I'll be damned! And he was so sure this
wouldn't happen to him. He thought that if he'd been
going to fall in love he would have long before now. I
told him that was dumb, that it could happen anytime, but he really believed it never would."

"It's pretty farfetched to mention 'love' in con-
junction with our relationship, Betty. Nothing's happened. Or almost nothing." And most likely nothing
ever would, she could have added. She couldn't shake
the notion that a real romance with Boyd belonged in
the pie-in-the-sky category.

"I'll bet something will happen if Boyd wants it bad
enough," Betty confided. "He won't give up.
Bullheadedness is my brother's middle name."

Audrey grinned. "And he told me the middle B
doesn't stand for anything."

AFTER SHOWERING, shampooing her hair and brushing her teeth, Audrey felt like a new person. It was
wonderful to wash away three days' accumulation of
grime. From Betty's duffel bag she took out clean
jeans, socks and a long-sleeved velour pullover. They
didn't have much in the way of cosmetics with them,

but there was lotion and lipstick. She felt human again.

She and Betty were sitting on the bunks, fluffing their wet hair in an attempt at drying it, when Boyd knocked on the door. "Are you decent?" he called.

"Come on in," Betty yelled.

He was carrying a shaving kit and some clean clothes under his arm. As he stepped into the room, his eyes fastened on Audrey, and he felt a flush creep up his neck. "Don't you look nice."

"Thanks. Quite an improvement, huh?"

He opened his mouth to say something else, then noticed his sister's amused expression and decided against it. "Hope you saved me some hot water. And if I were you two, I'd stay inside for a bit. Most of the hands are bathing in the creek, and modesty isn't in their vocabulary."

The bathroom door closed behind him. Audrey heard some rustling movements, then the sound of the shower. It occurred to her that this was the second time in the short space of eight days she had listened to Boyd take a shower. When he emerged from the bathroom a scant twenty minutes later, he was dressed in different clothes, was clean-shaven, and he looked marvelous. Suddenly she wished it were she and Boyd who would have the bunkhouse all to themselves that night instead of Betty and Jesse, and it had nothing to do with her concern over Betty's relationship with the disgusting man.

"Ah, that feels good," Boyd said. "Can I toss these dirty things in with yours?"

"Sure," Betty replied and indicated the duffel bag on the floor by the bunk where Audrey sat. "Over there."

Picking up the bag, he stuffed his clothes in it, then turned to Audrey. "Want to go for a ride?" he asked tersely.

"A ride?" The thought of climbing up on Ranger again wasn't the most appealing prospect in the world, but getting away with Boyd was.

"Actually, a drive in the truck. There's something I'd like to show you."

Audrey glanced at Betty, who encouraged her with her eyes, then back at Boyd. "We'll miss supper."

"No, we won't."

She assumed that meant they wouldn't be gone long, and that disappointed her. "All right," she agreed.

"Better bring your jacket."

Driving off into the fading daylight, they chugged and bumped along a rutted road that seemed to lead to nowhere. Then they topped a rise and Audrey saw what must have been their destination—an earth-colored adobe cottage that blended in with the terrain so well it virtually was camouflaged. The truck rumbled to a halt in front of the house. It was neat and well-kept, Audrey observed. Then she noticed some evidence of construction work, so perhaps it had been restored, for the house obviously was not new. She turned to Boyd with a questioning expression.

"This is where my grandparents began their married life," he explained.

Audrey looked at the structure again. "This was Bert and Margaret's house?"

"Yep. I'm in the process of renovating it. One of these days it's going to be my house. I want you to see inside, but first there's something else I want to show you while it's still light."

They got out of the truck. Boyd took Audrey's hand and led her to a spot some distance from the adobe house, to a small cemetery enclosed within a picket fence. "I thought you might like to see this. It's our family plot. Every Benedict since Bernard B. has been buried here. There's Granddad's grave."

Bert's headstone was simple, as were all the others. Audrey shoved her hands into her jacket pockets and stared at the headstone, overcome with emotion. A lump formed in her throat as she thought of the changes the elderly man had wrought in her own life. The money, of course, but more than that. Bert had inadvertently introduced her to Boyd, and while she had yet to decide if that was a blessing or a pity, she had to admit he was an exciting addition to a life that had been lonely and barren too long.

A couple of minutes passed before Boyd said, "It's getting dark. Ready to go?"

She nodded. "Yes."

Turning away, the two of them walked toward the adobe structure just as the last rays of daylight slipped below the horizon. The house, Boyd explained as he ushered Audrey through the front door, had no electricity at present, but it was stocked with kerosene lamps. He walked through the rooms, lighting the lamps, while Audrey followed. The walls had been painted recently, and the bathroom fixtures seemed new. It was a small place—living room, kitchen, two bedrooms and a bath—but it had charm. The tile floors were magnificent and would be horrendously expensive in today's market. When she commented on them, Boyd told her the tiles had been brought up from Mexico in a horse-drawn wagon in 1928 when there hadn't been a paved road or a telephone in the entire valley.

Furniture almost was nonexistent. There was a single bed in one of the bedrooms and a sofa in the living room. The main room also had a pueblo-style beehive fireplace and the exposed wooden beams called *vigas*. The kitchen still had an old-fashioned pump at the sink and an ancient cast-iron woodburning stove. "You're going to live here?" Audrey asked incredulously. As charming and picturesque as the cottage was, it was a bit on the primitive side.

"Sure am," Boyd replied proudly. Picking up one of the lamps, he motioned for her to follow him out the back door. They stepped onto a long back porch, a third of which had been enclosed to make a storeroom. Opening the door to it, he pointed to several large cartons that contained new appliances. "I've already bought almost everything I need to modernize. Winter's the slowest time around the ranch, so a couple of the men have offered to help me with the place after Christmas. There's a lot of work to be done, but I hope to be in here next summer. I need some space of my own. Living in the main house suits Brent fine, but it doesn't suit me."

"Well, it certainly is . . . private," Audrey affirmed, although she thought "isolated" might have been a better word.

Boyd led the way back into the house and set the lamp on a small kitchen table. "You're thinking it's in the back of beyond, but it's not nearly as remote as it seems. That road outside leads directly to headquarters, and it takes maybe ten minutes to drive there. Sit down and I'll rustle us up something to eat.''

''We're having supper here.''

He nodded. ''I stock quite a larder. Sometimes when I'm working on the place I spend several days at a time here. I have plenty of kerosene and there's running water. Admittedly, when I want to bathe I have to heat the water, but I've never minded that. I probably could live here with the place the way it is...plus electricity, of course. I won't, but I probably could.''

Audrey thought it amazing that a man like Boyd, who was accustomed to the very finest of everything, would enjoy such a back-to-basics existence. She seemed to be learning something new about him every day. She sat down at the little table and eyed the monstrous stove, which was an ornate relic of a bygone era. ''Do you know how to use that thing?''

''The stove? As a matter of fact, I do, but you can't turn a wood stove on and off the way you can an electric or gas one. It takes some time and patience, and it gets hotter'n blazes. To my grandmother, 'slaving over a hot stove' had real meaning.'' He indicated a propane-fueled countertop cooking unit, the kind used by campers and other outdoor types. ''I use that most of the time. I don't cook gourmet meals here.''

Opening a cabinet door, he removed a coffeepot and filled it with water from the pump. Audrey was certain that once she left the Triple B she would either be hopelessly addicted to strong black coffee or never want another cup of the stuff as long as she lived.

She found it fascinating to watch Boyd work. While waiting for the water to boil, he studied the array of canned goods in the cabinet, chose three and expertly opened them with his pocket knife. When the coffee was set aside to steep, he dumped the contents of two cans in one pan, the contents of the third can in another and set them on the stove. "Dinner in five minutes," he said, "and it's the specialty of the house."

The "specialty" turned out to be nothing more than canned Spanish rice to which chunks of Vienna sausages had been added. The concoction was served on paper plates, and Audrey couldn't believe how good it tasted. But the highlight of the meal, as far as she was concerned, were the green beans he had heated up. They were the first vegetable she had tasted in four days.

"How is it?" he asked after a few bites.

"Delicious."

"You're not just saying that?"

She shook her head. "No, it's really very good." She didn't add that at the moment she could have eaten dog food if that had been all that was available. "It's an unusual combination. I never would have thought of it. How did you?"

"Necessity. I was working here late one night last summer and was hungry. This was all I had. Turned out to be not half-bad."

"Do you spend a lot of time here?"

"Haven't been able to lately, but once roundup is over I'll be able to tackle the place in earnest."

"How long have you been working on it?"

"Off and on for two years. It was a mess when I started. Granddad built it in 1926, and this was really out in the boondocks then. When he and my grand-mother moved into the main house, this was abandoned for years. One of our foremen lived here some time ago, but he was single and didn't do a thing to it."

"Thanks for showing it to me. In some odd way it suits you."

"I wonder if it would suit someone else."

"Someone else?"

"I don't intend spending the rest of my life alone, Audrey. I wonder if a woman could live here and be happy. You, for instance. Do you think you could?"

Audrey had raised her coffee cup to her lips. Now she set it down without taking so much as a sip. Staring at the black liquid, she strove for nonchalance. "Oh... I suppose I could... given the right circumstances."

Across the table, Boyd's eyes impaled her. "And what would those 'right' circumstances be?"

"I'd have to live in a place like this—or anywhere on earth, for that matter—with the right man. That's all most women want."

"Oh? Describe this right man to me."

"That's impossible."

"Why? Haven't you met him yet?"

Audrey opened her mouth, then quickly closed it again. Her fingers tightened around her cup, and she clutched it so hard she wouldn't have been surprised if it had shattered in her hand. Sucking in her breath, she held it for several heartbeats. They were very far removed from the rest of the world, and considering all the unmanageable emotions he aroused in her, that probably wasn't a good idea. She had longed to be alone with him, but now that she was, she felt as awkward as a young girl on her first date.

Boyd never took his eyes off her. She was as disturbed by his proximity as he was by hers, and that knowledge sent the blood coursing hotly through his veins. With great deliberation, he reached across the small table and pried her fingers from her cup. Encasing her hand, he tugged slightly, then more insistently. Audrey's luminous eyes widened as he, seemingly without effort, pulled her from the chair, around the table, and settled her in his lap, wrapping his arms around her. He pressed her against his chest and placed his lips at the hollow of her throat. "The truth of the matter is," he murmured, fanning her skin with his warm breath, "you have met him. 'Fess up."

"Boyd," she whispered in a voice that didn't sound like hers, "this is crazy. We barely know each other."

"Oh, Audrey, spare me that old chestnut. How long does it take two reasonably intelligent adults to know they were meant for each other?"

"I . . . don't know. Longer than a week."

"Eight days," he corrected.

"That's . . . not very much time. Boyd . . . please . . . don't . . ."

Beginning with a shower of quick, light kisses on her throat and the underside of her chin, he assaulted her senses. One of his hands strayed from her back to the side of her breast, paused enticingly, then moved to her waist, along the curve of her hip and came to rest on her thigh. His mouth traced her jawline, nibbled on her earlobe, kissed her cheek, then captured her mouth.

Audrey thought she was strangling. Every fiber of her being sprang to life when his lips closed over hers, and she didn't want to think about problems or consequences or anything pertinent and important. For years, ever since the embarrassing fiasco with Jesse, she had been cautious in relationships with men, so cautious that her heart had remained untouched. Now she realized how much she had longed for something, someone who would make her feel alive and feminine and desirable. Boyd's touch lit a spark, then fanned it into a roaring blaze. Just thinking about the pleasure he promised made her giddy and weak. She ached for emotional release, and he could deliver it. Was there anything wrong with that? Both of them were adults, single...and very, very willing. Where was the harm?

As his kiss grew more insistent, Audrey responded to every pressure of his lips, his hands, his body beneath hers. She trailed her fingers sensually along the back of his neck, hearing him groan, feeling him shift impatiently in the chair. His hand left her thigh and brushed across her breast, as lightly as the touch of a butterfly's wings. The gentleness was more exquisitely tormenting than more overt fondling could have ever been. An involuntary sound escaped her throat.

The moment the sound was uttered, Boyd's hand closed over her breast and he raised his head slightly. "Audrey, I swear to God I think I'm in love for the first time in my life. I want you, and I have from the moment I saw you that day in the hotel."

Audrey fought to regain her breath. "That's probably your imagination."

One corner of his mouth lifted in a half smile. "You've turned my life upside down, inside out.

That's not my imagination.'' Holding her tightly, he pressed her more insistently against his lap, giving her proof of his arousal. "And neither is that."

She started to remind him that he was talking about sex, but she checked herself. Of course he was talking about sex, and she was thinking about it. She was very close to wanton abandon in her desire for him. "Oh, Boyd," she breathed. "This has just happened too fast. It's impulsive, and I've never been impulsive. I really don't trust anything I'm feeling."

"Funny. I trust what I'm feeling. I think it's more honest than anything I've ever felt in my life."

He kissed her again. This time the kiss was a long, drugging one that stripped her of what little restraint she had left. He was masterful at the art of seduction, leading her to wonder vaguely how many other women had been treated to this expert onslaught of sensuality. Not that it mattered. She was on the receiving end now, so she was going to relax and enjoy it. Her insides had turned to liquid, and the feeling was wonderful. It had been a long time coming.

Then reality set in, as it invariably did with Audrey. She wasn't going to have sex with this man whom she scarcely knew. It was unthinkable. A man could enjoy a woman, then forget her, but a woman—most at any rate—got emotionally involved. Audrey didn't think she was willing to risk that. One of her first impressions of him was of a man who would be hard to forget. She didn't need that complication, thanks. Loosening her grip on him, she all but jumped to her feet.

Caught off guard, Boyd was stunned. "Hey..."

"Let's clean up this mess. We really should be getting back to camp."

He couldn't believe it. "Audrey, what in hell happened?"

She gathered up the paper plates and cups, moving in jerky little motions. "What do you do with the trash?"

Boyd reached for her. "Sweetheart, come here."

Audrey faced him squarely. "Oh, Boyd, I'm not your sweetheart! How could I be? When roundup is over, and from talk around camp I gather that will be in two more days, we'll go back to the ranch house, and no doubt I'll be leaving. Our relationship is . . . transient." Her eyes begged him to understand. "Look, I know there are women who take lovers whose names they don't even know. . . ."

"You know my name."

". . . men they know nothing about, but I'm not one of them. Sorry."

"Seems to me I recall telling you that I think I'm in love."

"You can't possibly know that. Don't you see?"

"Maybe I'm dense, but no . . ." Then he saw Audrey's implacable expression and decided he was wasting his breath. "Son of a bitch!" he muttered under his breath.

"But it's really been . . . fun," she offered.

"Fun?" he cried incredulously.

"An adventure. I'll never forget my time here, never."

Boyd rolled his eyes toward the ceiling. "An adventure yet! That doesn't do much for my masculine ego.'' Placing his hands on his thighs, he shoved himself out of the chair.

Audrey couldn't determine if he was angry, disgusted, disappointed or what. Her insides fluttered like a covey of quail on the wing. ''What...do you do with the trash?''

He threw open a drawer and produced a brown grocery sack, which he unfolded and held open. His eyes never left her as she threw the plates, cups and empty cans into it. ''Lady,'' he said, ''you sure know how to spoil an evening.''

The drive back to camp was accomplished in almost total silence. Audrey slumped in the passenger seat, while Boyd stared resolutely through the windshield at the clear, black night. Thoughts spun inside both their heads.

Audrey kept reminding herself that calling a halt to the sexual encounter had been the sensible thing to do. Nothing had happened to indicate that more than the desire of the moment had been involved. She and Boyd hadn't known each other long enough to have established any kind of solid relationship. She didn't care if he was angry; she had been right.

Boyd's thoughts were more complex. He probably hadn't handled tonight so well. As powerful as his desire for Audrey was—and it *was* powerful—he wanted more than just her body. It still astonished him that he'd finally found someone he wanted to build something enduring with. No, he probably hadn't handled tonight so well.

But tomorrow would be different.

CHAPTER ELEVEN

AUDREY DIDN'T SEE Boyd at breakfast the next morning. It occurred to her that he might very well have been avoiding her, which was just as well. She felt terrible about last night but had managed to convince herself that she definitely hadn't teased or led him on. And she was more certain than ever that getting sexually involved with him was just asking for trouble.

Later, however, all her sensible inner resolve melted like ice on an August day. When the riders had mounted and stood waiting in a semicircle, it was Jesse, not Boyd, who rode before them and gave out orders for the day.

"Where's Boyd?" Betty asked with a frown.

"He said we'd have to do without him today," Jesse explained. "Said he had some things to take care of. Okay, let's ride."

Peculiar what a difference his absence made. Although the now familiar work went smoothly and quickly, Audrey thought the day would never end. She missed having Boyd ride along beside her from time to time, missed simply knowing he was nearby. When the crew returned to camp that evening she was in miserable spirits for no reason at all. As soon as she'd tended to Ranger she made straight for the old bunk-

house without taking part in any of the camp cama-
raderie. She thought she felt a headache coming on.

Later, after she and Betty had showered, they sat on
their bunks and waited for Skeet to announce supper.
"Do you suppose you'll be going back to Phoenix
when this is over, Audrey?"

"I guess so. I've been gone quite awhile. I really
should get back."

"You're going to stay over the weekend, aren't
you?"

"Weekend? I hadn't thought about it. Why?"

"You mean, no one's mentioned Tri-County to
you?"

"No. What is it?"

"Tri-County Fair and Rodeo. It's held at the end of
roundup every year and is the biggest event in these
parts, for sure. All the ranches in the valley compete
for everything from best chili cook to best guitar
picker. The Triple B's won the majority of the events
three years running."

"What do you win?"

Betty grinned. "Braggin' rights for another year.
But the rodeo's the best part. Ever been to one?"

Only hundreds. "I went to the Parada del Sol in
Scottsdale last year," she evaded.

"Well, Tri-County's nothing like that. It's strictly
amateur, but exciting, since you know all the contes-
tants. Oh, Audrey, you have to stay for it!"

It sounded like fun, but Audrey seriously doubted
that Boyd would want her prolonging her stay. "Well,
Betty...we'll see."

At that moment there was a loud rap on the door.
"Come in," Betty called, and Boyd stepped into the

room. Audrey's heart leaped straight up into her throat and stayed there. Her almost-headache magically vanished.

"Well, well," Betty said sarcastically, "look who's showed up now that all the work's been done."

Boyd barely acknowledged his sister's presence. His eyes were riveted on Audrey. "Will you come with me?"

Audrey started to ask, "Where?" Then she decided she didn't care. "Yes," she replied simply and reached for her jacket.

"Don't hurry," Betty called after them.

There wasn't much mystery about their destination, but she asked anyway. "Where are we going?"

He kept his eyes on the road. "I'm taking you to dinner."

"At your house?"

"Um-hmm."

"Boyd, about last night ... I ..."

Still without looking at her, he reached for her hand and raised it to his lips. "Hush, Audrey."

As the pickup rumbled down the road toward the adobe house, Audrey reflected on her perverse nature. All day long, when she hadn't been too busy to think, she'd congratulated herself on her good sense where Boyd was concerned. No deep involvement. That was the bottom line. Yet he'd shown up, done little more than crook his finger, and here she was.

Sighing, she glanced at him surreptitiously, enjoying the view of his attractive profile. Apparently he held no grudges about last night. In fact, he seemed to be in a pretty good mood. Even as she watched, he puckered his lips and began to whistle.

The minute Audrey entered the house all her questions about his activities that day were answered. A cheerful fire blazed in the beehive fireplace. A colorful area rug was on the floor in front of it, and the sofa had been moved in closer. The aroma of something wonderful permeated the rooms. Drawn to take a peek at what it was, Audrey gasped when she entered the kitchen. The little table had been set with a cloth, china, silverware and candles. A bottle of wine rested in a bucket of ice.

Turning to a grinning Boyd, she folded her arms across her chest and eyed him warily. "This is what you were doing while the rest of us were out in the sun and dust working our buns off?"

"Um-hmm."

"What are you up to? Did you bring me here to seduce me?"

He feigned hurt. "I brought you here to woo you. There's a difference." Gesturing toward the living room, he said, "Please have a seat, and I'll get you a glass of wine."

Trying desperately to hide a smile, Audrey reversed direction. "Plying me with liquor won't work," she threw over her shoulder.

She didn't distinctly hear what his comment to that was, but it sounded suspiciously like, "We'll see."

AUDREY WAS PREPARED to call it the most glorious evening of her life. Boyd, it seemed, had spent all day scurrying back and forth from the ranch house to the adobe one, procuring whatever was needed for this cozy setup. He'd brought a portable cassette player so Merle Haggard could serenade them while they sipped

wine in front of the fire. Later, he served dinner with
an exaggerated flourish, and the food, prepared and
packed by Maria, was fantastic. There even was a
salad. After days of chuck wagon fare, that salad was
quite possibly the best thing she'd ever eaten. Audrey
was sure no one had ever gone to so much trouble for
her. Boyd was pure delight.

They finished the meal, then washed and repacked
everything. Wiping his hands on a dish towel, Boyd
refilled their wineglasses, and they returned to the living room and sat on the sofa in front of the fire.
"How am I doing?" he asked seductively.

"You must be doing all right. My head is spinning,
and I don't think the wine's responsible."

"Good. Drink up."

"I really don't think I need any more."

"Whatever you say." He took the glass from her
hand, set it on the floor out of the way and placed his
beside it. Settling back on the sofa, he pulled her into
a tight embrace, and the sensual assault began. He
held her face against his chest, and the smell of her
freshly shampooed hair filled his nostrils. He thought
how clean she always smelled, even after a day on
horseback. Odd how simply holding Audrey brought
him such pleasure. He wasn't sure he had ever experienced a thrill from just holding a woman. He felt her
arms slowly go around him, her palms flatten against
his back, and he wanted the moment to go on forever.

Audrey was thinking the same thing. Resting her
head against his chest, she listened to the rhythm of his
heartbeat and thought how wonderfully warm he felt.
The evening had been pure delight from the beginning. He had successfully created the atmosphere he'd

intended. She felt safe, comfortable and content, locked in an impregnable capsule with Boyd, far away from the rest of the world. Sighing, she melted against him, became as pliable as putty and waited for his next move.

He curved a forefinger under her chin and tilted her face to receive his kiss. Mouths fused, tongues touched, arms tightened. As the kiss deepened, his hand moved to the front of her shirt, flicked at a button and slipped inside to cup a full breast that felt like a velvet pillow. His thumb made circular motions, teasing the nipple to erect hardness. All he wanted was to make Audrey feel good; hearing her low moan he guessed he was succeeding. His kisses became fierce and hungry.

Audrey didn't feel good; her insides felt like the belly of a volcano on the brink of eruption. A hot dizziness whirled inside her head, overcoming all rational thought. She felt a tingling warmth between her legs and a tightening of her womb. Her body yearned, almost cried out for fulfillment, and there didn't seem to be a thing she could do about it.

Boyd lifted his head and looked into those incredible eyes, now glazed with desire. "I'm waiting," he said huskily.

"For...what?"

"To hear that song and dance about what a short time we've known each other."

"Oh, that. Well, I...I guess that doesn't seem so important to me anymore."

"God, Audrey, all I do anymore is think about you. Please...put me out of my misery."

His entire body seemed to encase hers. Audrey arched into it, clutching him. "Yes," she whispered. "Yes, yes."

With some difficulty Boyd got to his feet and pulled her with him. He would have liked to scoop her up into his arms and dramatically carry her to the bedroom, but in his present condition there was some doubt in his mind that his weakened legs would even carry him. He held her tightly against him, and together they somehow negotiated the width of the living room and the length of the small hallway.

During his fit of housekeeping that afternoon he had changed the sheets. Audrey stared at the bed as though she'd never seen one before. Boyd came up behind her, slipped his arm around her waist and kissed the back of her head. Slowly she turned in his arms and slid hers around him. For a long wordless moment they simply stood locked together, lost in erotic sweetness. Then she raised her face, and the look he gave her seemed to melt her bones. It was absolutely insane to feel so much for a man she'd known such a short time, but there it was, real and insistent and undeniable. It shook her down to her toes.

Smiling, she closed her eyes and settled into the niche of his hips. Boyd's hands wandered over her back and down her arms. They drove her wild with desire, and with the passion came the first persistent stirrings of another emotion. Audrey wasn't prepared to call it love yet, but it was a caring tenderness she'd never experienced before. She knew that making love with him was going to intensify the feeling. She wouldn't be the same again. Boyd had played havoc with her senses from the beginning. What was left of her rational mind wondered if this had been inevitable from the moment she'd stepped through the door of the Durango Suite.

Then he broke the embrace slightly, stepping back to tug her shirt free of the jeans and fumble with its buttons.

"Boots first," she managed to say.

He mumbled something, and she stepped back to sit on the edge of the bed and offer him a leg. Tugging, he removed one boot, then the other. When he sat down beside her, she returned the favor. Then with shaking fingers they divested themselves of their clothes. Somehow the task was accomplished, and they were under the covers of the small bed, clinging to each other.

Boyd's stomach muscles were so tight they hurt, and the pounding of his heartbeat drowned out all other sounds. His mind and body were poised toward one goal, to make Audrey want him as much as he wanted her, not just tonight but again and again, for every night they could manage to be together. How to excite her the way she excited him? With no knowledge of her pleasure points, he moved cautiously. His hands sought and touched, rubbed and petted, while he muttered incoherent, guttural sounds from deep in his throat.

Audrey squirmed. "I can't hear you. What are you saying?"

"Nothing, nothing," he whispered. "You're on fire."

"Yes. Oh, Boyd..."

"I've been on fire for days." Boyd curved her against him, and the sensation of her warm flesh against his sent a thousand sparks shooting through him. Restlessly his hands explored, touching. The body he'd admired so often was as perfect as he'd expected it to be. His arousal complete, he ached to take her, yet sensed the need for restraint. He'd pushed her awfully far awfully fast. One insensitive move and he risked putting an end to something that had just begun. And he wanted her to remember this forever.

Taking his time, he nuzzled her neck, licked a nipple grown hard with desire, then buried his face in the valley between her breasts. Audrey arched against him, moaning softly. The fire burned out of control. Finally there was nothing to do but give in to it. Deftly he maneuvered her beneath him. Poised above her, he looked down into her heavy-lidded eyes, thrilled by the desire he saw on her face. Audrey felt his hard, throbbing maleness pressed against her stomach, and her arms tugged at him impatiently.

"Boyd...please..."

He filled her with as much gentleness as could reasonably be summoned at a time like this. The gentleness overwhelmed her. It was she who became reckless and abandoned, binding him with her legs and arms, wanting him as she had never wanted a man, moving against him again and again, faster and faster. Her inherent sexuality, so long held dormant, flowered and bloomed. Pure pleasure held her in its grip. Wishing the ecstasy could go on and on, she nevertheless drove toward the climax, caught in a whirlpool of passion. Her fingernails bit into his shoulders as she cried his name. He tensed, then shuddered and collapsed on top of her.

It was some time before either of them stirred. Boyd moved first, rolling off her, then bringing her close. "Audrey..."

"Mmm..."

"You... stunned me."

"To tell the truth, I stunned myself."

"I have the worst feeling I'm never going to be able to do without you."

Audrey couldn't help wondering if either or both of them had left themselves wide open to heartache because of this. It was a sobering thought and unworthy of the moment. What was that damnable trait of hers that prevented her from simply letting life happen? Why did she always have to think, ponder and analyze? "Don't say too much," she said.

Her remark brought a frown to Boyd's face. Propping himself on one elbow, he stared down at her. "You're not sorry. Tell me you're not."

Tracing the shape of his mouth with her forefinger, she said, "I'm not sorry. It was wonderful. You were magnificent. I wouldn't have dreamed I could be so... uninhibited."

He chuckled. "You were pretty magnificent, too."

"Really?" Not once in her life had she ever wondered what kind of lover she'd make. Did women think of such things?

"Really."

"What makes a woman good in bed?"

"Good God, what a question!"

"That's no answer."

"Well...I don't know, Audrey. A lot of things, and none of them have anything to do with... er, prowess or technique. I guess so much depends on how the man in question feels about her. If he cares, then she's ... wonderful.''

"That's nice," she said, sighing.

Boyd grew solemn, thinking of so many things. The tragedy in her past, for one thing, if indeed it had been her father Skeet had told him about. And, too, something about her involvement with him troubled her, which in turn troubled him. Did she fear complications? He would have liked to tell her how he felt, that this was so right for both of them, but she might not believe words uttered in the aftermath of passion.

Oddly, Audrey wasn't apprehensive in the least. She had no regrets. She felt relaxed, sated, filled and at peace. Even if this proved to be the only time she and Boyd ever had together, she wouldn't regret it. But she didn't want him making promises he couldn't fulfill. Something Betty had told her came back to her now: "As Benedicts, Boyd and I are supposed to marry well, the way Brent did." In other words, Audrey Hamilton might be acceptable for an affair but not for anything more permanent.

Oh, what a time for that! Pushing aside all thoughts of the future, of anything but the moment, she settled against him. "We should get back to camp."

"I know."

"Do you suppose there's been talk about us?"

"I don't know, and frankly, I couldn't care less."

"Everyone seems to think we'll finish up tomorrow. Do you?"

"Yeah, probably." He looked at her. "Then the next day, home."

Neither of them had to voice their thoughts. They both knew they were thinking the same thing. The end of roundup meant the end of this idyll. Then it was back to reality and the workaday world. Back to the Greenspoint.

"Boyd?"

"Hmm?"

"Can we come back here tomorrow night?"

He kissed her shoulder. "It's a date."

THEY DIDN'T LEAVE CAMP until after supper was served the following night, and it was very late when they returned. Lost in the sensual discovery of each other, Audrey and Boyd had tarried in the adobe house, loath to leave, each wondering when they would be in it together again...if ever. Their lovemaking had been even more intense than before, increasing their need for each other.

On the way back to camp, Boyd was swamped by sadness and worry. He didn't think he could bear to say goodbye to her. His spirits were somewhat restored, however, when Audrey said, "Betty has asked me to stay through the weekend for the fair and rodeo."

It was hard to believe he'd been so preoccupied that he'd completely forgotten Tri-County, the celebration of the end of roundup. "Are you going to?" he asked expectantly.

"I'd like to."

He breathed a little easier. That would give them an extra day or two. It wasn't much, but he accepted it with gratitude. For now it would have to be enough.

CHAPTER TWELVE

"WELL, SON, what's the tally?" Buck stood on the back porch of the ranch house and watched the milling herd being driven into the pens.

"Fifteen hundred head, I figure," Boyd answered. "Murdoch came up with the same number."

"Not bad. Respectable. Any problems?"

"Not a one."

At that moment Audrey and Betty rode up to the corral, dismounted and began unsaddling their horses. "How did she do?"

"Audrey? She did fine."

"Surprising."

"She's . . . ah, quite a woman." He noticed how his voice took on a peculiar quality when he spoke of Audrey, even casually. She had become everything to him, and the knowledge still shook him a bit. He wondered about his father's reaction to the news that he was head over heels in love with a woman he'd met less than two weeks ago. His grandfather might have understood; his father never would. Benedict men, so tradition had it, did not act impulsively when it came to affairs of the heart. They gave the same care to choosing their women that they gave to choosing breeding stock. In Buck's eyes particularly, the two weren't all that dissimilar, and there was no question in Boyd's mind that his father was going to consider this latest development impulsive.

But it's the sanest thing I've ever done, he thought confidently. It felt wonderfully liberating to, for once, do something not rooted in careful thought.

Buck didn't seem to notice any peculiar inflection in his son's voice. The two men stood and watched as the young women walked toward the house. "Welcome home," Buck said, obviously addressing his daughter.

"Thanks, Dad." Betty gave him a perfunctory hug when she stepped up on the porch.

Audrey stood to the side, taking care not to look directly at Boyd. She was too afraid her heart would be in her eyes. Then Buck turned his attention to her. "How was it?"

"I enjoyed every minute of it, Mr. Benedict."

"Good, good. Well, Audrey, I think I have some good news for you."

"Oh?"

"It seems some Phoenix socialite shot her husband last night. Not fatally, fortunately for the gentleman in question, but it's had the effect of making Dad's will yesterday's news. I thought you'd be pleased."

Audrey tensed. She didn't know what to say. Was she being dismissed? Overcome by a terrible letdown, she felt like Cinderella at five minutes past midnight. Chancing a sidelong glance at Boyd, she saw his startled expression. Her gaze flew back to Buck. "Oh, well, I . . ."

Betty came to her rescue. "Dad, Audrey's promised to stay through Tri-County. She worked hard on roundup, and she should be able to enjoy the celebration."

"Well, of course," Buck said, shrugging. "I certainly didn't mean to imply that you should leave, my dear. You'll be missed. I just wanted you to know that there's no objection when you want to leave."

"Thank you, Mr. Benedict. I really would like to stay for the rodeo, but then I must get back to my job. Has my office called by any chance?"

"Peter did telephone day before yesterday. He seemed rather surprised when I told him you couldn't be reached."

"I'll bet. I suppose I should check in with him."

That small exchange took Boyd aback somewhat. For three days he had been living in something of a dreamworld, but now reality came crashing down on him. Audrey would be leaving soon, perhaps within a few days. It was going to be hard to find time alone with her now that they were back at the house, but they needed to talk, to make some plans. And before too many more days had passed, he was going to have to sit down and have a talk with his father. Buck would need some time to get used to the idea of Audrey as a big part of Boyd's life.

He stared after her as she and Betty went into the house, aching to follow, to go to her room with her, talk to her. This was going to be damned difficult. After a week of being with her all day, riding with her, eating with her, making love to her, he resented every minute he had to be away from her. But Buck was speaking to him, so he regretfully gave his father his attention.

Inside the house, Audrey went straight to her room, though it crossed her mind that she should look up Elizabeth and say hello to her. She didn't act on impulse, however. Elizabeth was seldom home in the afternoon, for one thing, and she was too tired and dirty for another.

The first thing she did was call Peter, who sounded impatient. "When in the devil are you coming back, Audrey?"

"In a few days. The Benedicts have asked me to stay and attend some sort of celebration this weekend, and since they've been so nice, I hated to say no." And that was only a tiny fib.

"Have you forgotten the United Hardware Dealers?"

Audrey put a hand to her mouth. She had. After spending months luring the organization's annual convention to the Greenspoint, she had forgotten about it completely. "Of course not."

"They'll be here Tuesday, two hundred strong, and I expect you to be here, too."

"Then I will be. Don't worry, Peter. The groundwork's been done. Everything will go smooth as glass."

They said goodbye. Then Audrey stripped off her clothes and headed for the shower, where she gave her hair a good scrubbing and used a conditioner. Afterward, she wallowed in the luxury of once again having at hand all the things she had always taken for granted—a blow dryer, a curling iron and a full array of cosmetics. And once her hair and face had been done, she put on panty hose, slip, skirt, blouse and low-heeled pumps. The transformation felt fabulous.

When she had finished, she checked the time and discovered it was a bit early to go to the sun room. Propping her elbows on the dressing table and resting her chin in her hands, she wondered what Boyd was doing. Showering and getting dressed for dinner, too, probably. She felt oddly bereft at being deprived of his company for even a short time. How could she possibly have grown so used to him in a week? She'd been so immersed in him she'd forgotten the convention, and two weeks ago it had occupied huge chunks of her time and thoughts. She didn't know how she was going to do without him once she got back to Phoenix. Life had such a way of sneaking up on you when your back was turned. After all those years of working hard to keep her life uncomplicated, he had shown up out of nowhere and complicated it good.

THE FOOD THAT NIGHT tasted wonderful but still, dinner was a palpitating ordeal. Seated on Boyd's right at the table, Audrey felt the strain of being so close to him without being able to touch him. And from his uncharacteristic silence and tight-lipped expression, she suspected he felt it, too. They didn't dare look at each other, and the steady stream of banter that was floating around the table just served to make her more uncomfortable. She was glad she wasn't expected to contribute much to the conversation. Save for a few light comments about her experiences as a "tenderfoot cowhand," she remained silent.

Audrey had never been so glad to see a meal come to an end. She tried to think of a good excuse for not joining the family in the sun room for their customary postprandial session, but a headache was the only thing that came to mind, and that sounded pretty lame for someone who had just come from a week of roughing it in the great outdoors. Gamely, she followed the others as they filed en masse out of the dining room.

Lagging behind, Audrey was crossing the foyer when a strong arm went around her waist and spun her around. Startled, she gasped his name. "Boyd! You scared me to death."

He placed a finger on his lips to silence her, then took her hand and pulled her to the front door.

"Where are we going?" she whispered.

"Hush. You'll see."

"Won't the others wonder where we are?"

"Let 'em."

Grasping her hand firmly, he led her out onto the front porch, sprinted its length and loped across the side yard toward the barn. Audrey's feet all but left the ground as she frantically tried to keep up with him. He didn't slow his pace until they had gone some distance from the house. Audrey's chest heaved as she fought to catch her breath. "I repeat, where are we going?"

"And I repeat, you'll see."

Clutching her hand tightly, Boyd led her around the corral to a secluded area behind the barn where an enormous stack of hay stood. Scooping her up into his arms, he tossed her onto the hay, then fell on top of her.

Laughing lightly, she slipped her arms around his neck. "Lord, Boyd, what's gotten into you?"

"God a'mighty, you look gorgeous tonight. It was all I could do to keep my hands off you during dinner. I kept wanting to reach over and..."

Audrey wiggled against him and held him tight. "That might have raised a few eyebrows."

"I imagine so." Bending his head, he kissed her soundly. "Hmm. Twenty-four hours without that is about as long as I can stand."

"What are you going to do when I leave?"

"I don't even want to think about it." He kissed her again, crushing her farther into the hay. This time when he raised his head, she was covered with the prickly grass.

With one hand, Audrey brushed it away from her face. "Oh, this stuff is awful, coarse and scratchy. How in the world did a 'roll in the hay' ever come to stand for..."

"For what?"

"You know."

"Tell me." His hand went to the hem of her skirt, slipped under and moved upward, stroking and petting until it found its destination. Her panty hose were only a slight hindrance.

His hands tugged, and Audrey gasped, even as the first thrill of desire rippled through her. "Lord, no! You wouldn't, not here!"

"Why not?"

"Someone might see us. Boyd, please..."

"No one's going to come out here."

"How...can you be sure?"

"Twenty-seven people could walk by this haystack right now and never know we're here. At least they wouldn't if you'd be quiet."

"Boyd..."

"Hush." He effectively silenced her with his mouth. His lips were soft, coaxing, demanding. Their persuasive power stripped away her resistance. She felt herself relax to allow his wandering hands free access to her pliant body. They petted and stroked her with sure yet tantalizing touches. Her heartbeat accelerated, then hammered inside her chest. Beneath her skin an undeniable glow crept through her body. It amazed her and would always amaze her how easily and masterfully he could arouse her. There was such a delicious thrill associated with Boyd's touch.

With a feeling of pure satisfaction Boyd sensed her growing ardor and sought to intensify it. His mouth left hers, and his tongue made an impatient foray across her cheek and down the smooth column of her throat. With his hands he nudged her legs apart, then settled his hips between them, claiming the secret niche he now thought of as his.

"This...really is indecent," she whispered.

"Hush."

"In our clothes and..."

That was the last thing Audrey was able to say for a very long time. His body probed hers, and she became its welcoming sheath. Soon they both were moving to pleasure's rhythm, satisfying a desperate longing.

SOME TIME LATER they strolled arm in arm across the moonlit grounds, lost in the wonder of what had transpired between them. Neither of them saw the man who lounged against a tree trunk in the distance, but he saw them. He watched intently as the couple stopped in the shadows and shared a kiss before continuing on toward the house. He alertly noticed how their arms dropped when they reached the front porch, and how they separated before going through the front door.

Jesse smiled. So Audrey had a thing going with Boyd. Good! To Jesse's mind it was his ace in the hole. Throughout roundup he'd stayed as far away from her as he could. She despised him and wasn't very good at concealing the fact. Not wanting to arouse suspicions, he had prudently given her a wide berth. Though he no longer worried that Audrey might influence Betty against him—Betty was too besotted to believe anything Audrey might say—he'd still been afraid she might squelch his plans in ways he couldn't foresee.

Now he could stop worrying. If Audrey had the means to ruin his plans, he now had the means to do the same to her, and she would know it. One peep out of her, and he'd run to Boyd and his old man as fast as his legs would carry him. Things couldn't have been working out better.

THE POPULATION of the peaceful little village of Agua Linda tripled for one day every year. Some of the local merchants declared that they usually made more money during Tri-County Fair and Rodeo then they did at Christmas. By the time the Benedict clan arrived on Saturday morning, the main street of the town was teeming with activity. Buck, Elizabeth, Sara and Brent rode in the blue Cadillac, while Boyd drove Audrey and Betty in one of the ranch's pickups. They parked at the fairgrounds on the outskirts of the community, then strolled around to take in the sights. Dozens of judgings were taking place, of everything from livestock to sweet pepper relish, and at noon a chili cook-off was held. Audrey was just as proud as the rest of the Triple B hands when Skeet Drummond won first place.

Betty didn't linger long with the family. She soon left them with a promise to join Audrey and Boyd at the rodeo that evening. Ostensibly she was joining some friends, but Audrey correctly guessed that the "friend" was Jesse. She and her conscience waged a constant war over Betty's infatuation with the man, but Audrey knew that if she couldn't bring herself to tell even Boyd about her past, and she couldn't, she wasn't apt to reveal it to any of the other Benedicts.

The family was well-known, she noticed. No one passed without speaking. Audrey was not yet aware of the fact that her old friend, Bert, had been the virtual patron of Agua Linda, and the mantle had been passed to Buck. Almost every institution in town was owned or controlled or heavily endowed by the Benedicts, and that included the bank, the newspaper, the cattle association and a nearby private school. Audrey was introduced to more people than she ever could remember. More than a few of them obviously recognized her name as that of the woman who'd inherited all that money, but no one would have dreamed of asking pointed questions.

The day passed lazily. By midafternoon it was obvious that Elizabeth and Sara had had about all of the festivities they could take. Not long afterward, Buck and Brent and their wives returned to the ranch, leaving Audrey and Boyd to enjoy the rest of the day by themselves.

And they well might have been alone instead of among thousands of people. They had eyes only for each other and kept to themselves as much as possible. Away from the restrictive influence of his family, Boyd's entire manner changed. He knew he was wearing his heart in his eyes, but he didn't care. He was wildly in love with the beautiful woman at his side. There were problems, of course, but he'd deal with them when the time came. His immediate worry was that Audrey might slip out of his life as quickly as she had come into it. He suspected he was going to be a very busy man in the upcoming months, tending to business as usual while hurrying to Phoenix often enough to keep the flame burning.

He wondered how long it would take to convince Audrey to marry him, while smiling at the thought. How strange to know with absolute certainty that he wanted to marry her. Two weeks ago he hadn't known she existed.

The day wound down to evening. Audrey and Boyd sat in the pickup, eating hot dogs, drinking beer and waiting for the rodeo to begin. Audrey sighed contentedly and rested her head on the back of the seat. "It's been a glorious day. It's going to be awfully hard to climb in my car and drive back to Phoenix Monday."

Boyd's hand went to her nape and massaged gently. "I'll drive you. I don't like your being on the highway alone."

They exchanged knowing smiles. "A lame excuse is better than no excuse at all, I suppose. Will you really go with me?"

He nodded. "And once I deliver you safe and sound, I might have to stay a few days. I think it's time the family took more of an active interest in the Greenspoint, don't you?"

"Oh, indeed. Much more active." Audrey was flooded with happiness. She still wasn't prepared to say where all this was going to lead. It seemed highly unlikely that she and Boyd were going to walk arm and arm into the sunset to live happily ever after, so she didn't think about it much. She was seizing the moment and tomorrow be damned, something she hadn't done in her entire life. The inner loosening that brought on was wonderful.

They finished their food, crammed the napkins and cans into a paper sack, and Boyd left the truck to go in search of a trash bin. Audrey waited and scanned the scene through the windshield. Dusk had fallen. More and more vehicles were arriving by the minute, and the stands were beginning to fill up. Boyd finally returned to the truck, but just as he opened the door on the driver's side he was accosted by three cowboys. Audrey recognized them as Triple B regulars.

"Hey, Boyd, got a minute?" one of them called.

Boyd closed the door and turned in their direction. "Sure, Joe. What can I do for you?"

The men approached, and the man named Joe spoke up. "We're wonderin' if we can talk you into signin' up for the bronc ridin'."

Boyd laughed. "Afraid not, fellas."

"Aw, come on, Boyd," another man cajoled. "You were the best dadblamed bronc rider in the valley."

"That was some time ago. I'd better pass. But thanks for asking." He reached for the door handle, but Joe put a detaining hand on his arm.

"Hey, listen...there's no way the Triple B is gonna win this thing if we don't win the bronc ridin'. The Bar H bunch is probably gonna take the ropin' event, so we need to throw our best in the bronc ridin'."

"Well, now, boys, I'm flattered as all get out, but I haven't ridden in five or six years."

"Come on, Boyd. If Lefty Jarrell can ride a bronc, you can, too."

Boyd paused and frowned. "Lefty Jarrell? Is Lefty riding tonight?"

"Yep, and the money's on him."

"The hell it is! Lefty's as old as I am."

"Older," Joe said, pressing his advantage. "And he never was half as good as you were."

Audrey could see Boyd vacillating, and a sudden fear clutched at her. Surely he wasn't seriously considering such a foolhardy stunt. A wild horse was the meanest animal on earth, one who had soured under the saddle and would rather be shot than ridden. Bronc riding was terribly dangerous, and it definitely was a young man's sport. Bronc riders "retired" before thirty, if they lasted that long.

Her worst fears were realized when she heard Boyd say, "Okay, Joe, go sign me up. I'll get Audrey settled and meet you back in the chutes."

The three men hurried away to carry the news to the other Triple B hands, and Boyd walked around the truck to open Audrey's door. "Boyd, please don't do this," she beseeched.

But the adrenaline was flowing, and his eyes were bright with the challenge. "Don't worry about me, honey. I grew up riding broncs."

"It's dangerous, and you know it! Please, for me, don't."

He paid no attention. He merely shoved his hand into his hip pocket. "Here, you'd better hold these for me," he said, handing her his wallet and the truck's keys.

"Boyd, please..."

"Don't worry about me, Audrey. I know what I'm doing. Let's go find Betty."

As they crossed the parking lot, Audrey continued protesting, but then they were joined by some of the other cowboys, so she had no choice but to keep quiet. Once they spied Betty in the stands, Boyd patted Audrey on the shoulder, said he'd see her later, then walked away with the men. Filled with apprehension, she climbed the steps and took the seat Betty had been holding for her.

"Where've you been?" Betty wanted to know. "We've looked all over for you. Where's Boyd?"

Audrey saw that Jesse was sitting on Betty's right. She acknowledged him with a curt nod, then sat down on Betty's left. With a jerk of her head in the direction of the chutes at one end of the arena, she said, "He's entering the bronc riding."

Betty's mouth dropped. "He's what?"

"You heard me. Some of the men talked him into it."

"Oh, God, Jesse," Betty moaned. "Did you hear that? Go down there and put a stop to this!"

Jesse snorted derisively. "Are you kidding? Do you honestly think I'm going down there in front of the other guys and tell Boyd not to ride a bronc? He'd fire me on the spot. No way!"

Audrey's fear intensified when she saw the horrified look on Betty's face. It became almost paralyzing when Betty cried, "He must be crazy! He hasn't ridden a bronc in five or six years. Has he been drinking?"

"A couple of beers, that's it."

"Well, we've got to do something." Betty got to her feet. "Come on, Audrey..."

But Jesse grabbed her arm and pulled her down. "Don't make an ass of yourself, sweetheart," he muttered. "Boyd's a big boy. He'll be furious if you go down there and make a scene in front of everyone. I'm bettin' he can go the full eight seconds and then some."

Resigned, Betty turned to Audrey. "He's right, you know. There's nothing we can do, except cross our fingers and pray my dumb brother doesn't get his fool neck broken." She bit her lip. "Besides, he once was the very best amateur I ever saw."

Audrey noticed the lack of conviction in Betty's voice. The evening that had promised to be so fun-filled turned into an endurance run. Everyone around her, with the possible exception of Betty, was having a grand time, but she sat woodenly through the barrel races, the clowns' antics, the calf roping, and the bulldogging events, barely seeing anything. Had she been granted one wish, it would have been that the bronc riding would have been canceled altogether.

Naturally, the wish wasn't granted. An eternity later, the loudspeaker announced the bronc riding event. Audrey forced herself to watch the first four riders, which wasn't too difficult since they were strangers to her. One young cowboy barely cleared the chute before he landed rump first on the ground. The fourth contestant was the man named Lefty Jarrell, whom she had heard mentioned in the parking lot. To loud applause, he stayed on six and a half seconds. Then she heard Boyd's name come over the speaker, and a great roar went up from the crowd.

Fear-induced nausea rose up in her throat. "I...don't think I can watch," she told Betty.

Betty's mouth set in a grim line. "If my brother lives through this, I might personally try to blister his butt."

Audrey was certain she'd never be able to watch, but seemingly hypnotized, she discovered she couldn't take her eyes off the arena. Had it been anyone but Boyd out there, she might have thought it a spectacular sight. With a rolling motion as powerful as dynamite and as unpredictable as lightning, horse and rider came out of the chute. While the crowd roared and whistled its approval, the horse pulled every trick he knew in an attempt to dislodge his hated burden. Boyd rolled with him, hanging onto the rigging with one hand while the other arm flailed about freely. Most of the spectators were on their feet, and Audrey learned that night just what an eternity eight seconds could be.

"God, what a ride!" a man behind them exclaimed. "Benedict always was one ridin' machine!"

Then the eight-second buzzer sounded, and the crowd's applause became deafening. Audrey almost collapsed with relief. It was over. *When I get him alone, I'm going to kill him for putting me through this!*

The thought had no sooner formed, however, than the noise around her changed from unrestrained cheering to a collective gasp from hundreds of throats. Audrey thought she heard Betty scream. Her eyes flew to the arena where Boyd and the horse still flailed around. *What is he doing? Why is he still on that horse? Why the devil doesn't he dismount?* A split second passed before she realized what was happening.

Dear God, he was hung up, caught in the rigging and couldn't dismount! Audrey's hand went to her throat. If she thought she'd been afraid before, it was nothing compared to the stark terror that now raced through her. That horse was going to beat him to a pulp!

CHAPTER THIRTEEN

BOYD DIDN'T PANIC. He had been hung up before, and he knew there wasn't anything he could do but ride with the flow. Instinctively, he stopped using his spurs. Freed of that irritant, even the cussedest horse eventually would slow down enough to allow its rider to work free and get off. But an eight-second ride on a bucking bronc was grueling enough; getting beat around the arena for three or four minutes was a severe jolt to the system.

By now the horse was wild with fury. The frustrated animal kept banging his body against the fence, so Boyd knew his right leg was going to take a beating. At this point, since he couldn't work himself free, the one thing he didn't want was to be thrown and dragged on the ground. He'd once seen a young cowboy killed that way. It was fast becoming a catch-22 situation. The horse's wild antics were scrambling his insides, but he had to stay on until he could get free of the rigging.

It was amazing how many things a person could think about while being tossed in the air. It occurred to him that Audrey was watching all this. He was dimly aware of the clowns who were frantically trying to distract the horse. Two cowboys had jumped the fence and were attempting to help. Not too smart of them, but Boyd fervently hoped they would succeed. He'd drawn one goddanged mean horse, so maybe he'd win the dumb event after all.

By the time he had finally worked free and hit the ground, he knew there wasn't an inch of him that wouldn't be black and blue by morning. His head had struck something during the fall, and it was exploding. He vaguely wondered if he had any broken bones, and he hoped there was a doctor in the crowd. He had a moment to be grateful for two pairs of strong arms lifting him before he closed his eyes and slipped into unconsciousness.

Since accidents weren't uncommon at rodeos, a makeshift infirmary had been set up behind the chutes. It was nothing more than a tent with a few cots in it, and the physician on hand was a local doctor who always attended Tri-County Rodeo to take care of just such situations. Audrey, Betty and Jesse had hurried out of the stands and were waiting near the tent. When Audrey saw the unconscious Boyd being carried by two cowboys, she thought she would faint. His mouth was slack; his arms dangled. Blood spurted from the cut over his eye. He looked so awful she was sure he was dead. As her vision blurred sickeningly, she felt Betty's arm go around her shoulders. "He's going to be all right, Audrey. I just know he is," she said, but her voice didn't carry the conviction Audrey would have liked.

She didn't know how long they stood outside the tent, waiting. Probably not as long as it seemed. They had been joined by several Triple B men who, along with Jesse, congregated in a tight circle apart from the two women. Their murmuring, concerned voices reached Audrey's ears. *They think he's dead, too,* she thought, and tears welled in her eyes. *How could I have let this happen? I should have stopped him. I've never even told him I love him.*

At long last the doctor emerged from the tent. He scanned the anxious faces, recognized Betty and smiled. "He's all right. A bit battered, but nothing's broken. He's just going to have to rest and let everything mend. But I think I should warn you—he's going to feel like walking death tomorrow."

The cowboys broke into happy whoops, while Audrey all but collapsed with relief and gratitude. Betty hugged her impulsively. "Go on in and see him, Audrey. We're going to have to take him home. I'll bring the truck around. Are the keys in it?"

Distractedly, Audrey reached in her jeans pocket, withdrew the keys and handed them to Betty. Then, as the young woman walked away, she went in to see Boyd.

A kerosene lantern illuminated the inside of the tent. The air was heavy with the smell of disinfectant. Boyd was lying on one of the small cots, his hands folded on his chest. Fearfully, Audrey moved toward him, and when she peered down at his prone figure she uttered a choked gasp. She didn't think she'd ever seen anyone who looked so terrible. The gash over his eye had stopped bleeding and was beginning to swell. His right pant leg had been slit to the thigh, revealing angry red skin and dried blood. The knuckles of the hand that had been caught in the rigging were scraped raw. He was so still it frightened her. Placing a hand on his shoulder, she whispered, "Boyd?" When there was no response, she shook him gently. "Boyd?"

His eyelids fluttered. He coughed and opened his eyes. "Hi, hon," he murmured, then groaned. "God, do I have a granddaddy of a headache!"

"Headache?" she cried. "You're lucky that's all you have. I . . . thought you were dead."

"Well, I'm not. Messed up a little, I guess, but quite alive. At least, I think I'm alive."

"Ohh!" Audrey sank to the ground and placed her head on his chest. Fairly controlled until now, she began to cry. "Oh, God, I thought you were dead!"

"Don't cry. I'm all right."

"You're not all right! You'll probably be dead by morning. Anyone who'd do something so stupid ought to be dead."

As rotten as he felt, Boyd managed a small smile. "You should have been a nurse, Audrey. You have the most soothing bedside manner."

"How could you possibly do something so incredibly dumb?"

"Hey, I made a good ride. Getting hung up is just something that happens every once in awhile. Don't cry. Calm down and help me up."

Audrey's head came up with a jerk. "Boyd, I think you need to go to a hospital."

"I'm not going to a hospital. The doctor says I haven't broken anything."

"How can he possibly know that? I don't see any X-ray machines. You should go to a hospital and let someone check you over good. There might be internal injuries. I really think—"

"Dammit, honey, don't think. Just help me up and take me home."

THERE WERE SEVERAL unfamiliar cars parked in front of the ranch house when the pickup arrived, and the house was ablaze with lights. Boyd groaned. "I guess the folks have a house full of company. They usually do on the night of Tri-County. I don't want to have to answer a lot of damned fool questions. Betty, go in and see what's going on."

Betty, who had driven the truck home, switched off the engine and opened the door. "Right. I'll be back in a jiffy."

The trip from Agua Linda had seemed to take forever. Audrey knew Boyd was in more pain than he would admit. She had seen him wince at every bump in the road. But he was adamant about not going to the hospital, so she just prayed that that doctor at the rodeo had known what he was doing.

"I wish there was something I could do," she said lamely. "I know you're hurting, and I feel so helpless."

"Just stay close by. Oh, and you might give me a kiss. Isn't that supposed to cure everything?"

Smiling, she kissed him tenderly. "Promise me you'll admit it if you start feeling really bad. No suffering in silence."

"Promise."

Betty returned and opened the door on the passenger side. "Everyone's in the sun room, so I think we can get the patient in his room without anyone seeing us."

The two women gave Boyd a hand and helped him into the house. The threesome had crossed the foyer when Elizabeth came out of the sun room carrying an empty tray. At the sight of her son she let out a startled cry and almost dropped the tray. "Boyd! Good heavens, what happened to you?"

"The idiot forgot he isn't twenty anymore," Betty scoffed.

"It's nothing, Mom, really," Boyd hastened to assure her. "Just a little accident. I'm fine."

"How can you be fine when you look so dreadful? Do you need medical attention?" Elizabeth looked from her daughter to Audrey. "Isn't anyone going to tell me what happened?"

"Betty will fill you in," Boyd muttered. "Don't worry, Mom. I've seen a doctor, but I've got to get off this leg."

Betty stayed behind to explain everything to a clearly unappeased Elizabeth, and Audrey let Boyd lean on her while she helped him to his room. Once there she hurried to turn down the bed. "In you go."

"I don't want to go to bed," he protested. "I want a drink and a shower."

"Oh, Boyd, the shower can wait. I'll get you a drink if you want it, but you really should be in bed."

"I'm not getting in that bed without a shower. I'm too filthy."

She frowned thoughtfully. "Well, I guess you probably will rest better if you're clean. But you won't be able to stand in the shower. I'm afraid you might fall. Let me run a bath for you."

"I hate taking baths," he grumbled.

"If you insist on getting cleaned up, you'll simply have to take a bath."

"Whatever you say, dear," he said with a grin and sank to the edge of the bed. The grin faded immediately as he held his injured leg rigidly in front of him.

"You're going to have to help me with my boots. This son of a bitch leg is throbbing like crazy."

Audrey looked at him sympathetically. "You're really going to have something to moan about when that water hits it. Maybe you should reconsider that bath."

"Don't worry, I'm tough. Get these boots, will you?"

Audrey straddled his leg, presenting him with her backside. She held his leg between her knees, tugged on the boot, and it thudded to the floor. She repeated with the other, and that boot joined its mate on the floor.

Boyd's hands wandered seductively over her buttocks. "You have the cutest rump I've ever seen. Why don't you take a bath with me?"

Audrey straightened, moved away and shot him a disgusted look. "In this house? Don't be ridiculous."

"We'll lock the door."

"And, of course, no one would wonder why the door was locked."

At that moment Buck charged into the room, concern written all over his face. "You okay, son?" he asked anxiously.

"Yeah, Dad, fine."

"You look like hell."

"So everyone tells me."

"Betty told us what happened. Your mother's plenty worried about you." Buck crossed the room and leveled a stern look on his son. "Have you lost your mind? Don't you know bronc bustin's for kids?"

Boyd grinned. "Reckon my memory was refreshed tonight."

Buck turned to Audrey for the first time since entering the room. "A doctor saw him?"

She nodded. "He said nothing's broken, but Boyd's supposed to get a lot of rest."

"Mmm." Buck's gaze returned to his son. "Maybe having to spend a few days in bed will teach you a lesson. Maybe next time you'll think twice before you climb up on one of those fool things. You sure you're all right?"

"Fine, Dad."

Buck appeared to have his doubts. "Let someone know if you need anything. Now, I've got to get back to our guests. I'll swear to God, I thought you, of all people, had better sense than to do something that crazy." With that he left the room.

Audrey breathed a sigh of relief. What there was about Boyd's father that kept her on edge she didn't know, but she never fully relaxed around the man.

Boyd muttered disgustedly, "Lord, you'd think I was the only guy who'd ever gotten bunged up in a rodeo. Close the door, hon, will you? I want to get undressed."

Audrey closed the door, then crossed to the bathroom. "I'll go draw the water."

Boyd's very masculine private bathroom was much larger than the one in the guest room. Audrey turned on the tub's faucet full force, checked the water temperature, then returned to the bedroom. Boyd had shed his shirt and was struggling out of his jeans and undershorts. He chuckled dryly when he saw the rise of color in her cheeks. "Nothing you haven't seen before. Why are you blushing?"

"I don't know. I…oh, Boyd…how awful!" If the sight of his magnificent nude body was unnerving, its condition was alarming. His bronze skin had turned black and blue in an astonishing number of places. "You must feel dreadful. Are you sure you want to get in that water?"

"It looks worse than it is, Audrey, and I definitely want some soap and water. I told you, I'm tough."

"You'll put something on those cuts when you get out of the tub, won't you?"

"Yes, yes. You're going to make a nagging wife. I can already see signs of it. You'd better go turn off that water before you flood the place."

Audrey turned and went back into the bathroom to shut off the faucet. Boyd came in behind her and grabbed a nearby towel rack. She held his other arm tightly as he eased down into the warm liquid. The first stinging drops elicited a violent oath. Then as he settled down, he murmured a satisfied "Ahhh!"

"You all right?" she inquired with concern. When he nodded, she released his arm and said, "Now I'll go get you that drink. But don't try to get up until I get back."

The party was still going on in the sun room. Audrey realized that the bar was in there, and she didn't particularly want to barge in on Buck and Elizabeth and their guests. Standing unnoticed at the door, she managed to catch Betty's eyes and mouth "Boyd wants a drink." Betty nodded in acknowledgment and walked to the bar, while Audrey waited in the hall.

"How's the patient?" Betty asked when she brought the drink.

"Mildly cooperative. I know he's in terrible pain, but—" she winked "—he's tough."

Betty snorted. "Yeah, aren't they all? Come and get me if you need help with him. Otherwise, I'll see you in the morning."

Returning to Boyd's room, Audrey walked to the bathroom door and listened. She heard nothing. "Are you still there?" she called.

"I'm here, and my skin's getting wrinkled. I waited in case you wanted to dry me."

"Funny man. Can you get out by yourself?"

"I'm not crippled."

"Don't forget to put something on those cuts. Can I get your pajamas for you?"

"I sleep in the raw, Audrey."

She couldn't help smiling at the growled masculine curses coming from the other side of the door. She waited until it opened. Boyd stood before her with a towel wrapped around his waist, scowling at a bottle of antiseptic in his hand. "This damned stuff hurts!"

"Poor thing. I thought you were tough."

He handed her the bottle and a wad of cotton. "You do it for me."

"All right. Go sit on the bed."

First she gingerly dabbed the gash over his eye with the medicine, then blew on it. Inching the towel up past his knee, she knelt at his feet and carefully treated his wounded leg. "I hate hurting you," she said as she heard him suck in his breath. "Believe me, it hurts me worse."

Even though absorbed in the nursing task, Audrey was acutely aware of the way he looked, of the strength in his legs, of the dark hair covering them.

Without realizing she was doing it, she stroked his powerful calf muscles with her free hand. As for Boyd, he hardly noticed the antiseptic's sting, for he was intent only on the lovely woman at his feet and her gentle touch.

When Audrey was certain she had tended to all his cuts, she pressed her face into the side of his leg and kissed it. A tender fire was burning in his eyes when she recapped the bottle and glanced up. Their eyes locked together in silent communication. His gaze never wavered as he took the bottle and cotton from her and laid them on the bedside table. Placing his hands under her arms, he lifted her to sit beside him. Audrey sighed contentedly as his arms encircled her.

"Kiss me," he commanded.

She complied with sweet insistence. Their mouths fused together. The kiss was a deep, draining one, and when they parted, Audrey's mind reeled with the wonder of his power over her. All he had to do was touch her.

Boyd's hand hovered near her breasts, then closed over one and felt her expected response. Through the fabric of her shirt his fingertips molded the hardened bud. "Do you think we know each other well enough by now?"

She moaned softly. "Awfully pleased with yourself, aren't you?"

"What do you think?" His crooked smile was delightfully wicked.

"You're really terrible. Here you are, practically at death's door, and you're thinking about sex."

"You're damned right I am. Aren't you?"

"We aren't alone. I shouldn't be in here with you as it is."

"In an hour or so everyone will be asleep, and it's just a short walk from your room to mine."

"I couldn't do that, not even if we were alone. You need to rest. I might hurt you."

"I'll risk it."

Audrey's arms crept up the wall of his chest, and her hands locked behind his neck. "Boyd, promise me you'll never do anything as stupid as getting on that horse again. You could have been killed."

"You were worried."

"Of course I was worried! I was frantic."

"Good. That means you care a lot more than you want me to think you do."

She kissed him tenderly, then gazed at him with luminous eyes. "How could you doubt I care after what's happened between us?"

Cupping her face in his hands, he looked at her adoringly. "Audrey, love...this wasn't supposed to happen to me. I thought I was immune. But now that it has happened, I'm not going to waste a lot of time denying it."

Lost in each other, neither of them heard the door open. Buck's voice shattered the sweet eloquence of the moment. "Boyd, I'd..." He stopped short when he saw the couple seated on the bed. "Oh, excuse me...."

Audrey disentangled herself from Boyd's embrace and jumped to her feet so quickly she nearly lost her balance. Straightening, she stood some distance from the bed with her hands clasped tightly in front of her.

Buck looked at his son, then at Audrey and back to Boyd. "The guests have left, and your mother and I are going to bed. I thought I'd best check on you before calling it a day."

"Thanks, Dad. I'm fine."

A heavy silence fell over the room. Buck made no move to leave. Audrey didn't know why she felt so embarrassed, but she did. Something in the man's expression made her heart sink. Instinctively she realized that Buck wasn't going to leave until she did. Not knowing what else to do, she walked to the dresser and picked up the drink, then placed it on the nightstand. "I'm going to bed now, Boyd," she said stiffly. "Drink that, then be a good boy and get some rest." With as much poise as she could muster, she sailed past Buck and offered him a small smile. "Good night, Mr. Benedict."

"Good night, Audrey."

Out in the hall she put her hand to her racing heart. *That man doesn't approve of me,* she thought with certainty and dismay. *I don't know why, but he doesn't. Well, I'm not too sure I approve of him, either. So where does that leave Boyd and me?*

Unfortunately, she feared she knew the answer to that one.

CHAPTER FOURTEEN

LONG AFTER ELIZABETH had fallen asleep, Buck stood at the window of their bedroom, deep in thought. He had been surprised, to say the least, over barging in on Audrey and Boyd during what obviously had been a tender moment, and Buck wasn't fond of surprises where the family was concerned.

Contrary to what Audrey believed, however, he wasn't particularly alarmed or displeased. Now that he'd had time to think it over, he realized that the young woman from Phoenix passed all his rather rigorous criteria. She was pretty, educated, poised and charming. Elizabeth spoke highly of her, and Buck had learned to trust his wife's first impressions of people. Added to that was the fact that his own father had held Audrey in high esteem. All in all, Boyd might have made an excellent choice.

But Buck didn't like something going on that he wasn't right on top of. If his son was seriously interested in Audrey, he needed to know more about her. Perhaps a phone call to Peter Sorenson was in order. And it might be wise to have a heart-to-heart talk with Audrey herself before this thing went any further. It was imperative that she knew exactly what would be expected of her. Then Buck would decide whether to bestow his blessings on the relationship or stop it dead in its tracks.

The future, in his estimation, was much too important to be entrusted to the willy-nilly ways of young people who thought they were in love.

WHILE AUDREY was getting dressed the following morning there was a knock on her door. "Come in," she called. The door opened and Maria entered the room.

"Pardon, *señorita*," the housekeeper said shyly.

"Yes, Maria, what is it?"

"The *señor* would like to see you in his study as soon as you've had breakfast."

Although three men lived in the house, when Maria said "the *señor*" there was no question in anyone's mind to whom she referred. A tremor of trepidation swept through Audrey. A private conference with Buck Benedict was not her idea of a good way to start the day, and she didn't have to spend any time wondering what the subject under discussion would be.

However, she had anticipated something like this. Not for a minute had she thought Buck would let the cozy little scene he had stumbled upon last night go uncommented on. "Thank you, Maria," she replied calmly. "Tell Mr. Benedict I'll be along as soon as I finish dressing. I'm not really hungry this morning."

"*Sí*, very good." Maria said as she backed out of the room.

In spite of her apprehension, or possibly because of it, Audrey didn't hurry. She finished dressing and applying her makeup, then took the time to check on

Boyd, who, thankfully, was dead to the world. Standing over him, her heart constricted sharply. In sleep, he looked peaceful, almost boyish, and she longed to crawl into the bed with him, to wrap her arms around him and take comfort from the feel of his body. How incredible it was to have grown so fond of him in such a short time. She had expected love, if it came to her at all, would develop gradually over months or years. Yet, for better or worse, Boyd had changed her life dramatically in two weeks. Giving herself a shake, she quietly left the room and went to Buck's study.

The door was closed. She tapped lightly, heard his summons and entered the room. The study was unlike any other room in the house. It was a cozy, completely masculine retreat furnished with sturdy, leather-upholstered furniture and dominated by a massive mahogany desk. Dozens of framed photographs and official documents lined the paneled walls. Buck sat behind the desk in a chair that faced the door. Seeing Audrey, he got to his feet and smiled. "Come in, my dear, and have a seat. Maria tells me you haven't had breakfast. Please, at least have some coffee and one of these cinnamon rolls. They're very good."

A coffee service had been set up on a small table in front of one of the windows. The smell of coffee and freshly baked cinnamon rolls was irresistible. "Thank you," Audrey said. "That sounds wonderful."

She walked to the table, but Buck was there first, pouring coffee and putting a roll on a small plate. "The rest of the family has brunch later on Sunday morning, but I've never been able to sleep in, no matter what the day. I've noticed that you're an early riser, too. I like that. Morning's the most productive part of the day."

Then, instead of motioning her to a chair, Buck slipped a hand under Audrey's elbow and guided her around the room, pointing out and explaining the various mementos on the wall. "We haven't had much of a chance to visit while you've been here, Audrey, and I regret that. I always like my guests to leave the Triple B knowing something of its history. I'm not exaggerating when I say that the history of this ranch parallels the history of Arizona. Here, for instance, is the original deed to the ranch. You'll notice the date...."

Most of what he told her she already had learned from Boyd. Still, it was interesting and the photographs were fascinating. The Benedicts had been or were acquainted with a lot of famous people. There were pictures of one Benedict or another with every President since Harry Truman. Audrey made appropriate comments when they seemed called for, but her mind was on something else altogether. Buck appeared to be going out of his way to put her at ease. Why?

When they had covered the room, Buck asked her to be seated. Then he sat behind the desk once more, folded his hands and regarded her intently. "Audrey, I hope you'll forgive my being blunt, but I'm not accustomed to small talk or beating around the bush. Unless I'm mistaken, and I don't think I am, you and my son seem to have become rather fond of each other."

Audrey had to give him credit for his direct approach. "Yes, we have. We ... er, get along well."

"He must have been taken with you from the first."

At this Audrey had to smile. "As a matter of fact, our initial meeting was a bit on the testy side. But you can understand that, considering the circumstances that brought us together."

"Yes." Buck pursed his lips thoughtfully. "Dad's will was something of a shock to all of us, but I want you to know that no one in this family begrudges you your inheritance."

"Thank you, Mr. Benedict."

"Do you mind my asking if you and Boyd have discussed any future plans?"

"We've only known each other a couple of weeks, Mr. Benedict. I assure you things have not gone that far." .

"Yes, but I know my son. I've been waiting a good dozen years—a bit impatiently, I might add—for Boyd to show some kind of unusual interest in a woman. Now he has. I don't think he's going to let any grass grow under his feet. You know, Audrey, I'm fond of thinking I'm aware of everything that goes on in this family, but this came like a bolt out of the blue. Are you certain you don't find my questioning offensive?"

"No, not at all," she said decisively, which was only a tiny white lie. Vaguely she wondered why Buck was talking to her instead of to Boyd. She also wondered what Boyd would think about this little tête-à-tête.

As if reading her mind, Buck explained, "I'm having this little chat with you, my dear, because, while Boyd is fully aware of the family structure and what is expected of him, you probably aren't. The woman my son marries will immediately take on certain obligations."

"Most wives do."

"Yes, of course, but I'm speaking of special obligations. Before I tell you what they are, I want to assure you that I have nothing against you. On the contrary, I find you a charming young woman, and you certainly are adaptable. That's very important. Also, my father obviously thought highly of you, and I trusted Dad's judgment. So if you're thinking I don't approve of your relationship with Boyd, forget it. This has nothing to do with that."

Audrey didn't understand why Buck's words had the effect of making her feel even more tense and edgy. She couldn't imagine what all this was leading to, but she was beginning to be very curious about those "special obligations." There was more to this conference than simply getting acquainted, she was sure. "Thank you," she said and waited with suspended breath.

"Like all fathers, I suppose, I have had some grand plans for my children. Parents seem to do that sort of thing in spite of better intentions. Not all of my plans have been realized. I'll confess to having been disappointed in the past. There's the matter of grandchildren, for one thing. There have been Benedicts in Arizona, in this house, for a very long time, and I'm anxious for the line to continue. Do you have any objections to motherhood?"

Good Lord, Audrey thought, *this really is a bit much!* "Not at all. I think I would love being a mother."

"Good, good. One never knows about modern young women. And, of course, Boyd's wife would be expected to do a certain amount of important entertaining, but given the job you do for us at the Greenspoint, I doubt you would find that distasteful. Peter Sorenson tells me you're a natural at that sort of thing."

Audrey's eyes widened slightly. "You've spoken to Peter about me?"

"I telephoned the hotel this morning on the chance he would be there. He was. Do you mind my asking Peter about you?"

Would it make any difference if I did? "You own the hotel, Mr. Benedict, and I work there. You have every right to ask about my performance."

"You might enjoy knowing your employer was effusive in his praise."

"It's not difficult to do a good job when you like your work as much as I do."

"Indeed. But I'm wondering how the prospect of public life would appeal to you."

"Public life?" Audrey didn't understand.

"Yes. I'd like to see Boyd go into politics."

"Does he know that?" Never once had Audrey heard Boyd say anything to indicate he wanted to do something other than what he was doing now.

"Well, we haven't discussed it in so many words, if that's what you mean," Buck admitted, "but when the time comes, I don't expect him to resist. The family has always functioned as a single unit. What's good for one is good for all, that sort of thing. Brent and I agree that Boyd is a natural for politics. He can charm the birds out of the trees if he sets his mind to it. Naturally, he'll need the right kind of wife at his side. But again, you have beauty and poise, and you know how to deal with important people. I'm not worried on that score.''

To Audrey, the term ''public life'' brought one thing to mind: notoriety. She felt an unpleasant shiver race up her spine.

''Right now,'' Buck went on, his eyes alive with anticipation, ''I'm planning to launch Boyd's political career in a couple of years or so. Some state office, I'm not sure which one, but something with high visibility. We have party connections, and his name is well-known, so I don't expect problems. From there it should be a cakewalk to the governor's mansion.''

Audrey couldn't believe it. ''Mr. Benedict, are you telling me that if your plans work out, Boyd will someday be...Governor of Arizona?''

Buck smiled and nodded. ''Why not? And I'll confess something else to you—that's only the beginning. The next logical step is the U.S. Senate, and after that... Why not reach for the sky? Audrey, if these plans work out, someday Boyd might very well be President.''

Audrey gasped. ''President? You mean...of the United States?''

Buck nodded. ''Again, why not? It will take some time, of course. The groundwork has to be laid. But the year 2004 will be an election year. Boyd will only be fifty-two and will have put in a goodly number of years in public service. By then his name should be a household word. Yes, I'm thinking 2004 might be the perfect time.''

The revelation was so astonishing that Audrey was speechless for a minute. Then she said, "Isn't that terribly ambitious?"

"Of course it is, but it's no pipe dream. It could happen. So now you understand why I'm so interested in the young woman my son marries. The right kind of wife can be a tremendous asset to a man with political ambitions."

Or a horrible liability, Audrey thought and had not the slightest doubt into which column she belonged. "Mr. Benedict, are you . . . absolutely sure Boyd will want all the things you want?"

"It's more or less assumed that my offspring will follow my wishes. They never disappoint me. Or at least, almost never."

Audrey guessed the last remark was prompted by Boyd's failure to marry Linda Ames. If he had "disappointed" his father once, he might be willing to again. That hope stirred briefly. "I was led to believe you Benedicts shunned publicity."

"It's more accurate to say we like to control what's written about us. I have no objection to publicity if it's the right kind. I trust you realize the sort of life Boyd's wife would be forced to lead. Virtually every move she makes will be duly noted and commented on. Every aspect of her life will come under close scrutiny. Rarely will she awaken to a day she can completely call her own. Some women hate that sort of existence; some thrive on it. Tell me, Audrey, do you think you could cheerfully live in the goldfish bowl we tend to put our First Ladies in?"

The hope died. Whom was she kidding? She'd seen nothing to indicate that Boyd wouldn't go along with anything the family, meaning Buck, wanted him to do. If his father wanted him to be the governor or a senator or the President, he would give it his best shot. A hopeless despair washed over her for a minute, the feeling of being forced to give up something wonderful she had just found. It would have been nice, she thought, if it actually had worked out. Boyd, this house, this family. They really were a nice group of people, even the man sitting before her. Buck no longer seemed the formidable figure of authority he once had; he was just a man who took his responsibilities seriously. I could have fit in. Boyd's father and I might even have become friends.

The despair was quickly replaced by resignation, however. If nothing else, she was a practical person who accepted the inevitable.

"Well, my dear?" Buck prompted.

Sighing, Audrey leaned forward and placed her cup and plate on the desk. Then she got to her feet. "I'm going to be completely honest with you, Mr. Benedict. I could never live that kind of life. Not in a million years."

Buck sat back, slightly startled. He would have understood had she expressed uncertainty; in fact, he would have been wary if she hadn't. But the last thing he had expected was a flatly negative answer. In a curious way he was disappointed. Audrey had seemed to him the kind of woman who could field whatever life threw her. "You seem awfully sure of that."

"I am, believe me, I am. I know my own nature. Thank you for the coffee and roll, Mr. Benedict. I really enjoyed our visit. Now, if you'll please excuse me, I...think I'll be leaving before the day is over.

That way I can be ready for work bright and early tomorrow morning.''

''I've upset you.''

''No, not really. Just brought me back to reality. It's all right if I leave, isn't it?''

''If that's what you want, Audrey, I have no objection.'' Buck glanced at his hands a moment, then back at her. ''I'm sorry. I didn't mean to be discouraging. I simply thought it fair to warn you of what lies ahead.''

''Yes, and I do appreciate it, Mr. Benedict. You'll never know how much. I'll see you again before I go.''

Leaving the study, she hurried back to her room and closed the door. Squeezing her eyes shut, she fought back tears. She'd been a fool to fall for Boyd. Hadn't she always suspected it would be an unwise thing to do? One of these days she was going to have to trust her gut instincts. She'd always known that a woman with her past couldn't fit in with such a prominent family. She was certain that Buck's ''controlled publicity'' did not include a woman whose father had been sentenced to a federal penitentiary.

Sadly, she had to put an end to her involvement with Boyd, and it was going to be the hardest thing she'd ever done. Audrey sat on the edge of the bed, thinking and planning her next move. She couldn't tell Boyd she'd simply decided she didn't care for him. He'd never believe that.

She had to get back to the Greenspoint immediately, to put some distance between them. Oh, Boyd would follow when he was able, she was sure of it, so the break wouldn't be quick and easy. But he was a busy man and could spend only so much time in Phoenix. As the days and months passed, the visits would become fewer and farther between. Love couldn't flourish without nourishment. The thing would die a natural death.

Now, the immediate problem was telling Boyd she was leaving.

"WHAT?" BOYD ROARED, sitting up straight in bed. "Audrey, how can you even think of leaving? Look at me. I'm a beaten and broken man!"

Audrey stood by the edge of his bed, looking at his shocked face. She was determined to keep the mood lighthearted. Under no circumstances must Boyd suspect she meant this to be the beginning of a permanent break. He would get suspicious and start asking questions she dare not answer. "You just got through telling me you feel fine."

"I lied. I feel terrible. How can you desert me when I'm in this condition?"

"You wouldn't be in that condition if you hadn't been showing off."

"You have a cruel, mean streak that hasn't surfaced before."

"Look, Boyd, I'm simply going back to work, that's all. You've always known I'd have to one of these days."

"But not now. You have to stay here and nurse me back to robust health. I'll call Peter...."

"Please, don't. I've already talked to him, and he needs me. There's a big convention coming up...hardware dealers. I worked for nine months to convince them to hold their meeting at the Greenspoint, and Peter's going to expect me to be there to run the show."

"Oh, forget that damned job! You don't need it."

"Yes, I do, Boyd, but even if I didn't, I owe it to Peter to be there to run the show this week. It's not as if I'm leaving the country. I'll be three hours away."

Boyd flung back the covers, forgetting he was stark naked. "I'm going with you. Get me some clothes." But when he moved his injured leg, he groaned and fell back against the pillow.

"Don't be ridiculous," she chided, discreetly covering him again. "The doctor said you were going to feel terrible today, and you have to worry about infections and things like that. You're going to stay here and recuperate. Besides, I'm going to be so busy the next few days I wouldn't be able to spend much time with you. Please cooperate, love, and get well. I've got to go pack."

"That's it, huh? Just like that. You're sailing out of my life...."

Audrey rolled her eyes toward the ceiling. "Spare me the melodrama. I'll be back in a few minutes."

It took her less than thirty minutes to get ready to leave. She merely tossed her things into her suitcases, then sought out the rest of the family members, as well as Maria and Tina, to say goodbye and thank them for their many kindnesses. Finally she returned to Boyd's room.

He had put on a robe but still was propped in bed, and he wasn't alone. Betty was at his bedside, but the moment she realized Audrey had come to say goodbye, she hurried out of the room and shut the door. Audrey wished she hadn't. Leaving was difficult enough; she didn't want it to become emotional.

She walked to the bed, hating that subdued solemn look on Boyd's face. She held out her hand to him. He took it, but neither of them said a word for several uncomfortably long minutes.

"Ready?" he finally muttered inanely.

"Yes."

"I'd ask you to stay, but we've been through that."

"Like I said, I'm only hours away. You can telephone me anytime."

"Phone calls are highly unsatisfactory."

"I know. Please take care of yourself and get well."

He grunted. "I guess I'll have to if I'm going to be shuttling back and forth to Phoenix." He gave her hand a tug. She bent and accepted the melting kiss he placed on her mouth. "Remember that."

Audrey had to get out of there fast. "Oh, Boyd, you can be very sure I'll do that."

His eyes impaled her. "Be careful on the highway and call me the minute you get home so I'll know you arrived safe and sound."

She was getting too choked up to speak. Nodding silently, she gave his hand a squeeze, then turned and hurried out of the room.

Betty was waiting in the hall and walked her to the car. "I'm going to miss you. It's been fun, almost like having a sister. And from the look on Boyd's face a minute ago, that might come to pass one of these days."

"I wouldn't count on that, Betty. And I'm going to miss you, too. Come to Phoenix and see me one of these days."

"I just might do that."

"I'll show you the sights, we'll eat out and go shopping, all that stuff."

"Sounds like fun."

Again Audrey grappled with her conscience, thinking about Jesse, but in the end she drove away without a word, trusting that Buck's considerable influence would keep Betty out of the unscrupulous man's clutches. It was the best she could do.

CHAPTER FIFTEEN

THREE DAYS LATER Boyd sat in his bedroom brooding. He was in a rotten mood and had been ever since Audrey left. The slightest thing seemed to tee him off, something Betty had mentioned to him several times. He thought it damned peculiar that he'd never noticed what a humdrum existence he had led before Audrey came along.

He had called her every night, which probably wasn't a good idea. Hearing her voice only served to make him feel more alone and bereft. For two weeks he had been with her almost constantly; then in the blink of an eye she was gone. Of course he'd known he would miss her, but he hadn't known just how much. He reminded himself of a simmering kettle of water that had almost reached the boiling point.

From their phone conversations he'd gathered that Audrey was completely tied up with that damned convention. It was always late when he reached her at home, and she usually sounded bone-tired. He envied her the activity. His own enforced idleness coupled with her absence had him as restless and edgy as a caged tiger.

That was going to change. Today he felt much better. The swelling had gone down over his eye, the cuts were healing nicely, and the bruises would fade with time. His mind was focused on the upcoming weekend. He ought to be almost as good as new by then, and the convention would break up Friday afternoon. He was going to be in Phoenix this weekend if he had to be carried there, and he and Audrey were going to talk seriously about the future. Maybe he was rushing things, but being without her for three days had convinced him he didn't want to contemplate a life that didn't include her.

He lounged in the easy chair in his bedroom. He had done more walking today than he had since the accident, and he was genuinely tired. Deep in thought, he at first didn't notice when Betty walked into his room. Then she made some sort of noise, and he looked up. "Hi," he said.

"Hi. You're feeling better, aren't you?"

"Much."

"That's good. Got a minute?" Betty asked crisply.

"I seem to have plenty of them. What's up?"

Betty closed the door and went to sit at the foot of the bed, facing him. It was then that Boyd noticed the expression on his sister's face. She obviously was upset, and that surprised him. Betty, without a doubt, was the most serene individual he'd ever known. "Something wrong?"

"Plenty." Betty's mouth set in a tight line. "Dad and I just had 'words.'"

Boyd chuckled sympathetically. "Ah, well, you know Dad. What unpardonable goof did you commit?" He naturally assumed it had to do with the running of the ranch. To his knowledge, that was all Betty ever thought about. She'd probably made a decision Buck didn't agree with.

Betty heaved an agitated sigh. "Somehow Dad found out I've been seeing Jesse privately, and he doesn't like it a bit."

Boyd frowned. "Murdoch? How long's this been going on?"

"Months. Almost from the time he first came here."

"Well, I'll be damned! I never noticed."

"You wouldn't. You don't think of me as a woman. And for the past two weeks you haven't noticed much of anything but Audrey. Have you talked to her?"

"Every night."

"You've really fallen for her, haven't you?"

Boyd grinned. "Like the proverbial ton of bricks."

"I hope you remember who told you it would happen one of these days. That's why I thought I could talk to you, Boyd. Maybe you'll understand how I feel." Betty got to her feet and began pacing around the room. "Dad's ordered me to stay away from Jesse. No daughter of his is going to get involved with a common cowhand, not when there are so many fine, upstanding young men from good families out there. Dad wants to know why I gravitate toward the ordinary." Betty uttered a derisive snort. "I don't think I can stay away from him, Boyd. And why should I have to? Jesse wants me to marry him."

Boyd let out a low whistle. "That serious, huh?"

"Yes, that serious."

"Did you tell Dad that?"

"No, the coward in me surfaced, just like it always does when Dad gives me one of his lectures. I don't know what I'm going to do. If I keep on seeing Jesse, I'll be openly defying Dad, something I've never done.

Oh, I think it's so unfair of him to put me in this position. Lord, I'm twenty-three and still under his thumb."

"To some extent we all are. That's the way things have always been done in this family."

"Tell me about it." Betty stopped pacing and went to stand in front of her brother, her eyes bright and earnest. "What . . . what do you think would happen if Jesse and I married against Dad's wishes?"

Boyd had some ideas, none of them particularly pleasant. "I'm not sure," he said carefully. Like his sister, he often thought their father sometimes put them in untenable positions, and he, too, felt that was unfair.

"I just might do it," Betty said defiantly. "I just might."

"I'd think long and hard about taking such a drastic step, if I were you. Try to be patient. I can't say I've ever regretted being patient when dealing with Dad. Sometimes he talks first and thinks later. He might come around in time."

But Betty was in no mood for patience. "Wait and see, you mean. That's so easy for you to say. Tell me, dear brother—if Dad disapproved of Audrey, if he ordered you to stay away from her, would you be willing to 'wait and see'?"

The question brought Boyd up short and made him think again of the things Skeet had told him that night at camp. He had no idea if the man named Jack Hamilton was Audrey's father, but suppose he was? What would Buck have to say about that? Boyd was only too aware of his father's preoccupation with "good" marriages for his children, and Buck had some pretty straitlaced, old-fashioned notions about what constituted "good." To date, none of his notions nor his authority had been challenged, but Boyd wondered what would happen if they were.

"Well," Betty challenged. "Would you?"

"I'm not sure. No, that's not being honest. I don't think I would wait, Betty. I'm not saying that would be the smart thing to do. I'm only saying, I don't think I could stay away from her."

"Then you must understand what I'm going through. That's the way I feel about Jesse. Dad doesn't have the right to keep us apart."

"I'm sorry, sis, I really am. I wish I could be more help to you," Boyd said, feeling terribly inadequate. Yet, he couldn't come right out and advise Betty to defy their father. "This is one time I'm not going to give you any advice. This is something you're going to have to work out for yourself, because you're the one who'll have to live with your decision."

"Yeah." Betty sighed again. "I didn't really expect you to solve the dilemma. Guess I just wanted someone to talk to. I wish Audrey was here."

"So do I."

"I'll bet you do, but I wish she was here for a much different reason. Right from the start, I could talk to her, like I'd known her for years, almost like she was a sister. Strange, huh?"

"No," Boyd replied, "not so strange. I know the feeling."

THE HARDWARE dealers' convention had been a resounding success. At the closing meeting a motion was made and passed to make the Greenspoint a yearly tradition. Audrey couldn't have been more pleased, but the work it had entailed had taken its toll on her. Not only had she had to oversee the arrangements for all the meetings and luncheons and the closing night's banquet, she had had to orchestrate the outside activities for the accompanying spouses. She had put in four straight thirteen-hour days, and she couldn't say she was sorry to see the affair wind to a close.

Late Friday afternoon, when the last of the conventioneers had checked out, she went into her office, sank wearily into the chair behind her desk and kicked off her shoes. "I feel like I could sleep for a week."

Helen was closing up for the day. "Yeah, I can imagine. You've been so busy I've hardly had a chance to talk to you. I'm dying to know about everything. In fact, I'm about to burst with curiosity. I'll buy you a drink before I go home, and we can talk."

Audrey didn't have to wonder what the "everything" Helen wanted to talk about was, and she was no more willing to talk about her inheritance now than she'd been three weeks ago. "Thanks, Helen, but will you give me a rain check? I'm pooped."

"Sure. You working this weekend?"

"No."

"Got big plans?"

"I'm not sure. Maybe." Boyd had called every night since she'd been back, and he'd vowed he would be in Phoenix by Saturday. However, she hadn't heard from him today, and something could always happen to keep him from making the trip. She had mixed emotions over the prospect of seeing him again. She missed him twice as much as she'd thought she would, and the nightly phone calls were an exquisite torment. Then she would be reminded of the necessity for making a permanent break with him and would start hoping something would prevent him from coming to Phoenix. The more time that elapsed between visits, went her theory, the easier the final break would be.

But the theory was full of holes. It would never be easy. From the phone calls she could tell that Boyd thought things were just beginning, and she suspected he would be a persistent suitor. How would she ever muster the courage to call it off? The thought of hurting him was more than she could bear, just as the thought of all that loneliness stretching before her filled her with a kind of emptying despair.

What a mess you got me in, Bert. She imagined her old friend had thought that bequest would make life easier for her. He could never have guessed it would bring on problems and complications galore.

"How about you, Helen? What's on tap for your weekend?"

The secretary shrugged. "Not much. I'll take my mom shopping tomorrow, which is always an ordeal, since she finds it so hard to part with a dollar. Then..."

At that moment the telephone at Helen's elbow jangled; she lifted the receiver to her ear. "Manager's office... Yes, sir... No, Mr. Sorenson has gone for the weekend. Yes, sir... Well, I'm very sorry, but perhaps in the meantime you could take a shower.... Yes, sir, right away." Replacing the receiver, Helen shot Audrey a disgusted look. "Some guy in the Durango Suite is pitching a walleyed fit and wants to see the manager this minute! He says the stopper in one of the bathtubs doesn't work.''

Audrey groaned. "Oh, for Pete's sake!"

"You heard me suggest he take a shower. He said he always takes a shower, but when he pays two hundred and fifty bucks a night for a room he expects everything to work, and he's pretty steamed that it doesn't.''

"One of those, huh? Takes all kinds to fill up a world."

"You look so tired. Why don't you scoot out of here? I'll sic the night manager on our disgruntled guest.''

Audrey stuffed her feet into her shoes and stood up. "I'm going to take you up on that. Good night, Helen. Give Maintenance a call before you leave and have a good weekend.''

"You, too, Audrey."

Halfway home Audrey remembered the depleted state of her refrigerator, so, as tired as she was, she suffered through the usual Friday night mob at the supermarket. It was after seven when she finally unlocked her apartment door. Just as she pushed it open, a figure stepped out of the shadows in the hallway, startling her so much she almost dropped the sack of groceries. Wide-eyed with fright, she whirled around and found herself staring into a pair of familiar smoke-colored eyes. "Boyd!"

"Hello, love. Allow me." Relieving her of the groceries, he pushed her inside, kicked the door shut and set the sack on the nearest table. Then in a fluid motion he pulled her into a strong embrace. After giving him a long, thorough kiss that took her breath away, he held her at arm's length, his eyes sweeping her from head to toe. "Let me look at you. I'll swear you've gotten more beautiful."

"Oh, Boyd," she breathed in a shaky voice, "you said Saturday. Why didn't you let me know you were coming?"

"I suddenly decided about three hours ago that I couldn't wait until tomorrow, and I knew the chances of reaching you by phone were slim. So I just got in the car and headed this way." He paused and the smile on his face faded. "It's all right, isn't it? You said the convention would be over. You don't have plans for tonight, do you?"

"No, no." She touched the cut over his eye. It had just about healed. "How are you? You said you were doing fine, but I don't trust you to tell me the truth."

"Honest, I'm fine." He executed a little dance step. "See, almost as good as new. Miss me?"

"Yes," she admitted truthfully. "Very much." At that moment Audrey conveniently decided the break would have to be a gradual thing...very gradual. Going back into his arms, she kissed him tenderly and settled pliantly against him. "I'm so glad you're here."

"I'm glad I'm here, too. For five days I've been a man with a problem. All the time I was sailing down that highway I was making plans. I intend being here for breakfast in the morning." His eyes smoldered. "How does that sound?"

"Do you have to ask?" Audrey pushed all problems to the back of her mind. Their hips locked together, and her memories stirred. The familiar scent of his after-shave filled her nostrils. She laid her cheek against the smooth fabric of his shirt and smiled like a contented child. "You feel so-o-o good."

His hands moved downward to cup her buttocks and pull her up to meet him. "Yes, I definitely have a problem, and I think we'd better go into the bedroom and solve it right away."

Audrey's breath escaped in a part moan, part sigh. "That seems like the only sensible thing to do." Reluctantly she stepped back. "But first, those groceries have to go in the refrigerator."

The task was accomplished quickly. When Boyd closed the refrigerator door after the last of the food had been stored, he turned to her, and she glided back into his arms. "Now, where were we?" he asked.

"On the way to the bedroom, as I recall."

"Lead the way. I'm right behind you."

Boyd had to make a conscious effort to calm himself. If he didn't, what would follow would come close to ravishment. His fingers shook as he unbuttoned his shirt and unzipped his pants. The sound of Audrey's clothes being discarded intensified his desire. He supposed he should go to her and undress her slowly, layer by layer, but neither of them needed foreplay. Five days apart had been all the enticement they needed.

Somehow they both were naked and under the covers. As wonderful as Boyd's lovemaking had been before, Audrey thought it even more so that night. Tender at first, and so beautiful she wanted to cry, it grew strong and urgent, the great, hungry rhythms driving them with mind-boggling passion. The mutual climax was explosive, shattering, indescribable ecstasy. Mutual. That's the wonder of it, she thought as she lay weak and numb in his arms. Her mind drifted somewhere between dreams and reality, and she clung to him with what little strength she had left, dreading the moment when she would have to release her hold on him.

How on earth am I ever going to end it? He's everything I ever dreamed of, longed for. It isn't fair.

"Are you asleep?" Boyd's quiet voice penetrated the sensuous fog.

"No."

"You were so quiet."

She shifted, seeking a more comfortable position. "I was thinking."

"About what?"

"Oh . . . everything and nothing."

Rolling over, he propped on his elbow and looked down at her. "I've hated every damned minute of this week. Audrey, we have to talk."

"Not now."

"Yes, now. Listen, hon, I know you have qualms about this, and I think I understand. It's happened pretty fast. But I don't have any doubts at all, none. I'm awfully old to be falling in love for the first time, but I'm so sure this is right for both of us."

Audrey closed her eyes for a moment, then opened them and gazed at him lovingly. "Maybe that's what bothers me. Most men your age have been in and out of love half a dozen times. How can you trust that what you feel for me is really love? You don't have anything to compare it with."

"I don't know. I just do. There's been a good, sound reason for just about everything I've done in my life, and when you think about it, that's pretty damned dull. Maybe the fact that I fell head over heels in love with you practically at first sight is precisely why I trust this. I didn't think love was ever going to happen to me. Now that it has, I'm impatient.''

Audrey traced the outline of his mouth with the tip of her forefinger. ''And that's a mistake.''

Boyd's head went back to the pillow. He drew her into the circle of his arm, but his mind whirled with a jumble of thoughts. Something was wrong or, at least, not quite right, but he couldn't pinpoint what it was exactly. He was pretty confident that Audrey cared for him as deeply as he cared for her, but for some reason she was reluctant to give in to her feelings completely. He didn't know what was bothering her, but he did know that something pretty complicated was going on in that head of hers.

But he would try to get to the bottom of it later. Right now he was a very contented man. Feeling her stretched out beside him erased the emptiness of the past week and left him sated with happiness. Brushing her temple with his lips, he asked, ''Hungry?''

''Um-hmm. I was too busy to do more than grab a milk shake at lunch. I could eat a horse.'' Sitting up, Audrey hugged the sheet around her breasts. ''However, I'm afraid we'll have to settle for the deli stuff I got at the store.''

Throwing the covers aside, Boyd swung his legs off the bed, stepped into his trousers and slipped on his shirt without bothering with shoes and underwear. ''Sounds fine to me. Now that I think about it, I'm close to starving myself.''

AN HOUR OR SO LATER they had finished dinner and were sitting on the sofa, sipping the last of their wine, when Audrey thought to inquire about the rest of the family. "How are your folks?"

"Fine."

"And Betty? I miss her."

Boyd turned serious. "Betty's not so fine, I'm sorry to say."

"Oh? What's wrong?"

"It seems my sister has gone and gotten involved with one of the ranch hands. You remember Jesse Murdoch, don't you? Somehow word got around to Dad, as it usually does. He's not happy about the relationship, and that's putting it mildly. Things have been a little touchy around the house for the past few days."

Audrey raised her glass to her lips, and her heart skipped a beat. This was exactly what she had hoped.

"I don't know what's going to come of all this. Apparently Betty and Dad had another row last night. She came to my room in tears…first time I've seen her cry since she was a kid. She swears she's going to marry the man, no matter what. Once they're married, goes her theory, what can Dad do?"

"What does your mother think of all this?"

Boyd chuckled. "Whatever Dad does. I'm trying to stay the hell out of it, but I've never seen my sister so determined. She just might marry Jesse, who knows?"

Dismayed, Audrey set her glass on the coffee table and stared across the room for a minute. Betty was just too nice a person; Audrey's conscience finally won the battle. "Don't let her, Boyd."

"What?"

"Betty thinks the world of you and really cares what you think of her. Maybe she'll listen to you. Don't let her marry the man. It would be the worst mistake of her life."

He stared at her, deeply puzzled. "Hon, why would you say that? You don't know a thing about Jesse."

"Yes, I do. I knew him years ago."

"Years ago? You knew him in Texas?"

"Yes. He…used to work for my father. Please take my word for it and don't ask too many questions. Jesse Murdoch is a scoundrel."

"He must have recognized you."

"Oh, he did."

"Yet neither of you gave the slightest inclination you'd known each other before."

"No, which makes me only a bit less of a scoundrel than Jesse. You see, I've known about Betty's involvement with him since my first day at the ranch, and I chose to say nothing. I could tell you I did that because Betty swore me to secrecy, but…that wouldn't be the truth."

Boyd felt his muscles tighten. He noticed the way Audrey's eyes shifted away from him, the firm set to her mouth. Something about this turn of conversation disturbed her. It wasn't much, but it was his first glimpse into her past, and though she'd asked him not to question her, he had to. He set his glass beside hers on the coffee table, then turned and took her hands in his. "Audrey, I wish you would tell me about your life before you came to Phoenix. I've always known there was something you wanted to keep hidden, but I love you, and I think I have the right to know all about you."

Audrey looked down at their entwined hands, studied the crisp dark hairs on the back of his. It was a comforting sight. She thought of walking hand in hand through life with him, and her heart ached. Words wouldn't come.

"Audrey?"

"Yes."

"I wish you would trust me enough to talk to me. Whatever it is can't be that bad."

Confusion assailed her. How little he knew. Once he heard the truth, he'd realize, as she did, that they couldn't have a future together. That was what made it so damned hard to tell him. It would have been nice to make the magic last a little longer.

But that was selfish and dishonest. Boyd deserved to hear the story. Then he would know the inevitable split had nothing to do with her feelings for him, and she at least could prevent Betty from making a disastrous mistake.

However, she wondered if she actually could get it out. Everything had been bottled up for so long, and it wasn't the kind of thing anyone would relish telling.

"I . . . don't know where to start."

"The beginning's always a good place," Boyd said gently.

Audrey settled back against the cushions, tucked her feet under her and began talking. Surprisingly, once she began, she couldn't stop. It all tumbled out, and with the telling came a great loosening within, the releasing of a burden. Her voice was flat and monotonous, and she felt as though she was relating a story she had seen on television or read in a magazine, something that had nothing to do with her.

CHAPTER SIXTEEN

"I WAS BORN with the proverbial silver spoon in my mouth," she began.

"I would have bet on it," Boyd said.

"It was my paternal grandfather who started it all. He owned a company that manufactured aircraft parts, and he made a fortune during World War Two. He died at a relatively young age, and that made my father a very young millionaire. Then, not long after I was born, the company came up with a gadget that could sense the temperature of fuel. They called it FP44, patented it and sold it to the air force and navy to use on their jet airplanes. Since the company was the only source for the device, the income from FP44 was enormous."

"I can imagine," Boyd murmured.

"I led an idyllic life. We had a beautiful home in Dallas, another one on the Gulf Coast and a ranch. It wasn't anything like the Triple B, of course, but it was a working ranch, a basic cow-calf operation. That ranch was my favorite place on earth. I could ride a horse long before I could ride a bicycle."

"I would have bet on that, too. From the beginning I suspected that you had either lived on a ranch or spent a lot of time on one."

Audrey looked at him in mild surprise. "Really?"

"Really. You ride too well, for one thing. And you never asked enough questions. Most real greenhorns are curious as hell when they get on a ranch for the first time. And there was the time you handled the wounded calf without flinching. Just a lot of things made me think ranch life wasn't entirely foreign to you."

She nodded and sighed. "My mother hated the tomboy in me. She worked so hard to turn me into a lady. I was sent to the finest schools. She took me all over Europe and the Far East and taught me all the social graces. I guess I was something of a pampered princess, and I might very well have grown up to be a real snob if it hadn't been for the down-to-earth influence of the ranch. If there are disadvantages to growing up with a lot of money, I didn't know about any of them."

"That kind of life is pretty far removed from being the assistant manager of a hotel," Boyd commented, alive with interest. "Even a hotel as classy as the Greenspoint."

"I know. Sometimes it amazes me that I was able to make the transition at all. It wasn't easy at first."

"What happened, hon?"

Audrey struggled with her memories. "It was about five years ago when everything started coming apart. One day, out of the blue, some FBI agents showed up in Dad's office with a search warrant. Someone had called over the Fraud, Waste and Abuse Hotline. Dad was accused of fraud on the FP44 contract. The informant claimed he was keeping two sets of books and charging the government far more than the actual cost of manufacturing the gadget. Naturally, Dad pleaded innocent. He acted downright indignant, in fact, but after an investigation that went on for months, the federal attorney took the case to the grand jury and got an indictment. The trial lasted two months and was a nightmare for Mom and me.''

She faltered at this point, and it was on the tip of Boyd's tongue to tell her to forget it since the revelation obviously was so painful for her. He couldn't, though; he was too fascinated.

Taking a deep breath, Audrey continued. ''The defense based its case on Dad's reputation and character, on his wealth and 'good works.' Why, our attorney kept asking the court, would a man of Jack Hamilton's stature steal from the government and jeopardize a contract that brought his company millions of dollars a year? There simply was no motive. Dad could have conducted business like a straight-arrow saint and made more money than he ever could spend.''

''I was thinking the same thing,'' Boyd said.

''So did everyone else at first. Public sentiment ran strongly in Dad's favor for a long time. Then the federal attorney dropped his bombshell. The government's investigation revealed that years before, unknown to anyone, especially Mom and me, Dad's business had been on the verge of bankruptcy due to some bad debts and unfulfilled contracts. He had gotten overextended at the bank, and he had poured money into the ranch. In turn, it made almost nothing. Meanwhile, Mom and I were living like the millionaires we thought we were. I can't even imagine how much money it must have taken to keep up that lifestyle.''

Audrey paused and frowned. "I also can't imagine why Dad didn't tell us. Maybe he thought his financial troubles would diminish him in our eyes, but he should have told us. We could have tightened our belts and maybe none of it ever would have happened. It was all so useless."

Her voice trailed off. Boyd patted her hand in a sympathetic gesture; she collected herself and went on. "Anyway, Dad miraculously had come up with a great deal of money to plow back into the business until it was financially solvent again. This was just about the time the alleged fraud began taking place. The evidence against him just mounted and mounted. In the meantime, a government audit of the company had been going on, and its figures indicated that Dad had been defrauding the government out of approximately a million dollars a year for ten years."

Boyd expelled a ragged breath. "Ten million?"

"Yes, ten million. Then the prosecution produced a surprise witness, Dad's comptroller. As it turned out, he had been in on the scheme. He was terrified of going to jail, and he confessed everything, even turned over the second set of books in return for immunity from prosecution. That pretty well iced the cake. The fraud had been so skillful, so clever, it might never have been discovered if it hadn't been for the informant. The verdict, of course, was guilty."

Boyd was silent and tense. So Skeet's information had been correct. He'd always harbored the suspicion it would be. He couldn't take his eyes off Audrey. In one way he was sorry he had asked about her past. None of this was any of his business, nor did it have any bearing on the future and what they'd found together.

However, he had asked, and now that she'd begun talking, it was as though a dam had burst to let the river flow through. Boyd didn't dare speak for fear the river would dry up. Apparently Audrey needed to talk about it.

"The whole thing was awful, and it killed my mother," she said stoically. "She had been an absolute rock throughout the trial. No one had been more confident of acquittal than she, but when the comptroller confessed, she broke down. Mom had had high blood pressure for years. She had a stroke the night the guilty verdict came in and died a few days later." Her voice turned wistful. "She was the gentlest person I've ever known, a lady down to her fingertips. I don't think she ever did an ungracious thing in her life. Your mother reminds me of her."

If Boyd remembered right, Skeet had told him that Jack Hamilton never made it to prison. He'd never felt so much for anyone as he felt for Audrey at that moment, but he seemed to be held in the grip of a morbid fascination. He had to know everything, whether he had the right to or not. "Your father, hon…did he go to prison?"

Audrey wiped at her eyes, but when she removed her hands her eyes still were dry. "He was sentenced, but he never got there. He had some sleeping pills the doctor had given him while the investigation was going on. He…took a handful of them and died of heart failure."

Boyd was astonished that she could talk about it at all, much less talk about it in that unemotional monotone. "Audrey, what about you? What was happening to you all this time?"

"You can imagine the notoriety," she said dully. "Back in Texas my father was almost as well-known as yours is here. The press hounded us for months. My mother's funeral was turned into a circus. The day Dad killed himself, a couple of reporters tried to force their way into the house. The servants and I were literally prisoners. The cook couldn't go to the grocery store, and I couldn't go to work. My boss was wonderful about it at first, but finally, out of fairness to him, I quit...over the phone. I didn't even go back to clean out my desk. One of the women in the office mailed my personal things to me."

"No wonder you reacted the way you did when I mentioned the media."

Audrey nodded. "We finally had to have police protection, and one of the policemen did our shopping for us. On top of everything, none of our life-long 'friends' came around."

"But why?" Boyd exclaimed. "You hadn't done anything."

She turned to him with the saddest pair of eyes he had ever seen. "Boyd, I'm glad you've never been in a position to learn how people can behave when the chips are down. You'd be surprised how many of them honestly believe that the apple doesn't fall far from the tree."

He shook his head slowly. He couldn't even imagine the enormity of all she'd been through. He doubted he would have survived it as well as she had. Now he could add tremendous admiration to his love for her. "So you left Dallas then?"

"No, not right away. The furor eventually died down, and I began hoping I could return to some sort of normal existence. But there was another shock in store—the small matter of income tax evasion. Dad had made roughly ten million dollars more than he'd reported. His estate owed...oh, I can't remember, some enormous sum, far more than was available, since the legal fees were astronomical. Part of the sentence had been to prohibit the company from ever doing business with the government again, so that put it under. The ranch was confiscated, then the houses, just about everything I thought was mine."

"By that time I was numb. I began having terrible headaches and stomach upsets. My whole system just went out of kilter. What was worse was my mental state. I began to despise the father I'd always loved so much. Our family doctor feared I was on the verge of a nervous breakdown, and he urged me to go away and start over again somewhere else. But I didn't have the slightest idea how to go about doing that. I was twenty-three and had never had to hang up my own clothes or boil water. Suddenly I had no one, and very little money, just a small savings account Dad had opened for me when I was in school. To this day I don't know what I would have done if my friend's phone call hadn't come when it did."

"The friend in Phoenix?"

She nodded. "I guess she was too far removed from the scene to feel 'tainted' by our friendship. She asked me to stay with her until I could get my head on straight. It was a godsend. After a few months in Phoenix my health returned, I took the temporary job at the hotel, and the rest you know." She sighed.

emotionally drained. "For someone who'd never given a dollar a thought, I did pretty well. I learned to take care of myself, to pinch pennies and make do or do without. I discovered there's a great deal of personal satisfaction in becoming self-sufficient. My life was wonderfully uneventful until the day you showed up with that incredible news about Bert's will."

Boyd felt almost as drained by the account as she was. He put his arms around her and hugged her tenderly, momentarily too overcome to speak. Then he remembered what had gotten this conversation started in the first place. "Audrey, what did Jesse Murdoch have to do with all this?"

"He was the FBI informant."

"Jesse?"

"Yes, Jesse," she said bitterly. "He worked on our ranch, as I told you. It seems Dad and his comptroller held their secret planning sessions there, in a small office located at one end of the bunkhouse. That was where the second set of books was kept. That was how cleverly they covered their bases. If anything happened, there was no evidence in Dad's offices or in any of our houses, and who would think to look in the bunkhouse? Anyway, Jesse accidentally overheard part of a conversation between Dad and the comptroller, just enough to arouse his curiosity. Being the kind of man he is, he nosed around until he found those books. They didn't mean much to him, but he suspected something shady was going on. From that time on he merely kept his eyes and ears open. He'd known about the double-dealing for a long time before he went to the law."

"What made him finally decide to do it?" Boyd asked.

Audrey averted her eyes for a moment. This was going to be the hardest part of the whole ordeal, telling Boyd she'd once had the bad sense to think she was in love with Jesse. It was like owning up to some terrible weakness of character, and Boyd's opinion of her had become the most important thing in the world.

Still she had come this far; she really had no choice but to go on. Somehow she managed to tell him everything she knew about Jesse, concluding with, "He turned my father in out of spite, nothing else. Dad fired him at my request, and Jesse's parting shot was a visit to the authorities. I'm not saying Dad shouldn't have been punished, but Jesse's motives were something less than admirable."

It came as something of a shock to Boyd to hear Audrey say she once had been in love with the man his sister wanted to marry. The shock passed quickly, however. That had all happened so long ago, and it was to Audrey's credit that she had sent him packing the moment she'd learned his true colors.

"You can't let Betty marry him, Boyd, you just can't!" Audrey exclaimed fervently. "Please call her and tell her not to do anything foolish."

Boyd agreed that Betty would be making a terrible mistake if she married Jesse, but how was he going to prevent it? He certainly wasn't going to be the one to repeat Audrey's story; that would be betraying a confidence. But without that story, his pleas to his sister would fall on deaf ears. Betty would simply think he was acting on their father's behalf.

Getting to his feet, he shoved his hands into his pockets and walked to the terrace door, deep in thought. Suddenly he turned to Audrey. "I'm not sure she'll listen to me, Audrey. She's got her heart and mind set on marrying the man. But I'll bet she'd believe you if you told her everything you've just told me."

Twisting around, Audrey fastened pleading eyes on him. "Do you have any idea how difficult that would be for me? Can you imagine what your father would think?"

Boyd returned to sit beside her. "Tell Betty in confidence. No one else has to know about this."

Audrey rubbed her temples and thought carefully before speaking. "The story might help Betty, but it won't do a thing for us."

"What are you talking about?"

"Boyd, listen to me. I know you want to believe that you and I have a future together, but now that you know the whole story, I'm sure you realize it's impossible."

Boyd sat back and eyed her quizzically. "No, I don't realize that at all! What are you saying, Audrey? Surely you don't think I feel any less for you because of something your father did. No one else has to know a thing about any of this...no one but Betty, of course, and she'd never tell anyone."

"You're not thinking straight, my love. What about all your father's plans for you? People in the public eye can't afford family skeletons. It would all come out, believe me. I'd be nothing but an embarrassment to you when you run for governor."

He looked at her as though she was speaking a foreign language. "When I do what?"

"Your father and I had a long private talk the day I left the ranch."

"Oh? This is news to me. Suppose you tell me what the talk was about."

"You, mostly. You and your future. You see, he was beginning to suspect there was something going on between us. After that scene he stumbled onto in your room the night of your accident, I'd think it strange if he didn't suspect it. He wanted me to know what I was getting into."

Boyd's eyes narrowed. So this was the complicated something going on in Audrey's head. What the devil had his old man said to her? It galled him no end that his dad had talked to Audrey. Buck B. Benedict was not yet in charge of the world, in spite of what the man himself thought. He doubted that the private talk had been pleasant for Audrey. Talks with his father seldom were.

"This is very interesting. Suppose you tell me what you'd be 'getting into,' other than the love affair of the century."

"Please, be serious. Your father told me about his plans for you—first a high-visibility state office, then governor, maybe the U.S. Senate…and eventually the presidency."

Boyd almost choked. "Presidency!" he roared. "Are you talking about…the White House, Washington, D.C.?"

Audrey nodded solemnly. "In 2004, I think he said. Boyd, a woman with my background cannot be First Lady of the land!"

He stared at her for a split second, disbelieving. Then when he saw that she was completely serious, that she was indeed relating something his father had actually said, he fell into a fit of convulsive laughter. Audrey had never seen Boyd really amused, and the sight was something to behold. The laughter began deep in his chest, rumbled up and spilled out. He fell back against the sofa's cushions and laughed so hard his entire body shook. Twice he tried to collect himself, only to begin laughing again. Audrey thought it would never end.

Finally he was able to compose himself enough to speak. "God a'mighty, I've got to hand it to Dad. When he dreams he doesn't waste time on the penny-ante stuff. The presidency yet!" Then something occurred to him. "Audrey, was Dad the reason for your hasty departure last Sunday?"

"Yes. He was very nice, but once he told me about his political plans for you, I knew I was going to have to put an end to... us. I thought it would die a natural death, since we'd be apart so much. Then you showed up tonight, and it was as though we'd never been separated." Her shoulders rose and fell in a forlorn gesture.

Boyd took one of her hands, kissed its palm and held it against his cheek. "Listen to me, hon, and believe what I say. I am not, repeat not, going to be governor of Arizona, much less President of the United States."

"I'm sure you mean that now, but I've seen the way your family operates. Your father calls the shots. If he wants you to be the governor... You once told me you do what he wants you to do."

"But that's because he's never asked me to do anything I didn't want to do. I do not want to run for public office, period. It's not my thing. Now, can you imagine a President who didn't want to be President?" He then gave her a smile that melted her insides. "Besides, even if I wanted it, I'd want you more."

For the first time during that highly emotional evening, Audrey felt tears welling. "Oh, Boyd...you say the nicest things."

"No more talk about putting an end to us, hear? We've just begun, Audrey, and it's going to be the stuff syrupy novels are made of."

"It...doesn't seem possible. I've been alone so long."

"But no more. Now you have me to bounce off of." He gave her a quick kiss, then looked at his watch. "It's still early. Call Betty."

Audrey grimaced. "I really hate to, you know. She's liable to tell me to mind my own business."

"I know, and if she does...well, then we'll decide our next move. But I'm afraid you'll never forgive yourself if you don't warn her."

"You're right, of course, but I'm not going to tell her anything I don't think I absolutely have to. Okay?"

"Sure." Boyd dialed the number and got his sister on the phone. He didn't waste time with small talk. He merely asked Betty to hold on, then handed the receiver to Audrey. "She sounds like she's been crying," he whispered.

"Betty?" Audrey asked anxiously.

"Hi, Audrey," Betty said dispiritedly.

"You sound awful."

"I've just had a big fight with Dad. That can ruin anyone's day."

"Betty, I hope I'm not being presumptuous, but . . . Boyd tells me you and Jesse are talking about getting married right away."

"Yeah." Betty made a sound of contempt. "Dad doesn't approve, of course. Now he's threatening to fire Jesse if I don't put this 'nonsense' out of my head. I tell you I've had it, Audrey! I'm plain fed up. Dad can disown me for all I care. I'm going to marry Jesse and that's that!"

Audrey took a deep breath and tried to interrupt, but Betty started raving. "Granddad left me a small trust fund, and Jesse has some money saved. Between the two of us we can afford a small parcel of land. I don't mind starting on a shoestring. Money doesn't mean all that much to me, and I don't give a flip for the prestige that goes with being a Benedict. As a matter of fact, it might be nice to be Betty Nobody for a change. All I want is to marry Jesse."

"Oh, Betty, I wish you would give that some thought. I think . . . no, I know you'll be making a dreadful mistake if you go against your father's wishes."

"Audrey, please, not you, too. I'm up to here with my father's wishes!"

"But I have something I need to tell you. You see, I . . ."

At that moment, however, something went pop inside Audrey's head. "Have you told Jesse this?"

"About defying Dad, you mean? No, I haven't. Unfortunately, Jesse seems to think he'll be welcomed into the fold with open arms. I just haven't had the heart to tell him it isn't so.''

"I see." Audrey's mind whirled. "You know something, I think you should tell Jesse exactly what you just told me—the business about starting out on a shoestring and all. He might like knowing how you feel about money and being a Benedict. I think you should tell him everything.''

"Really? Why?''

"I'll...ah, explain later. Will you do that? Right away?''

"Well...I don't understand, but...I guess so, if you think it's a good idea.''

"Boyd and I will be there tomorrow.''

"Hey, that's great!''

"Promise you won't do anything rash until we get there.''

"Okay, Audrey. It's going to be good having you around again. I know you'll be on my side, and I damned sure could use a friendly face. Mom and Sara are no help at all.''

That remark made Audrey cringe. For a moment she felt a little on the devious side herself, then quickly remembered she was doing it only for Betty's own good. "I'll see you tomorrow. Don't do anything until you talk to me." Hanging up, she turned to a puzzled Boyd.

"What was all that about?" he asked. "You didn't tell her a thing.''

"I know, but maybe, just maybe... It would be so much better for Betty to find out for herself what a self-serving louse Jesse is.''

"I don't understand.''

"I know that, too. Let's just wait and see, okay? Betty's promised not to do a thing until we get there."

He shrugged and reached for her, drawing her into his arms. "I suspect that this is some sort of womanly reasoning that a dense male isn't even supposed to understand." He felt Audrey melt against him. "Tired?" he asked solicitously.

"Exhausted."

"Want to go to bed?"

"Um-hmm!"

Releasing her, Boyd bent and swept her off her feet. Audrey relaxed in the cradle of his arms as he carried her to bed. She had gotten a lot off her mind tonight, and the disburdening effect was wonderful, but in reality nothing concrete had been settled. There still was the problem of her past versus Buck B. Benedict. It wasn't realistic to hope Boyd's father would never hear about Jack Hamilton. Tomorrow when they got to the ranch, if Betty remained determined to marry Jesse, Audrey was going to have to tell her about the man, and there was no question in her mind what Jesse's next move would be. He would tell everyone within earshot about her father. As she well knew, Jesse was a man who liked getting his revenge.

But worrying about that could wait for tomorrow. She was so tired she was only dimly aware of Boyd setting her on her feet, slipping the robe off her shoulders and guiding her between the smooth sheets. Enough was enough for one day.

CHAPTER SEVENTEEN

THE FOLLOWING MORNING Boyd woke to an unfamiliar but decidedly pleasant sensation—the feel of Audrey's smooth, lithe body dovetailed into his. For long minutes he lay as still as a stone, not wanting to move for fear of disturbing her. She still slept soundly. Last night she had fallen asleep the minute her head hit the pillow, and she had hardly moved since. He knew that because his own sleep had been so fitful. Though he wouldn't have admitted it to Audrey, he was more than a little worried about what today held in store for them. If she was forced to reveal her past in order to save Betty from a disastrous mistake, things might get unpleasant. There was no need to wonder what Buck's reaction to the story would be.

Not that I give a damn, Boyd thought. But he knew Audrey would, and at the moment she was his only concern. No more pain and unhappiness for her. He wouldn't have believed it possible to love someone as much as he loved her. At last he had found a special woman who was more important than family or work, and nobody was going to come between them, least of all Buck Benedict.

But Boyd wasn't stupid. Saying he would openly defy his father if necessary and actually doing it were two entirely different things. Habits of a lifetime weren't easily broken. Plus, there was Audrey and her feelings to consider. He wouldn't dream of forcing her into a situation where she would feel unwanted and uncomfortable.

Well, wasn't he supposed to be the diplomat in the family? This might test his capabilities to the limit. Lying there, Boyd decided it was time to have a long talk with his father. He probably should have done it before now. Buck was going to have to understand what Audrey meant to him, and while he was at it, he would forever lay to rest the absurd political ambitions his father had for him. All he wanted out of life was to continue doing what he was doing, only now with Audrey by his side.

She stirred beside him just then, and everything else was forgotten. He buried his face in her hair, sniffing its clean scent. "Good morning," he said.

"Good morning," she murmured drowsily. "Mmm, this is nice."

"This is the first time we've spent the night together. I could get used to it. Want to make it a habit?"

"Mmm."

"May I assume that means yes?"

"Mmm." Audrey was waking by slow degrees. She stretched luxuriously, slithering her body along the length of his in an unconsciously erotic maneuver. Boyd's responses stirred immediately. Tightening his hold on her, he showered light kisses across her shoulders and back. She shivered and uttered a little giggle. "Do you always sleep so soundly?" he asked.

"Just about. It comes from hard work, a clear conscience and all that."

Rolling her over, Boyd threw a leg across her stomach, effectively imprisoning her. "I've been awake off and on for hours. A time or two the urge to rouse you was strong. I was amazed at my own willpower, but you just looked too peaceful to be disturbed."

"Admirable of you."

"Are you good and awake now?"

"Um-hmm."

"Want to play house?"

"You're a sex maniac!"

"Nice, huh?"

Her arms slid up his chest and wound around his neck. "I really do have a lot to do before we get on the road."

He moved over her. "So let's make love and get the day off to a great start."

THOUGH AUDREY OFFERED to follow him to the ranch in her own car, Boyd refused, explaining that it would give him a good excuse to return to Phoenix with her for another night. Several hours later they were heading south out of Tucson toward the valley. It was a beautiful day. The sun was shining, the temperature was in the high sixties, and Audrey was sure she'd never seen Boyd in better spirits. It occurred to her that his sunny good mood might very well change before the day was over, but she quickly pushed the thought aside. She wasn't going to borrow trouble, and she was confident she and Boyd together could handle anything that came along.

So, in spite of a vague uneasiness, she was feeling pretty good herself. Loving and being loved in return did wonders for one's disposition, she was discovering. And as they neared the ranch, she was overcome by a sense of coming home again. Three weeks ago she had barely been aware of the valley's existence; now she was thinking how nice it would be to grow old here.

When they pulled up and stopped in front of the house, the dogs barked, as usual, and Jorge greeted them, also as usual. But inside the house things were strangely quiet. "I can't believe no one's watching a ball game on Saturday afternoon," Boyd said with a frown.

They wandered in and out of rooms, looking for someone, anyone, but they couldn't find a soul. Finally Maria appeared and explained that Buck, Elizabeth, Brent and Sara had decided to spend the weekend in Flagstaff. Audrey breathed a sigh of relief over that news. Whatever happened, at least Boyd's father wouldn't be in the center of it, not yet.

"Where's Betty?" Boyd asked the housekeeper.

Maria shrugged. "*No se.* I haven't seen her in…oh, in hours, not since breakfast."

"She wasn't here for lunch?"

"No. I'm sure she hasn't been back here since very early this morning."

Audrey shot an anxious glance in Boyd's direction. What if her little scheme had backfired? "Isn't that strange for Saturday?" she asked.

"Not really," he replied. "Any number of things could have come up. Maybe she just went into Agua Linda or to Tucson for shopping."

"But she knew we were coming."

Boyd turned back to Maria. "Has anything . . . er, unusual happened around here since I left yesterday?"

Maria fastened a blank stare on him. In the way of longtime servants, the woman was aware of just about everything that transpired in the household, yet she pretended to be aware of nothing. When the situation demanded, she also could conveniently forget English, which she spoke and understood as well as Boyd did. *"No comprendo, señor,"* she responded with a childlike innocence.

Boyd smiled. "All right, Maria. If you see Betty, tell her we're looking for her."

"Sí," Maria nodded and scurried away.

"*'No comprendo,'"* Boyd explained to Audrey, "means 'I know but I'm not telling.' I'm betting there's been another blowup between Betty and Dad. She's either off somewhere licking her wounds or getting revenge. Let's just hope only hurt feelings are involved here. Maybe we should check her room."

Betty's room looked in order. At least there were no signs that she'd packed anything, which was mildly reassuring. "We're probably making a big deal out of nothing," Boyd said with a noticeable lack of conviction. "She'll show up before long. I'm going to get a beer. Want one?"

"No, thanks."

They went into the sun room. Boyd took a can of beer out of the refrigerator behind the bar and turned the television set on to a football game, while Audrey picked up a magazine and idly thumbed through it. An hour passed. Neither the game nor the magazine held much interest. Both of them glanced at their watches too often. Finally, Boyd got up, switched off the set and reached for his jacket. Audrey closed the magazine and stood up, too. "Where are you going?"

"Oh, no place in particular. I thought I'd wander around, check the horses or something. That was a lousy game."

She grabbed her own jacket. "I'll go with you."

THE FIRST THING Audrey noticed when they entered the barn was that the stall for Betty's horse was empty. That wasn't much cause for alarm, however. As Boyd had said, any number of things could have taken Betty away from the house.

"Let's see if we can find Jesse," he suggested when they left the barn.

Audrey nodded in agreement and stayed hard on his heels as he made his way to the bunkhouse.

They found Skeet Drummond sitting on his bunk, puffing on a cigarette and playing solitaire. The elderly cowboy was the only person around.

"Hi, Skeet," Boyd greeted.

"Howdy, Boyd." Then, seeing Audrey, Skeet scrambled to his feet. "Howdy, ma'am."

"Hello, Skeet. It's good to see you again. Please, don't get up."

But it wasn't in Skeet's nature to sit while a lady stood. "What can I do for you folks?"

"Seen Murdoch?" Boyd asked.

"Murdoch?" The old man squinted. "Jesse left."

"Left?"

"Yep. Drew his pay, collected his gear and jus' hightailed it outta here. Said it was time for him to be movin' on. Right after breakfast, it was."

Boyd glanced at Audrey, who was thinking exactly what he was. Betty hadn't been seen since breakfast either. Anxiety tinged his voice as he turned back to Skeet. "Didn't happen to say where he was going, did he?"

"Nope, and nobody asked. He probably don't know where he's goin' hisself. Hell, Boyd—s'cuse me, ma'am—you know how the drifters are. Ain't one of 'em that don't have a bad case of itchy feet."

"Murdoch's been with us for some time now. He's no drifter," Boyd said.

Skeet cackled. "The hell he ain't...s'cuse me, ma'am. He's a cowpoke, ain't he?"

"Yeah, guess you're right. Tell me, Skeet, did he leave alone?"

"Reckon he did. At least, there wasn't nobody else around while he was packin'. Can't rightly say I actually *saw* him leave, though."

"Thanks, Skeet."

"Don't mention it. Nothing's wrong, is there?"

"I hope not."

Boyd took Audrey by the arm, and they left the bunkhouse. Outside they stopped and looked at each other worriedly. "Oh, Boyd, do you think they've gone off together?"

"The two of them on one horse?"

She shrugged and bit her bottom lip. "It's just such a coincidence, both of them disappearing right after breakfast."

"Yeah, I know."

"If she's gone off with that despicable man, I'll never forgive myself."

"None of this is your fault, Audrey."

"Yes, it is! I should have warned her about Jesse last night. I should have warned her about him when I first learned about their relationship, but I . . . I just kept telling myself it was none of my business. Actually, what I was doing was protecting *me*, and that's not right."

"No sense worrying about that now, hon. You do thrive on guilt, don't you? Come on, I've got some more checking to do."

First, Boyd ascertained that only one of the ranch's cars was missing—the Cadillac. His family wouldn't have driven all the way to Flagstaff for the weekend, so the Cadillac no doubt was parked at the airport in Tucson. Further investigation revealed that all of the horse trailers were on the premises. "Betty's definitely on horseback, and that means she can't have gone far," he told Audrey, clearly relieved.

Suddenly she turned to him with a start. "Betty's makeup," she exclaimed.

"What?"

"Her makeup was on her dresser. She doesn't use a lot of it, but she does use some, and it was sitting on her dresser. Women don't go off without their makeup, they just don't." The thought made her feel a little better.

Boyd pondered that a second, then said, "I have an idea. Let's take us a little ride around the ranch and see if we run into anything."

"What are you thinking?"

"Oh, I don't know. Maybe a rendezvous somewhere, like Summerfield camp. Go get in the pickup. I'll tell Maria we're leaving for a little while. I'll also tell her to keep Betty here if she shows up."

THEIR HOPES that Betty and Jesse might be at Summerfield camp were quickly dashed. The camp was deserted, and there were no signs that anyone had been near it since roundup. "There's only one other place on the ranch I can think of that she might be," Boyd speculated.

"Where's that?"

"My house. If she isn't there, and if she isn't at home, then we'll have to accept the fact that she's gone off somewhere. And there's a strong possibility she's with Jesse."

Audrey's heart sank. She felt so responsible for all this, and it was anything but a good feeling. "She promised me she wouldn't do anything until I got here."

"Yeah, but she's nutty about the guy. I'm afraid he could talk her into just about anything."

But as soon as the adobe house came into view a wave of relief swept through both of them. Betty's horse was tethered outside. "Thank heavens!" Audrey breathed.

That was encouraging, but when they parked the truck and got out, she hesitated. "Boyd, at least we know she hasn't left the ranch, but we don't know if Jesse's in there with her. Maybe we shouldn't barge in."

"Sorry, hon, but I've got to know what's going on."

Betty was alone. They found her in the bedroom sitting on the single bed, and she obviously had been crying. She was startled and none too pleased to see them. "What are you doing here?" she snapped at Boyd.

"Looking for you," he snapped back. "We were worried about you."

"Well, as you can see, I'm here and I'm fine."

"You don't look fine to me."

"Stop worrying and go back to the house. Obviously I want to be alone or I wouldn't be here."

Boyd ignored her. "How long have you been here?"

"Almost all day."

"Had anything to eat?"

Betty shook her head. "Not since breakfast, but I'm not hungry."

"You got to eat something."

"Leave me alone!"

Audrey stepped forward. "Boyd, why don't you go make us some coffee?"

He hesitated, looking first at one woman, then the other. Finally he shrugged. "Okay. Coffee it is."

When he'd left the room, Audrey closed the door and faced Betty. "Want to talk about it?"

"Not particularly."

"Maybe you should. Sometimes it helps."

Betty's mouth twisted wryly, and her chin trembled. "I followed your advice, Audrey. Last night I finally told Jesse how Dad felt about our relationship. I also told him I was willing to give up everything to marry him."

"And?" Audrey prodded, though she was sure she knew what had happened.

"I thought he'd be happy, but he acted so strangely. He kept saying there had to be a better solution. Naturally I supposed he just hated to see me on the outs with my father. I kept telling him I knew what I was doing." Betty laughed a dry, hollow laugh. "I guess it finally got through to him that I was dead serious. He said he'd see me in the morning and we'd talk about it. But this morning when I went to the bunkhouse after breakfast, I discovered he'd...gone. Just packed up and went away without a word.''

"Oh, Betty..." Audrey went to sit beside her and put an arm around her shoulders. She'd never seen a sadder face, and her heart went out to the woman. "I'm so sorry...not that he left, since that's the best thing that could have happened to you. But I am sorry that you have to go through this."

"Can you beat it, Audrey? He just left. I'm having such a hard time believing any of it."

"I know, I know."

"He didn't want *me* at all. He wanted everything that came with me. How could I have been taken in by that kind of man? I thought I was a whole lot smarter than that."

"Lord, Betty, you're taking me back farther than I want to go."

Betty looked at her with a puzzled frown. "What?"

Audrey smiled ruefully. "What I'm saying is, I'll bet there aren't three dozen women in the world who don't have a Jesse somewhere in their past. Unfortunately, it seems to be carved in stone that we have to go through a Jesse as part of the education process."

Betty was struggling with her emotions. "It's just so...embarrassing."

"I know." *Someday,* Audrey thought, *I might tell her the whole story. Someday, but not now.*

"How do I explain?"

"You don't. Only a handful of people even know about you and Jesse, and no one's going to be thoughtless enough to ask any questions. I know it's hard, but try to be grateful that you found out about him before you married him. Somehow I don't think that a man with avarice in his soul would make a very good husband."

"Yeah." Betty sighed wearily. "This morning, once I realized he'd actually gone, I thought...I thought my heart was breaking. Now I think I'm just mad."

"That's a good sign."

"Trouble is, I don't know who I'm madder at...Jesse for being such a louse or me for being so stupid."

Audrey was reliving the whole thing all over again. "I know exactly how you feel."

Betty looked at her, feeling a rare kind of communion passing between them. "You really do understand, don't you? Was there a Jesse in your past, Audrey?"

"Oh, yes. You'll get over it, I promise. That's straight from the horse's mouth."

Betty lapsed into thought for a minute. Then heaving another sigh, she got to her feet. "I guess I'll go back to the house before it gets dark."

"Boyd always keeps food on hand. Don't you want something to eat?"

"Not really. I'll leave you and Boyd alone. I'm afraid I'm not very good company right now. I'll go home and find something to do. Enough of this sitting around feeling sorry for myself."

Audrey stood and hugged Betty impulsively. "Tomorrow will be better, take my word for it."

"Anything will be better than today. Thank God Dad won't be around tonight. I really don't think I could take him.'' Betty managed a small smile. ''You know something, Audrey. I'll bet anything I'm not the first woman Jesse's pulled this stunt on.''

It was with a great deal of effort that Audrey kept a straight face. ''You know something, I'll bet you're right.''

''I feel sorry for his next victim. He's bound to succeed one of these days.''

''Let's hope not.''

''Thanks for being such a good friend.''

''You're welcome.''

''I'll see you guys back at the house.''

Audrey walked with her to the door and stood on the porch watching her ride off. Then she went into the kitchen looking for Boyd. He wasn't there, but the back door was open, so she went outside. He was sitting on the porch steps, staring off into the distance. When she heard the door open, he turned and eyed her quizzically.

''Betty went home,'' she told him. ''I thought you were going to make coffee.''

''I didn't figure you really wanted coffee. That was just an excuse to get me out of the room so you two could indulge in women talk.''

Smiling, she sat down beside him. ''How perceptive you are.''

''How's Betty?''

''Older and wiser.''

''And Jesse's really gone?''

''Right. Long gone.'' Audrey laid her head on his shoulder and slipped her arm through his. ''Good ol' Jesse. It's hard to believe anyone could be such a thorough bastard. I think he's the only person I've ever known who doesn't have one redeeming quality. You just wonder what goes on in that head of his, how he can look at himself in the mirror.''

"Is Betty taking it hard?"

"Yes, but she'll survive. We always seem to. She's beginning to get mad, so the healing process has already begun."

They sat together in companionable silence for a few minutes until Boyd said, "I'm thinking that any minute you're going to tell me what the hell's going on."

"That's right. You don't know, do you? Last night on the phone Betty was in a real snit. She said she didn't care if your father disowned her. She was going to run off with Jesse, and they were going to start out on a shoestring. I could imagine how Jesse would love hearing that, so I told her she ought to tell him exactly how she felt. She did."

"You figured he would split, right?"

"Of course. Leopards don't change their spots...or is it zebras their stripes? I feel sorry for Betty, but in time she'll come to see this as the best thing that could have happened to her."

"And it's not too bad for you, for us, either."

She pulled away slightly and looked at him. "For us? How's that?"

"There's no need for anyone else to ever know about your father. Not my family, not anyone but you and me."

Audrey pursed her lips, thinking, hoping, doubting. "I don't know, Boyd. Is that honest?"

"It really isn't anyone else's business. It belongs in the past. Who needs to know?"

"But things have a way of getting out. What if someone from that past shows up one day, the way Jesse did? I could be an embarrassment for you and your family."

A smile of pure adoration crossed Boyd's face. "Audrey, I'm sure that you'll never be an embarrassment for me. And before long everyone in the family is going to love you so much they'll feel the same way I do."

Her head went back to his shoulder. "Oh, Boyd, maybe it's because things went so badly for me for so long, but…I'm almost afraid to believe everything has worked out this well."

"Believe it, and enjoy it."

Her gaze strayed across the grounds to the family cemetery in the distance. "Wouldn't Bert be astonished to see what's happened to us because of that last-minute whim of his?"

"Yeah, probably. Astonished and pleased."

"It so easily might not have happened. What if I hadn't stopped to talk to him that first day? He often said it was our little chats that brought him back again and again. If I hadn't taken the time to speak to him, he might never have come back to the hotel. You and I might never have met."

"Audrey, I know deep down inside that wherever you were, whatever you'd been doing, you and I would somehow have met each other."

"You believe in fate!" she cried.

"I guess I do. What else could have kept me single so long? I had to be free for you."

"That's such a nice thought. It appeals to me."

"Love me?"

"Of course I do. Common sense tells me it really isn't reasonable for me to know that so soon, but I do."

"Are you going to marry me?"

"Probably."

"Only probably?"

Her eyes sparkled merrily. "Oh, I'm sure I'll marry you eventually, but I think you owe me something first."

"Hon, what in the devil are you talking about?"

"A courtship," she explained patiently. "Boyd, we've only known each other a few weeks. Admittedly, we've spent a lot of time together during those weeks, but nothing about this relationship has been exactly orthodox. We've never even had a bona fide date. A woman likes to be pursued a little. Now it seems that all you did was smile at me a couple of times, and I was in your arms."

"It didn't seem that easy to me."

"I'd like to see you have to work at it, have to rearrange your schedule in order to be in Phoenix, become frustrated with longing, that sort of thing."

"This is a fey side of you I haven't seen before." He grinned that irresistible grin. "You want to be wooed, huh?"

"Yes, is that so unusual?"

Boyd pretended to think about it seriously. "I hope you realize that a courtship won't tell you much about what kind of husband I'll be."

Audrey snuggled against him, so happy she thought she would explode. "Oh, I know what kind of husband you're going to be—thoughtful, considerate, devoted, loyal."

"You make me sound like a Boy Scout." His arm went around her, and he drew her closer. "All right, one courtship coming up. Trouble is, I'm not sure how one goes about conducting such a ritual. Any suggestions? What do I do?"

Raising her face, she kissed him soundly. "Surprise me."

CHAPTER EIGHTEEN

HE DID. In fact, he overwhelmed her. Boyd Benedict's courtship of Audrey Hamilton would remain the chief topic of gossip among the Greenspoint's staff for some time to come. It began in earnest on Monday morning when Audrey returned to work. She had left Boyd sleeping soundly at her apartment, yet she had been in her office less than half an hour when Marie Collier, the hotel's florist, showed up with a lavish bouquet of pink carnations. Naturally, they were from Boyd.

What a sweet gesture, Audrey thought, reaching for the phone to dial her number and thank him. There was no answer, which meant he was on his way back to the Triple B. She had to wait for his phone call that night. "The flowers are just lovely, Boyd. I wish you could see them. I can't even remember the last time someone sent me flowers."

She thought she heard him chuckle. "Audrey, you haven't seen anything yet."

The next morning she discovered what he meant. Another bouquet arrived, then another the following day, and that continued every day of the week.

"I'm running out of creative ideas," Marie complained. "How do you feel about green plants?"

"How long is this supposed to go on?" Audrey asked.

"The gentleman said I'm to bring you fresh flowers every day until he tells me to stop."

"Oh, I don't believe this!"

"Hey, enjoy it, Audrey. How many women ever have something this exciting happen to them? Besides, your generous boyfriend has sure done wonders for my business."

Peter walked into Audrey's office on the fourth day of the barrage, glanced around and asked, "Did someone die?" But Helen was enthralled. "This is absolutely the most romantic thing I ever heard of! I could cry."

When Boyd showed up at her apartment Friday night he was carrying red roses and wearing a tuxedo. In formal clothes he was something to behold, but Audrey couldn't hide her exasperation. "It's a good thing I don't have hay fever. You're crazy, you know that?"

"You're right. I'm crazy about you."

"Boyd, this is ridiculous! Please stop wasting your money."

"Hon, you wanted to be wooed. Please let me do it my own way. Go put on your finery. I'm taking you to a place that's so expensive there are tassels on the menus."

And so it went. Each gesture was more outrageous than the last. Frugal Audrey was appalled at the way he was spending money, but since Boyd obviously was having the time of his life, she suffered through weeks of the onslaught. She hated letting all the lovely flowers just wither on her desk, so she found a senior citizens' center where they were more than appreciated. It wasn't long before she was wearing a magnificent diamond ring on her left hand, and the weekends with Boyd were a delight. More than once she wondered how much of what was going on his family was aware of. Not much, she suspected, since she hadn't heard from Betty. Mostly, however, she just enjoyed the thrill of the pursuit. It would have been an exciting experience for anyone, but was especially so for a woman who had been alone such a long time.

Still, she remained adamant about not rushing into marriage. She felt they had all the time in the world. She didn't doubt that they would marry eventually, but she was convinced they would never regret moving slowly.

Actually, when she was being completely honest with herself, she admitted to some lingering doubts about how she would fit into the Benedict family structure. She had thought and thought about it but had yet to pinpoint a niche where she would fit comfortably. That was the only unsettling aspect of an idyll she would remember the rest of her life.

In the end, it was the singing telegram that stripped away the last vestiges of her resistance. For weeks Audrey had been aware of Boyd's growing impatience with the delay, and she had more or less braced herself for some new excessive gesture on his part. But when four fresh-faced young men in red-and-white striped jackets confronted her in the lobby late one afternoon to croon a saccharine love song, to the delight and merriment of all onlookers, she could only hide her flaming face with her hands and shake her head in disbelief. This was too much!

Audrey intended calling Boyd the minute she got home that evening, but the call wasn't necessary. He was waiting at her front door, grinning from ear to ear.

"It's only Thursday," she admonished.

"I know, but I came a day early. I wanted to find out if you got the telegram."

"Of course I got it. So did everyone else in the hotel. It was the highlight of the day. They're all holding their collective breath, waiting to see what preposterous thing you'll come up with next."

He stood aside while she opened the door, then followed her inside. "That was it, the pièce de résistance. I can't think of anything else to do."

"Good."

"Are you going to marry me?"

Audrey tossed her handbag onto the sofa and turned to slip her arms around his waist. "Yes, you win. No more of this nonsense. I accept your proposal." She looked at him, her eyes earnest. "But first we need to talk about something."

"Okay. Talk away."

"My future," she said solemnly.

Boyd didn't understand. "Your future? You're going to be my wife."

"Beyond that, I mean. It's something I've been thinking about a lot lately. Boyd, I simply can't live the way your mother and Sara do. I suppose there was a time when I thought my own life would be like theirs someday, but that was another time, another world. I've been working for years now, and I've changed. I'm going to have to do something more meaningful than attend teas and bridge luncheons for the wives of prominent men."

"Got any suggestions?"

"Well, I've been thinking.... I know I'm a little rusty, but with practice I could probably help Betty around the ranch."

"Okay, we'll give it some thought," Boyd said decisively. "Hon, I never had any intention of turning you into Susie Homemaker. The ranch will be home, but you'll have full rein to do whatever your inclinations dictate."

Audrey melted against him, holding him tightly. "I'm so relieved everything's settled. Now all we have to do is get married. Do you suppose we can just slip away quietly and do it?"

Boyd laughed. "I'm afraid not, hon, sorry. Mom will never let you get away with that."

OF COURSE he turned out to be correct. Weddings were right down Elizabeth's alley. Once Boyd had told his family of their plans to get married, his mother was in almost daily phone contact with Audrey. The arrangements became more and more elaborate, and soon Elizabeth's invitation list contained the names of three hundred of the Benedicts' "nearest and dearest." With resignation Audrey entered into the spirit of the occasion, juggling the preparations with her job.

It was decided that the actual ceremony would be held at the Greenspoint. The hotel staff were the only family Audrey had, and she conceded that only a banquet room would accommodate Elizabeth's crowd. By any standard, it was going to be a stunning affair, exactly the sort of wedding Audrey's mother would have insisted on. And despite the Benedicts' protests, she paid for the whole show herself out of her sizable inheritance. She thought Bert would have liked that.

On the day of the actual ceremony, she stood in the small room off the banquet hall where she had dressed. Helen and Betty had just left, and in the distance Audrey could hear the organ music. She hadn't expected to be nervous, but she was. Her stomach was executing flip-flops. Too late she decided she should have eaten breakfast.

There was a knock on the door. "Come in," she called and turned, expecting to see Peter, who was walking her down the aisle. Instead, the commanding figure of Buck B. Benedict strolled into the room. Attired in a three-piece navy-blue suit, Boyd's father presented an even more imposing picture than usual.

Buck did nothing to still her stomach. Although she had been huddled with Elizabeth, Betty and even Sara for weeks, Audrey had seen precious little of Buck. She doubted they had exchanged more than half a dozen sentences since the engagement had been announced. She couldn't shake the notion that despite his overt politeness, Boyd's father wasn't completely pleased about the marriage.

"Mr. Benedict," she said quietly, though her pulses were pounding.

"Audrey, how lovely you look."

"Thank you."

"I hope you don't mind this intrusion."

"Of course not. It's no intrusion."

"I wanted to have a word alone with you. Things may get hectic later on."

"Of course."

"Boyd and I had a long talk last night. Is it true that you're concerned over what your...er, official job will be once you join the family?"

"Well, I...I'm not sure that *concerned* is the word...."

Buck interrupted. "I understand that you're not the least interested in the social end of it, but that's fine. Sara and my wife handle that admirably. And, of course, Boyd and Betty manage to keep the ranch running smoothly."

Audrey felt her breath catch. Was he trying to tell her there really wasn't anything for her to do?

"Yet," Buck went on, "it's important that we all contribute to the common good, so I have a suggestion for you. How about this hotel?"

Audrey's eyes widened. "The...Greenspoint?"

"Yes. Boyd and I agree that it's time we took more of an active interest in the place. Unfortunately, not one of us knows a thing about hotel management. You, on the other hand, do. I like the idea of having one of the family show up here a couple of times a week to keep an eye on things and report back. Does that appeal to you, my dear?"

Appeal to her? Audrey couldn't believe it! She had assumed the Greenspoint would become part of the past. "Oh, it more than appeals to me. I'd *love* the job!"

"Good, good. Then it's settled." Buck reached out and patted her shoulder, then, in a surprising move, leaned forward and placed a kiss on her forehead.

Audrey couldn't have been more astonished if he had slapped her. "Welcome to the family, Audrey."

For her it was a stunning moment. She was rendered almost speechless and felt dangerously close to tears. "Th-thank you."

Buck turned to leave, thought of something and faced her again. "You may be pleased to hear that my son let me know in no uncertain terms how he feels about my political plans for him. I won't say I'm not disappointed, but... When you get to be my age you better have learned to cope with disappointments. If you haven't, you're a fool...and I'm no fool." He shot her a smile. "I'll see you after you two are safely hitched."

He strode out, and a moment later Peter strode in. "What a beautiful bride you make, Audrey! Are you ready? The family's just been seated."

She picked up her bouquet and took Peter by the arm. "As ready as I'll ever be."

They reached the double doors just as Betty, as maid of honor, started down the aisle. Audrey and Peter stood on the threshold for the brief moment before the "Wedding March" began. Instinctively her eyes flew to the flower-bedecked altar and to the minister's left where Boyd and Brent stood, looking stiff and uncomfortable in the elaborate formal clothes. But the moment Boyd saw her, his face broke into a wide smile, and he shot her a thumbs-up gesture. At least half the wedding guests saw it and laughed. Beside her, Peter laughed, too.

Only Boyd would do something like that, Audrey thought as she began the long walk down the aisle. It was an auspicious beginning.

EPILOGUE

AUDREY AND BOYD had been back from their honeymoon in Mexico less than a week. Boyd was spending the day at the family's offices in Tucson, and Audrey was alone in the adobe house, arranging the furniture that had been delivered that morning. All the new appliances had been hooked up, and that night she was going to prepare her first meal on the new gas range. Up until now, Boyd had had to do most of the cooking since the old wood cook stove had completely baffled her. She couldn't say she had been at all sorry to see the cast-iron monstrosity carted away.

Glancing around, she noted with satisfaction that the house was beginning to look as if someone actually lived in it, and tonight they were having company. Betty was coming to dinner and bringing a man named David Lindsey with her. David was a young Tucson attorney who had recently purchased some acreage in the valley and was venturing into the horse-raising business. His name had been popping up more and more frequently in Betty's conversation, so Audrey held out great hopes for the relationship. But even if nothing came of it, this was the first time her sister-in-law had shown the slightest interest in a man since Jesse's hasty departure.

It was midafternoon when Audrey heard a car pull to a stop in front of the house. Since it was far too early for Boyd to be getting home, she hurried to a window to look out. A well-dressed, middle-aged man was emerging from a blue sedan and starting up the walk. As he neared, she recognized him as one of the family's lawyers. She had met him once before, months ago when he'd officially notified her of her inheritance, but his name escaped her completely. She waited for his knock, then went to open the door.

"Good afternoon," she greeted.

"Hello, Audrey," the man said, extending his hand. "I'm George Blackburn. Do you remember me?"

"Of course. It's nice to see you again."

"I stopped at the house, and Betty told me I could find you here. I was on vacation when your wedding took place. Otherwise I would have gotten this to you before now." He reached into his coat pocket and withdrew an envelope, which he handed to her.

Audrey glanced down at the envelope. There was no stamp, no letterhead, no return address on it. Only her name—Audrey Hamilton Benedict—was scrawled across it.

"It's from Bert," the lawyer explained.

Audrey's head came up with a jerk. "Bert?" she gasped.

George Blackburn nodded. "He gave it to me the day he made the final revisions in his will. He said the letter was for your eyes only. His instructions were to give it to you in person if you married Boyd. If either of you married anyone else, I was to destroy the letter unopened."

"Good Lord!" Audrey's heart began racing. A letter from Bert concerning Boyd and herself? How could that be? The lawyer had to be mistaken. It didn't make any sense. Then she remembered her manners. "I . . . ah, would you like to come in for coffee, Mr. Blackburn?"

"No, thanks just the same. I imagine you're anxious to read the letter, and I really must be getting back to the city. My apologies for the delay."

"That's quite all right. Thank you for coming all the way out here."

"Don't mention it. I'm sure I'll be seeing you again. Please give Boyd my regards . . . and belated congratulations."

The lawyer left, and Audrey hurried inside, alive with curiosity. She sat cross-legged on the sofa, and her fingers shook as she tore open the envelope. The letter had been written in a bold, rather unsteady script. Her eyes widened as she began reading.

My dear Audrey,
If you're reading this, then my plans have worked out exactly as I envisioned. How gratifying! I've known for some time now that my days on this old planet are numbered, and I decided that getting you and Boyd together would be my last hurrah. It took me a while to figure out how to do it, though. I wish I could have seen the look on your face when you found out about the money. Was Boyd the one who gave you the news? I hope you went right out and did something frivolous and extravagant with it, but knowing you, I'll bet you didn't. I also wish I could have seen the look

on Buck's face when the will was read, but that's another story entirely.

Back to you and Boyd. From the day I met you, I wanted the two of you to get together. Then as time went by and we became friends, I began planning to leave you a little stipend when I went to my reward. Gradually the two ideas melded into one. I reasoned that a modest sum would go unnoticed since I left a little money to a lot of people my family doesn't know. One day it dawned on me: I'd simply leave you enough to make everyone sit up and take notice. A hundred grand was bound to raise even a Benedict's eyebrows; at least it would make everyone curious about you. I figured Buck's curiosity would get the best of him, and if he ran true to form, he'd dispatch Boyd to the hotel to find out who in the devil you were. And once my grandson met you, I was sure my job would be done. I'm sure that's what happened, just as sure as if I were there to see it with my own eyes.

Why, you're probably asking yourself about now, if I wanted you and Boyd to meet, didn't I just drag him to the hotel and introduce you? A couple of reasons. One, I would have blown my cover, and I enjoyed the heck out of being anonymous. Two, Boyd's gotten a trifle touchy over my matchmaking attempts in the past. I didn't want to turn him off before you had a chance to turn him on.

So, my dear, I sign this with a great sense of personal satisfaction. You considerably brightened an old man's final days. I never made a million dollars that meant as much to me as the fifty bucks you loaned me. I trust you consider the debt repaid with interest. I hope you and Boyd reproduce like crazy and have a wonderful life together.

Affectionately,
Bert

P.S. Don't let anyone talk you into putting the money back in the family coffers. Take it and have a ball.

Audrey was crying so hard when she finished the letter that the print swam before her eyes. Setting it on the spanking-new, glass-topped coffee table, she went in search of a tissue, then slipped on a jacket and walked out the back door. She knew there were at least a dozen things she could have been doing in the house, but she was too overcome with emotion to concentrate on any of them.

Her misty eyes scanned the horizon. It was winter now, and the landscape was at its bleakest. Before they knew it, however, spring branding season would be upon them. The herd would be turned out to pasture to feast on the grass that grew thick and lush during the summer rainy season, and the cycle would begin all over again. It wasn't too much to hope that by the time next fall's roundup rolled around she would be too pregnant to be able to go along.

Without consciously realizing she was doing it, she crossed the expanse between the house and the cemetery, stepped over the picket fence and went to stand in front of Bert's grave.

"You conniving old darling," she sniffed. "I can't believe you did that, went to all that trouble! And to think it worked out exactly as you envisioned. Wait until I tell Boyd. He's so fond of saying that fate brought us together, that he would have found me no matter where I was. I can hardly wait to tell him that 'fate' has another name, and it's Bertram B. Benedict."

Audrey didn't know how long she stood there, half-laughing and half-crying, but she thought it must have been a long time. The air was becoming quite chilly, but she seemed rooted to that spot, almost mesmerized. She was lost in a private reverie, oblivious to everything around her, when she heard her name being called. Turning, she saw Boyd standing on the back porch, waving one arm high above his head.

"Hey!" he shouted.

"Hey, yourself!" she called back.

He motioned her toward the house. She waved to indicate she'd be right along, but first she turned to glance at the headstone again. "Boyd's home, so I've got to go now, Bert, but I'll be back . . . often. Thanks so much . . . for everything."

She stepped over the fence again and ran to the house and her future.

Harlequin Superromance

COMING NEXT MONTH

#274 CHANCES • Meg Hudson
Sharon Williams thought a leisurely train ride and a
long vacation in Miami would be the perfect way to
clear her muddled thoughts and straighten out her life.
But when a computer mix-up has her sharing quarters with
Scott Williams, she loses her privacy... and her heart.

#275 VISIONS • Sally Garrett
Eileen Mills discovers an inner strength she never knew
she had when she is widowed and left a single parent
struggling to save her family's potato farm. Handsome
journalist Dan Page helps her make another discovery—
broken hearts *do* mend when healed by time and loving.
Don't miss Book Two of Sally Garrett's uplifting
RAINBOW HILLS SERIES.

#276 A PERFECT GEM • Lynn Erickson
Working with attractive, fun-loving Graham Smith
on courier assignments is exciting for professional
bodyguard Jane Manning. That is, until the Amsterdam job.
Why is Graham acting so oddly when ten million in diamond
is at stake?

#277 STRONGER BY FAR • Sandra James
Jason Davalos is the only man who can help Kate McAllister
rescue her ex-husband from Mexican kidnappers. But
whether he will is another story. Jason hates her
ex-husband, yet Kate knows Jason once loved her.
That love is her one hope....

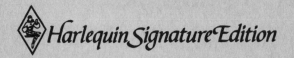

◆ *Harlequin Signature Edition*

Carole Mortimer

Merlyn's Magic

She came to him from out of the storm and was drawn into his yearning arms—the tempestuous night held a magic all its own.

You've enjoyed Carole Mortimer's Harlequin Presents stories, and her previous bestseller, *Gypsy*.

Now, don't miss her latest, most exciting bestseller, *Merlyn's Magic*!

IN JULY

MERMG